GEOGRAPHY OF REBELS

THE BOOK OF COMMUNITIES

THE REMAINING LIFE

IN THE HOUSE OF JULY AND AUGUST

—

Maria Gabriela Llansol

TRANSLATED FROM THE PORTUGUESE BY AUDREY YOUNG

INTRODUCTION BY GONÇALO M. TAVARES

AFTERWORD BY BENJAMIN MOSER

DEEP VELLUM PUBLISHING

DALLAS, TEXAS

Deep Vellum Publishing
3000 Commerce St., Dallas, Texas 75226
deepvellum.org · @deepvellum

Deep Vellum Publishing is a 501c3
nonprofit literary arts organization founded in 2013.

ISBN: 978-1-941920-63-3 (paperback) · 978-1-941920-64-0 (ebook)
Library of Congress Control Number: 2017938734

—

REPÚBLICA
PORTUGUESA

CULTURA
DIREÇÃO-GERAL DO LIVRO, DOS ARQUIVOS E
DAS BIBLIOTECAS

—

Funded by the Direção-Geral do Livro, dos Arquivos e das Bibliotecas.

Cover design & typesetting by Anna Zylicz · annazylicz.com
Text set in Bembo, a typeface modeled on typefaces cut by Francesco Griffo for Aldo
Manuzio's printing of *De Aetna* in 1495 in Venice.
Distributed by Consortium Book Sales & Distribution.
Printed in the United States of America on acid-free paper.

Table of Contents

—

ON THE WRITING OF MARIA GABRIELA LLANSOL

"At the level of movement, I went to Sintra, read Hölderlin" (MGL)

There is, in reading, a movement begun in the slight trembling/trepidation of the eyes, which continues down to the top of the feet, swinging beneath the table. There is, in the swinging legs of those who are reading, motionless, an impressive stride, a traversing: those who read, amble.

Any place, any country, nowhere is further away than the page I am reading. The page twenty centimeters from my eyes is, in the end, at a far greater distance; it depends on my willingness to perceive it, that is: to travel it. To perceive something is to travel it: to roam around; to perceive a page is to roam all around that page: we end up tired, we've gone too far. "At the level of movement," says MGL, "I went to Sintra, read Hölderlin."

Reading as a kind of physical activity, reading as a sport: athletics, soccer, gymnastics, reading an essay, handball, figure skating, reading a poem, reading a novel.

Devising a gym where the user chooses between aerobics, gymnastics, or reading a book of poetry; three movement classes, each lasting an hour.

Writing as a translation of reading. A translation that isn't only incorrect, or wrong; more than that: it is clumsy. I write trying to translate what I've read between two identical languages, but I fail, hence creativity; invention as evident failure, not in repetition but in the attempt to pass from one thing to a whole other side. I lost something in the passage, *in the transit,* or rather: I gained something, because a table that loses one of its four legs during a move invents, at that moment, another object with three legs. *"I write in full possession of my faculties of reading."* (MGL)

"The art of endangering bodies" (MGL)

Excerpts from Gonçalo M. Tavares's book *Brief Notes on Maria Gabriela Llansol, Maria Filomena Molder, and Maria Zambrano,* published by Relógio d'Água, 2007.

1.

On the writing of Maria Gabriela Llansol.

Em dashes, a new breath, distance between words, words on their own in a sentence that seems the result of a shipwreck. Words do not necessarily exist in a sentence, they have autonomy, their own biography—for instance, an adjective distanced by graphic signs from the noun it qualifies ceases to be an adjective and proudly becomes an individual word. Words have autonomy.

Signs introduce breath, rhythm. Oxygen, O2, between the words. One word, breathe; Two, three, breathe.

A writing on stage, theatrical.

2.

A sentence as a space, a space to occupy, a space very nearly for manual and hard labor, a space for engineering—beams, lintels, em dashes—it seems an inhabited house, Llansol's sentence, but a sentence left unfinished, a sentence under construction. The pillars are still there, of course, but perhaps it isn't a construction, but a reconstruction. The sentence is being recovered, as if it were a sentence with old materials being salvaged for a new time.

The lines are horizontal stakes; stakes that hold the ceiling when they are placed vertically and hold the sentence, hold the words, join the words, when they are placed horizontally.

3.
Characters that have the names of philosophers, of animals, that are Types, aggregates of sensations.

Character-sentences, characters that have a certain style to their sentences.

Characters that cannot be distinguished anatomically, but by the energy their name transmits to the remaining space, to the rest of the sentence.

4.
This is also about sudden illuminations infiltrating what seemed to be a sleeping beauty-sentence. A kiss that awakens the sleeping beauty, that causes it to leap up; not a quiet awakening, but a leap forward, leap upon leap, an excessive leap, beyond the limits of the leap—a leap forward. Thus Llansol's text. At times we seem to be in the calm, expected sea, and then suddenly, those sentences that make us stop, that demand we read with a pencil, underline, salvage the sentence from that place, from the book, carrying it to the everyday, to reality.

"telling them that, with such cold weather, those sitting in the middle of the horses' blood would win" (*The Book of Communities*)

Carry a sentence to reality and let it exist there. It won't be swallowed

or absorbed as if it were made of the same material as reality, or anything like that. The sentence will exist in reality as something that's
on top of something else, and does not mix. Not two liquids, but
two solids, one on top of the other. We carry Llansol's sentences with
us, those that leap—like an animal—from the text, those that leap as
certain animals leap from the earth that seemed flat and low. And we
carry the sentence with us to reality and and lay it down like someone
laying a blanket upon a stone. And this is the image—a blanket upon a
giant rock, a small blanket, with specific dimensions, a warm blanket,
a blanket that raises the temperature placed upon a rock of gigantic
proportions. Every sentence is a blanket.

They are small, they don't cover the entire world, they don't cover
the entire surface of reality, they are minimal, but they cover just a
little, they protect—as if they were hiding what is shameful in reality.
A kind of modesty and coldness, two problems solved with a sentence.
There are small squares of reality that are covered, that is, understood,
by certain sentences that come from books. There are many of these
sentences in Llansol.

"other children invented that there was a chair in this room with
torn stuffing where the sea could be heard, as soon as we put our ear
there; now, the springs are damaged." (*The Book of Communities*)

5.

What is literature for? For so much, but also for this—a sentence
sometimes allows us to understand one square meter of the world, one
square meter of reality, let's think about it like this—as if reality could
have this unit of measure. What is the unit used to measure reality, here
is a serious question. Time is typically assumed to be what is used to

measure reality, but we can think about space as a unit of measure.

One square meter of reality, two square meters of reality, one square centimeter of reality, ten thousand kilometers of reality.

And, yes, a sentence also has width, length, height, volume; it can be carried from a book to the world, to one square meter of the world. And this sentence will cover that square meter of reality, will understand that square meter of reality. It isn't much, they will say, for reality stretches out endless meters in all directions. True, it isn't much, but it is something.

Making square meters lucid, transforming the measurements of the world into lucidity. I look around and am able to understand because I brought the right Sentence with me. Sometimes, it is this.

To make at least a few square meters of reality lucid. Like someone carrying a small first-aid kit, carrying sentences from Llansol to the outside world, to the place and moment where you are alive.

6.

This edition of the Geography of Rebels trilogy, which includes *The Book of Communities*, *The Remaining Life*, and *The House of July and August*, and has been published by Deep Vellum thanks to the Espaço Llansol and Audrey Young, is a major event. A great writer like Llansol deserves such an edition in English. May readers enjoy this strangeness, which will, in time, I am certain, win them over.

—GONÇALO M. TAVARES

THE BOOK OF COMMUNITIES

To my mother
(Elvira)

This is how I read this book:

there are three things that strike fear: the first, the second, and the third.

The first is called the provoked emptiness, the second is called the continued emptiness, and the third is likewise called the glimpsed emptiness.

Now we know that Emptiness does not depend on Nothingness.

There are, then, three things that strike fear.

The first is mutation. No one knows what a human is. The limits of the human species are consequently unknown. They can, however, be felt. The mutant is extra-ordinary, bearing with it a new ordinary. This book is a process of mutants, physically perfect. It is a terrible process. It is advisable to fear this book.

There are, as I have said, three things that strike fear.

The second is Tradition, according to the spirit that moves where it breathes.

We all believe we know what Time is, but we suspect, with reason, that only Power knows what Time is: Tradition according to the Weft of Existence. This book is the history of Tradition, according to the spirit of the Remaining Life. Yet another reason for us not to take it seriously.

There are, I say for the last time, three things that strike fear.

The third is a bodywriting. Only those who pass through there understand what it is. And that it is of interest to no one.

Speaking and negotiating, producing and exploring, construct, in effect, the happenings of Power. Writing accompanies the density of the Remaining Life, of the Body's Other Form, which, I tell you here is: Landscape.

Writing glimpses, it cannot be used to confine. Writing, as in this book, fatally brings Power to the loss of memory.

And who knows what a Body With A Hundred Absent Memories of Landscape is.

Who can bear Emptiness?
Perhaps No One, not even a Book.

A. Borges
Jodoigne, January 4, 1977

Place 1 —

in that place there was a woman who did not want to have children
from her womb. She asked the men to bring her their wives' children
so she could educate them in a large house with only one room and
only one window; she wore a black shawl close to her face; she had a
distant way of making love: with her eyes and with her speech. Also
with time, for since the days of her great-grandmother, going back to
any era was always possible. Moving, she sometimes looked intently
at a place   the most beautiful in her house   the whole house
        because the whole house was beautiful and in that look began
either the time of children, or the time of men. Women, there was no
other, aside from her, never passed beyond the entrance, which led to
the land, land with a garden where they could walk. The men were
content because every time she said it isn't you I care about, it's the
next. So they convinced themselves that, in the moment before, they
had been the next. She sat in her room (everywhere) and picked up
words on a lightly curved forefinger, as if she served herself an aperitif
or a fish. She never thought that perhaps she was situated in the fragment of a cooled star or that she could, with a powerful plant, poison
        but, there being no other woman in the house, there were many
voices which, from different corners, all seemed to turn toward her

body and did not quiet when she spoke

there was a curtain in the window

which served as a place of spiritual retreat for the children who, at times, wished to leave for the woman, in turn, to receive new lovers there they copied the *Ascent of Mount Carmel,* by Saint John of the Cross, they laughed, they listened to the voice that slowly read what they had written and, in the end, even imitated their laughter   you must know that a soul   laughter   must generally pass first through two nights that the mystics call purgations   laughter   or purifications of the soul and that we here will call nights   laughter

because the soul walks as if at night, and in darkness; you must know that for these children this laughter did not signify derision; out of pure and extreme ignorance, other children invented that there was a chair in this room with torn stuffing where the sea could be heard, as soon as we put our ear there; now, the springs are damaged

the housecat came in   you live in the alternative of being a real cat or a royal object   and the papers slipped to the ground without her caring: papers, children, lovers, there would always be Saint John of the Cross: when she stood up because a child called her to the locutory in the garden behind one of the house's walls, she already knew the girl wanted to speak to her; she listened so raptly to what she revealed that, after two hours, she felt an ache in the nape of her neck and also in her skull; it seemed to her, as always when she spoke for a long time, that the words fell into her eyes, dilated and sunk them; the girl wanted an answer and she remembered that no precedents existed; despite this, she was going to think on it, to be with a few children and the papers, and perhaps Saint John of the Cross, whom she would find in any place.

Covered by the table and always ready to write, she dreamed about a group of men and Saint John of the Cross, discalced carmelite, sitting in front of an oven, roasting mutton; his forehead began to darken, red, between waves of scent; she understood, by the fixity of his expression, that he had entered the dark night and that either his book, or his hands, or his feet were now lying on the rack and they traversed flames and circumstances with unforeseeable results. And that he did not write: he had gathered his right fist inside his sleeve and because of the cloth's transparency only the image

of those who asked for the prisoner to be received could be recognized; sleepreading in the chair, tobacco smoke rose between his fingers, while the woman twisted her bracelet on her wrist:

never again bring me a message that doesn't know how to tell me what I want. The door closed with a soft

disturbance of air

which agitated the scarf

which wrote to look for the book; a short phrase, once found, was lost again; she raised her hand to ask a question, already forgotten; they looked in opposite directions, the question arose in the woman in the form of a smile; she hesitated on the s, as if she were going to write Saint; from the canonized body of Saint John of the Cross rose smoke and the question, the girl's sweet fire. He lay his hair against the back of the chair, looking up, and when he distinguished ahead he tapped his fingers through a long path of obscure contemplation and aridity; he had to go through many lines until he found it in the middle of the page after a horizontal white space that seemed another margin there on the page.

Place 2 —

"that you pierce the substance of my soul so intimately and tenderly and glorify it with your glorious ardor so that from now on, in your great kindness, you show me how much you wish to give yourself to me as in eternal life; if, before, my prayers did not reach you — when with the anxieties and exhaustions of love in which my spirit and my feeling suffered

My name is Ana del Mercado y Peñalosa.   When I go out, I tie a velvet ribbon around my neck. I am hopelessly devoted to writing   (and to disappearing in writing)   I do not like to read. I like to listen to music as if I myself had written it.
From this day forward, I can no longer separate reading from writing;   (if I could see the text being produced, I would return to reading once again).

I was born in Segovia where I have many possessions, I was widowed by Don Juan de Guevara.

Undressed, I pick up the deck

because of my cowardice and my great impurity and the weakness of my love, I asked you to kidnap me and take me with you as my soul ardently wished it because the impatience of love did not allow me to conform myself to the conditions of life in which you still want me to live, for some time yet; and, if the old forays of love, lacking the necessary quality to attain the effects of my desire, were not sufficient, now, when I feel so strong in love that not only do my spirit and senses not grow weary in you, but, to the contrary, my heart and flesh rejoice in the living God sustained by You in a great conformity of both parts of cards that I put on one of my knees and say diamonds or spades, red or black. If it's diamonds or hearts I will make love immediately. If it's spades or clubs I must wait five minutes looking intensely at an object that I myself choose, which could be a pillow, a lamp, a portrait, or one of the bouquets of flowers replaced every day by one of the tallest children who will succeed me indeterminately.

The time of hemorrhoids, or rather, the time of illness, the time of time: I always write with the notebook open on top of the book, which lets me compare the writing that comes from the deck of cards with that already printed. Eating afterward with half-closed eyes and listening to music give me great pleasure.

The children believe that memory rejuvenates me and Saint John of the Cross had a vision that I am the frame of a family portrait.

— which causes me to ask you what you want me to ask and not to ask you what you don't want me to ask, and I couldn't even ask it, nor does it even occur to me to ask it — as for the future, my requests are more effective and valuable in your eyes, as they come from You who impels me to make them, I beseech you with pleasure and joy (my judgment depends upon your countenance from this day forth — which happens when you receive and hear my prayers): tear the delicate fabric of this life."

Place 3 —

We always let night fall, before turning on the lights. Slowly, everything disappears in the place where it was, the children play games,
calling him and calling each other. At that hour they are completely
blind, they move between the pieces of furniture without knocking
them over or touching any of them; they can also remain quiet at my
side without me knowing and feeling myself alone awaiting a visitor

on the day
I was suffering from hemorrhoids, I stayed in bed all morning:
I dreamed that I was where, in fact, I was: in the atmosphere of my
room; topless, I looked in the mirror, which I chose to be an oval to
remind me of a face and I asked it who it would liberate; in front of
me, my body was very beautiful and I wanted to be photographed
within the frame; I also wanted to masturbate in front of that body, I
was somewhat aroused by my lover's slipper lying flat on the carpet.
My hemorrhoids cause the pain of a shaft being driven through my
body. This happened with lightness and brevity, I reached the end, I
looked for the notebook and the pen on the bed and I wrote   on
the day I was suffering from hemorrhoids

I had then a mirror vertigo in which the mirror, being always mirror,
appeared to me as a bier, a sick person in their bed, more precisely, Saint
John of the Cross, dying in Úbeda. But it was impossible that he was
dying because he wrote at my side and the pages of his complete works
fell, retroactively, around the mirror while everything happened with
lightness and brevity: I dreamed that, in my room, he was beginning
to write what he had already written.

I sat down at his side saying   what I write, I write for the first time.
My observation did not interest him. He lay down on my bed which
had become a spare cot and   began to die his death of Úbeda,
believing I would be capable of taking it as it had been
                                          we three wrote lean-
ing against the railing, dying on our feet, not knowing whose mouth
articulated what we said. Saint John of the Cross, fearful to suddenly
begin levitating, leave our company, and, not least, become ridiculous
because at that time all my lovers walked in the oratory, or rather, the
great entrance to the garden.
Ana de Peñalosa was still telling her story
the death of my only daughter, my second mourning
Don Luis del Mercado entrusted me with the education of my niece
Inés
it has been three years since I last abandoned my oratory
       between me and he who began to detach himself from the ground
            "a castle made entirely of diamond or a very transparent
crystal where there are countless rooms, as there are many mansions in
heaven: some above, others below, others on the sides; and in the center,
in the midst of them all, is the most important one, which is the one
where things of great secrecy take place": there was, then, the second
space in the house, the ceiling space, where Saint John of the Cross
went when he levitated: a subsequent mirror announced itself slowly:
a few wrinkles and white hairs, tender text and hard text; I no longer
ask for the youth of his face but for that of his writing: an admirable
woman is a bad mother: on that day she was the victim of two small
deceits that led her to pick up the pen and the book
she was listening to kyrie eleison, Christe audi nos, Christe exaudi nos

when, looking at the dresser   miserere nobis she had the impression
that on top of it, behind a glass, there was another candle
miserere nobis; she wondered in astonishment   miserere nobis
      how it could be possible; she realized it was a flask of beauty
cream made from plants   miserere nobis   the
other illusion   miserere nobis   was that she, in bed, went to
close the door to the room overlooking the great hall so they wouldn't
be able to see her through the window   miserere nobis: but, once
she was lying down, she saw that the window wasn't actually in front
of the bed   miserere nobis.

There was yet a small incident:

she was so absorbed that her cigarette went out in her hand and, wanting to relight it to swallow its smoke with the kyries, she remembered
that she had left the matches where Saint John of the Cross was, near
the ceiling or in the Chapel. She then concentrated on the writing and,
suddenly, at the top of the page, scratching at it with her fingers, she
found a match that she used to light the candle of an oratory, a table,
and a few abandoned images: she spent some hours there, in either an
intense or a vague sensation of writing: the house, the true and subsequent house, had yet to be made; changing rooms, another part will
be completed; I stop at the entrance to the new room which, for the
time being, is only space crossed by air with a few openings of sun and
the rest rain, humidity, cold because the climate is not Atlantic like that
of the house I left, moderately sweet and bitter; I sit down to the time
without movements and I become a faint apparition until a new cell of
the new house is written — it must be a cell with a tomb built upon
the place where I sat, a tomb of evident and aromatic dream where
I see you in many people and many moments of your life. Through

the small opening in the attic tomb overlooking the garden, voices could be heard and the beating of oars announcing that Saint John of the Cross was going to arrive. John's name furrowed the water and the boat's keel penetrated each letter as he conversed with the book, the book open on his knees being born from his mouth and covered by a particular quality of sun; voices could be heard and the beating of oars, his lowered eyelids still allowed him to utter his dreamed writing. When he put his feet on land I said to him

    good morning, actor of speech

    and he answered me:

    good morning, mother: next to the river was a courtyard surrounded by windows; the ground, washed by you morning and afternoon, was always shining, although one day I noticed the brightness had diminished and the plants lacked the just-watered splendor you gave them, I sat down with my white sheets of paper between my hands, meditating on the enigma, and I ended up writing that you would be in the moment of absenting yourself, almost opening the door, in the most remote room of the house, although you constantly desire to be hospitable. For three centuries, your courtyard influenced the lifestyle of the brothers and sisters who form the community: our rules encompassed the novitiate, the prayers, the style of dress, the slumber, the journeys, the silence, and the utterance of speech. The fast is not from meat, but from movement. At certain hours of the day, when all the sand fell in the clepsydra, those who are part of the community should become immobile and look attentively at the position in which they found themselves; when I stopped in the left wing of the house I thought, since Ana de Peñalosa had left, that all her rooms would be closed. But, obeying the rules, the door had been left completely open and two small birds listened to a mandolin from the old round birdcage; in the dresser drawers she left the clothing she wears to sleep at night; her day dresses hang from pegs placed at the entrance to the next room where there is a work table and a skull, eye sockets wound in ivy. The bed seems that of a young woman, with room for a single body, at its foot hung an engraving of a placenta enclosing a fetus only a short time before birth. The dresses are different colors, short and long, and one has the impression that they seem to describe her. I imagine her in the middle of the carpet, welcoming me, and say: good night, mother. We cannot run to each other because it's time to follow one of the rules. The light goes on in the birdcage and I make out my open book on her work table, underlined at the beginning of the *Living Flame*, her hand abandoned in it; I am fascinated by the stillness in the room and I notice that a single ring occupies her hand in the same way her hand occupies the page; I take her hand, infringing on the rules, and her hand contains a word with which she, also infringing on the rules

I did not descend the river by boat to attend your death but I found myself, by chance, on the bank of a river and, when the last memory of all of you blurred, I noticed the day and the greenery which, from the earth, penetrated the water; the blue boat oscillated toward the tree it had been tied to, and also oscillated toward the mouth of the river, and I then began to accumulate memories of the future in a great meditation; the river seemed to me to be the walls of this house which were sailing and each part, with its own function, was present but dissolved in the water, running. My habitual somnolence had abandoned me, waiting to see the gliding of the water, I felt I would be awake forever. But this state was more restful than sleep, without any of the dreams I did not want to have. It is the future, I thought. The river runs very fast, and what I was thinking transformed over time, which is shadowed and full of whispers, close to my feet; once in a while, the blue boat tied to the tree stretches the whole length of its chain and bends toward the bank covered in green plants where a salutary dampness begins to descend. Do you know this unforgettable place? The wind picked up and blows over me and through the tree, which lost the brightness I remembered; it became colder and I think only of the torrent whose speed is always increasing; at a certain point, as there is a small island in the middle of this turmoil, I begin to believe that, in the other branch of the river, the waters rise toward the source. Today the weather still hasn't changed and, within a few days, I will return. I don't know if you will be able to see me right away; it's better for you to busy yourself writing, even in my room because for some nights yet I will live in the garden and look at your illuminated windows; I will call them illuminated leaves. If you find a cradle in my room

I spent the night on the bank of the river, for nowhere else do I sleep with such serenity. The boat is still tied to the tree and I know it is morning by the sound of the water, by the hasty passage of the current, shadowed but without storm; the low tree trunks formed a kind of cavern; and the noise, beginning there, disappears at a distance, in the middle of the mass of water.

To find a place called Fontiveros, remember that I will be there, within a few days; I will get up and follow the river, leaving the garden. Knowing you well, I believe you will begin to descend the river, rigid as you are. The infantile

voices of your brothers   His waning face fought the current and it seemed as if he fled when, in fact, he left for the meeting he had arranged. A powerful sound came out of the water and commanded him to immobility. He knocked on the door and the midwife said to them: — Enter, please. — He sat down at the table and raised his head toward the ceiling, eyes closed. Ana de Peñalosa sat down as well, identical to her son. The lamplight fell on her hand and Saint John of the Cross's face rose, studying all the corners of the room. It seemed to Ana de Peñalosa that her illuminated hand had trembled and that her fingers had become light and tapered; her wrist, lying on the table, beat. It is the water's current, she thought. But she felt her fingers to be increasingly tenuous in such a way that when Saint John of the Cross lowered his head, her hand had disappeared, severed at the wrist, and in its place, lying flat, was the page: "There I told you I wanted to remain in this desert of Peñuela — six leagues before Baeza — where I arrived nine days ago. I am well, and in very good health, because the enormous expanse of desert is beneficial for body and spirit."

He leaned against the wall, retreating. In an instant, he crossed the place of Fontiveros, where the houses are a lime white that   ; at the same instant, in the garden of Peñuela, he remained in prayer all night and, in the morning, they saw him rise up from the earth the top of the table was rectangular yellow, the predominant color of the air in Fontiveros and, when it was made into water, it became, in the second layer, mirror; a wind like that from the river passed by, a wave rose up, a candle was lit within it (the room's lamp was extinguished, the daylight disappeared): in the candlelight, our faces and handwritings intertwine; they lay in shadow, our severed left hands of Ana de Peñalosa, and they replace the duplicate pages: the second layer broken, they both appeared in a fetal position, mouths dirty with the milk of words; raised in the air, the candle went out, the room's lamp was extinguished, the daylight disappeared.

Place 4 —

when the weather began to darken, this river flowed vertically. As it fell in the courtyard, it provoked a shudder in the layer of water already there. Alongside the drain form bubbles. Driven by the remaining water, they cut across the corner in a rapid movement that, gradually, decreases and stops; the bubbles now moved in a circular pattern and the noise of the rain, isolated in one or another drop, can be discerned, above all, at the height of the roof. I let out a sigh and the time it takes the isolated drops to fall became, each time, less brief. It brightened without, however, the sun emerging or the candle going out. Afterward, in the courtyard, it seems that someone is drinking water and that the sound is amplified, writing

John's overwhelming desire.

The midwife tells me she is going to sleep, that the wait has been greatly prolonged. I smile; and, having found it underneath the page, I held my severed hand to my chest; Saint John of the Cross, or my son, they write in vain on the blank page. Always blank   there was no writing: he then lay down upon the paper, his body taking on the proportions of a newly born child. I looked, ignoring. Nothing happened, only a wail was heard, between the table and the ceiling. Eyes closed, or open, I did not sleep; he disappeared on the page, and:

          where is my mother?

The rumble of the storm comes from the south of Fontiveros. It has certainly already crossed Úbeda and, before Segovia, will not find rest. We will keep each other company; I feel no pain, and John cannot be born from any part of my body; I have seen the leaves of Fontiveros in autumn, they are red or yellow and resonate through the streets when the air is charged with electricity or when he passes by with his hand writing

leaving the streets,

he found himself in the middle of the countryside.

Around one o'clock in the afternoon, the community returned and recited an antiphon; all of them, affectionately, kissed his feet and hands. It rained

when I was, by chance, sitting on the bank of the river, all I had to do was look at him for things to change by force of circumstances. In the countryside, I have to walk to be able to describe this path. I turn back to be able to begin and notice the leaves decaying from the dampness, which still hide the ground covered in herbs; to my right is a dense line of pine trees and a few buds rise up in bare shrubbery.

Those present

wanted to cut a lock of his hair, a piece of his habit, and I saw there were some who bit his ulcerous leg

when the path descends, precisely at the place where the sun is reflected, my leaves are drier; the brightness is tenuous, it disappeared when I raised my eyes and the leaves resonate for having aged and shriveled; most of the trees are bare, it is a winter landscape.

What had belonged to

him was distributed as relics: habit, cingulum, cilice, breviary

but the ivy remains as it was and I sit down on a stone in front of the low sun, as if it were summer

There were some who pulled the

nails from his toes, there were some who wanted to cut off a finger
I have been here for a few moments, I begin to smell the variety
of plants and herbs, the vegetal species are indescribable. This is the
moment I've been waiting for

Born without agony, John's face was full
of peace and contentment, of a particular beauty which isn't that of a
cadaver, he who had a face   ;
as in dreams, he must actually be eaten

and that was how he had been born,   I spent a restless night, waiting for
I put my hands on my temples and,   the moment when I will return to
in the mirror, saw that they had   this path; I could leave, but now it is
whitened   night and I want to walk it precisely
                                      at the same hour.

First homily:

it is the following day, but I believe the seasons are going to change.
I picked up a small branch and held it against the sun: it is speckled
with frost. The sun is still high in the pine trees, it casts a cold shadow
on the soil's tangled vegetation; my feet freeze and I see the nearly dry
herbs framed by a gleamless white, absent any light; it cannot be the
same hour as yesterday. In the middle of the path, a woodcutter has
piled up logs cut from trees; I do not know if I will continue or turn
around, but I cannot stop making my way along the path I walked;
now the sun hits the full height of every pine tree, from the bottom
of the trunk, and there is even a place that shines, on the ground.
Shrubs different from the pine trees seem covered with dry leaves that

do not fall because no one touches them; a log was covered in moss where the axe's blade passed, but I don't want to sit down on that green bench shining with the same frost; I am about to arrive close to the sun which, at my right, illuminates all the foliage lying on the ground beneath a pine tree; in my left hand the branch is still white and dusted in rime because the cold is glacial, and they still haven't changed. I reached the point in the path where there are more rotted leaves; then the frost reappears descending toward the village streets and I turn around with the sun rising behind me wanting to lie down here forever as you hear

Second homily:

always the same cold, delicate and intense. The outlying fields have been covered in frost: it is the early hours of the morning. At night I did not feel my usual desire to return to travel this path; but before I arrived I was filled with sadness; the frost increasingly thick and, gradually, the leaves are all white and a mineral whisper beneath my feet.
It is an illusion to believe that,
on either side of the path,
the branches were moving closer. It must be the shadow's effect. The logs from yesterday no longer fearfully obstruct; some of them rest along the sides, beneath the branches; I sat back on my heels. Someone approached and passes by, without wondering whether I am there; the brightness continues on the ground, it is very warm and makes the vanishing frost green again and leaves the grass bare. The sun moved toward the pine trees and no longer returns to illuminate sections of the descent. A few of the shrubs' stalks are red and they remind me

of our umbilical cord: I remove a branch from the middle of the path because it moves me to sorrow

Saint John of the Cross looked at the candle as if to ask it what, next, he was going to write: the wick was not at the center of the flame and the wax, luminous at its base, reminded him of sperm deposited in his mother's womb, his mother of the book; there were two shorter candles propped against the burning candle and the pages of the open book were connected by a furrow.

The *Living Flame* was not written indifferently, says the Prologue. If the words have a meaning: it exceeds all that could be conceived and splinters anything in which we would want to enclose it

He had crossed his legs beneath his habit and wrote between his eyes and his knees; Quasimodo's Sunday Mass was being sung by the Community and fine voices followed the movement of the pencil as his teeth chewed on it. He saw his mother at the peak of ecstasy and thought, without writing it down, about a boat or a mirror at the top of a wave; the page about his eyes was in the center of the wall and was a hundred times larger than his body. Then he was scared and the pencil seemed to him to be the tip of a breast, which he brought to his mouth. Ana de Peñalosa was suspended over the page, and he on her lap. She rocked him, but the amplitude of her voice was that of a chorus and in the shadow she began to perceive the different physiognomies of the brothers who were singing   you are looking for me, but I am looking for you all the more

Everything is being said and the rest of the commentary will not describe a moment in history. He hid his face in his hands, always watched by Ana de Peñalosa, and he perceived, within the closed book, the fire's speaking color.

Since the candle had gone out, he told his mother to bring him another candle tomorrow; he plunged into the darkness of the blind, into the silence where admiration becomes lost.

Place 5 —

While he waited, John, always at the center of darkness, sat down, and had a dream that, sleeping, he traveled the three paths simultaneously: the way of the river, the way of the pine trees, and the candlelight the flame lit, he half-closed his eyes against the cloud of smoke and concentrated on listening to the river passing by: it had a feminine voice, shrouded with murmurs that could only be heard once. He made an effort to deprive himself of the pleasure and sweetness of memory but it brightened without, however, the sun emerging or the candle going out; the boat remains tied to the tree and I know it is morning by the sound of the water, by the hasty passage of the current, shadowed but without storm; but I found myself, by chance, on the bank of the river and, when the last memory
of all of you blurred, I noticed the day and the greenery which, from the earth, penetrated the water; the blue boat oscillated toward the tree it had been tied to, and also oscillated toward the mouth of the river, and I then began to accumulate memories of the future in a great meditation
but the ivy remains as it was and I sit down on a stone in front of the low sun, as if it were summer ("I do not know how many days I will stay here because they threaten me, from Baeza, that it won't be very long. I am well, without knowing anything, and the desert life is

admirable"). The sun is still high in the pine trees, it casts a cold shadow on the soil's tangled vegetation; my feet freeze and I see the nearly dry herbs framed by a gleamless white, absent any light; it shouldn't be the same hour as yesterday. In the middle of the path, a woodcutter has piled up logs cut from trees; I do not know if I will continue or turn around, but I cannot stop making my way along the path I walked

The lit wick, as I watched over it, filled the candle with wax. A dog, or another animal, came over to me and left its skin on the ground. I looked at its bare body and, with my hand, caressed my mother. The parted skin and body brought me joy and sorrow and the animal, which could have also been a wolf or a bear, began to emit a melodious and powerful voice. I lay down on the skin and the fur, soft and manifold,

turned me into morning. He went over to the brazier and the heat of the flame beat at his chest. Hanging above the flame was the portrait of Ana de Peñalosa

(even though I would be happier here, I will leave when you ask me to)

which he then saw was Ana de Peñalosa herself; he wanted to enter the portrait and the fire. He pushed his mother's knees apart; the early morning seemed to him to be the silk fabric of her dress and the lips that had torn the silk savored, singing, the marvelous food that would guide him on his journey. He picked up the book but, when he went to cross through the opening, he realized they both could not pass; so he left it on the table, open to the place where, for the last time, he had slept. The homily resonated in his ears from the entrance, the shadows of the trees cast on the walls reminded him of the fear of becoming lost. He then raised his hand like a torch and ordered, turning around: follow me.

The scent of the herbs that were meant to carpet the opening spread through the air; rosemary and mint burned on the ground and, among them all, the feminine voice of the homily stretched out.

ANA DE JESUS

(in her room she opened the window and, to keep from falling asleep, welcomed the cold, particularly on her chin and her hand; she was bending over the paper, which she had divided into three columns; the smell of the food, rising from the kitchens, made the air delicious and bearable.

A bit of snow

but I do not close the window so it can be near, without the glass; in the meadow at the center of the cloister there is also a bird that runs and stops (disappears). The air is clean and the brightness begins to hit the furniture in the room, inviting us for a portrait.

I now watch the path advancing toward the main road, between two ruts: it is a path of grass; all is meadow.

It troubles me that I must abandon this place. — What will I do, really, away from here,

where night and day are so important? — They speak, expressing themselves through delicate changes in light. — I'm going to close the window because my throat's already hurting: a response to the cold. The weather has changed so many times and I haven't been interested in anything else   )

SHE HAD COME TO VISIT HIM. With her, she had brought her dog. She asked him about the book, where he was in the text: John of the Cross told her that he was going to die to be able to describe the moment of death; but, rather than looking at her, he looked at the dog, its eyes prominent and closed.

Ana de Jesus's voice had picked up speed. He did not understand why she spoke to him; he saw many trees and horses pass through the dog's eyes, a few of the horses stopped close to the trees and shook their manes, nostrils smoking. Dark birds flying low, and even imitating terrestrial animals, crossed the meadow, surprised. And, as the movement brought him a turmoil of ideas, among which that of death had taken form, he lay down on the pallet and communicated to Ana de Jesus that he was going to arrive.

The dog went over and stood beside him, stretched out over the stone; Ana de Jesus found that she was talking to herself or, then, to Ana de Peñalosa who, in the meantime, had come and sat down in front of the text.

— What is he writing? — asked Ana de Jesus

— He is writing me — replied Ana de Peñalosa, and she entered the maternal bed hearing the canticles, unable to fix her feet to the ground. Walking amidst quicksand, the introduction to those new surroundings did not end; she responded to all the doubts briefly because she had little time (she could not delay any longer). But the book had become precious, she had used it so many times that it was now impossible to close it completely. It lay on the work table with small gaps between the pages, its front and back covers turned inside out; her desire to sleep was constant, although she could not give into it because she had to keep watch over the canticles with open eyes and on feet that, enormous from writing, hesitated; she heard, as she reflected, a loud whisper, "greater than language can express and feeling imagine"; Ana de Peñalosa and Ana de Jesus took him by the

hand, clasped their fifteen fingers and three palms tightly; as the crowd
advanced to surround someone, who fled; their hands undulated over
the sheet and the bed and Ana de Jesus said, secretly, to Ana de Peñalosa
— ...it must be experienced.

Next to the body of the dog lying on the ground appeared the body
of the one they pursued; the room's walls receded within a dense fog:
I am not born, but
the book lay on the work table; raindrops came in through the window and spread across the words he had written for the Prologue of
the *Living Flame*
O most noble and pious Lady,
it was difficult
to do as you asked:
no one can speak
of the depths of the spirit,
unless they have a spirit
of fathomless depths.   In the meadow at the center of the
cloister there is a bird and a dog and, between them, I worked the
miracle of hiding the body of the one they pursued:
(Ana de Peñalosa said, "he entered into ecstasy")
I, Thomas Müntzer, reduced to a child's body, whose size does not
exceed that of my severed head after the battle of Frankenhausen;
I, Thomas Müntzer of Stolberg,
making the air's clear trumpets resound with a new canticle, attest that,
above all my contemporaries, I have consecrated myself, with ardent
zeal, to become worthy of acquiring a most rare and perfect science.
The men who had held power until now converse coldly
between the pages appeared the manuscript of a text that Saint John

of the Cross had neither written, nor ever seen
it was only a voice in which a voice was imagined
before nightfall, covered in a cursive handwriting, illuminated by the
red lamp that Teresa de Ávila hung from her throat
she is seated, reflected in the mirror and the silk of the dress she
removed;
on her naked lap,
the head of the day
which is unimaginable
radiates,
without annulling
the terrible voices
and descriptions
of the nocturnal
itinerary:
I spent the afternoon and early hours of the evening wanting,
still on that day
and before
it became morning,
to open the window over the river with the impression that I had
slept in the river
and had just arrived there:
there was a brightness so intense that none could bear it, unless it were
veiled; the bridge would come from above, overlying the sun. The
birds flew within the water (to the depths), the boat sailed seemingly
empty, although hands grasped the oars, which did not move; an even
more intense light accompanied the boat, like a fountain born in the
middle of the water; and, at times, words and phrases were inscribed

in the birth of that light, which tumbled down to the place where Thomas Müntzer was going, his ears and his mouth.

From the banks, the crowd continued to loose expletives; but the Living Flame, falling flame after flame, covered the body: the ululating voices lowered their tone, only the green of the meadows where there were many white and yellow flowers followed the boat

it stopped in front of the window where Saint John of the Cross wrote; Thomas Müntzer raised his chest dewed with water; the shouting became singular, irresistibly drawing the current; a bird, emerging from the river's depths, landed on his chest; the boat continued to glide alone, but traversed by flames:

Saint John of the Cross looked at the spiderwebs which, on the ceiling, edged the pale blue of the cornice and, at that moment, in the boat that was always descending the river (although always in the same place), Thomas Müntzer noticed that a horse swam nearby and that the crowd, reflected in its lustrous neck, had become a peaceful mirror.

Saint John of the Cross, turning to lower his eyes toward the page, as he had seen and not seen the ululating crowd, picked up Ana de Peñalosa's hand, which she had abandoned on the table, put the pen between her fingers (although I ignore where you are) and wrote:

"among all three there were three people and one beloved being."

He hid himself to write; but, first, he began by reading the book that held his infinite happiness

he remained at the beginning, but it had no beginning; it was its own beginning and, accordingly, there was no beginning; one in the other was like the beloved in their friend; and this love uniting them has the same value in them both, the same equality

as he was reading, he realized that he read standing, in front of his bookshelf

the art of fasting

distracted,

he looked at his ring finger on which Thomas Müntzer, while he had been headless on the boat, had placed a ring whose stone was his head

how could he hide himself to write

we will let him write, said the horse. We, John of the Cross and I, left for the river and the forest, on a morning of clouded sun; the horse wanted to go with us and we climbed up on its back; John of the Cross had several hands, the reins, and his hand on the horse's neck. It whinnied a few times: we put a garland of flowers on its head. We immediately saw Thomas Müntzer lying in the boat, his severed head appeared in front of us,

the darkness hung

we moved toward the atrium of the house where we could only arrive at night, after many hours of river and forest and always on the back of the horse that, trotting, whinnied words

we, felt the heat of its blood under our legs, and the wide house was already nearing

on the first night, we would camp in front of it without going in, awaiting the boat in which Thomas Müntzer's body traveled

we would find the summer house uninhabited, the lights on in Ana de Peñalosa's room

on the other side of the bank would be the desert, the river, and the forest.

Late in the evening:

— The boat still hasn't come. A pallet made of logs has arrived — In the place for his head lies a wreath of clovers.

He did not stop, nor the horse at his side.

— We passed in front of the house longingly, reading, throughout, by the light of the river, the writing made by the horse's hooves — Saint John of the Cross's feet left his sandals, rose up into the air — A woman in a large vestment appeared to us, the sun enveloped her and twelve stars crowned her head. She shouted painfully when a second sign covered the sky: an enormous dragon, red as fire, with ten horns on each of its seven heads, its entirety ornamented with a diadem; its tail lashed the stars and plunged them to earth; we returned to the horse's back. Thomas Müntzer went on foot and we held his hands as if they were reins. We shuddered at the idea of entering the desert where the river and the forest — …before we came, they were already there. — (Ana de Jesus, in the laundry, ironed, the embers, lucidly, crackled. From time to time she read a few lines of the manuscript left in front of her atop the peaches. She heard them move away without opening the door to the courtyard or running to the window but, in thought, she began to accompany them, to go to their meeting, or even overtake them on the desert path; she folded the clothing, as "with this positive hope that descended on them from above, the nausea of work diminished," or a mantle of sand, the noise she heard was that of footsteps approaching or moving away, she realized she was ironing with Thomas Müntzer's head, his eye sockets burning. She read without stopping, confused by the book the earth began to surround her, she breathed in the fire with delight, lions, prayers, and crowds lingered in Thomas Müntzer's skull, which he kept in his hand and on the ironing board.)

The boat finally moored and, from within, Thomas Müntzer's body emerged. He went over to Saint John of the Cross, who was a man of moderate stature, face grave, venerable, burnished and attractive. On this bank of the river he was sitting by the water's edge. A shadow drew the rest of the body he lacked, so they could talk:

— Nothing satisfies me when I am far from your company. — He put his hand in the water, which was then two hands seemingly severed at the wrists; he wanted to meet Thomas Müntzer — all he had to do was turn his head to see him. — Today, nothing satisfies me when I am far from your company. I went out to the island any number of times until I remained in this place. The crowd has moved away and no one will be able to prevent us from writing, we will penetrate further into the depths. — He had a pleasant manner and conversation. That same day he had reentered the community, after escaping from the prisons of Toledo where he had absconded down a rope.

— In this strange privation I have fallen into... — But when he saw Ana de Jesus leave the house through the trees with his skull in her hands and close to her mouth, and approach him, he leaned over in the position of someone reading:

— Those who feel weak should write to me with friendship; I, in response, will console them. If I make an error, I will abide by a friendly reprimand, in broad daylight and in front of a community, provided they do not subject me to force. But, under no circumstances, will I accept being criticized or judged without sufficient testimony, behind closed doors. Through my actions, I intend to improve the teaching of the evangelical preachers, as well as not scorn our brethren from the Church of Rome who are heavily burdened.

I want to demonstrate the justice of my principles; it would please me, if in your ignorance it does not seem ridiculous to you, it would please me, then, to be publicly confronted by my adversaries in front of men of all countries and all beliefs.

That's what I was like — said Thomas Müntzer. The weather had changed so completely that they seemed to be in another day; fog had fallen over the river, although without obscuring the visibility of the banks; it was cold but did not raise goosebumps, Thomas Müntzer studied Saint John of the Cross's face through the fog, his face moved smiling and uneven in the mist. — "But it is night." — No, it isn't night — replied Thomas Müntzer who had never read what Saint John of the Cross had written. — It is only the weather, which has changed unexpectedly: the temperature fell and condensation hovers over the river, rising over the mountaintops. My battle is already lost, I can throw my severed head into the river. — They watched Thomas Müntzer's head glide in the water; fish described swift circuits around it, the shadow had been completely lost when the sun went away; its motion produced a white foam that, at a certain point, taken by the wind, fell onto the banks of the river, disappearing in the place where it is said what the dark night consists of and how necessary it is to pass through it.

Place 6 —

Müntzer (Thomas), founder of the Anabaptist sect, born in Stolberg, beheaded in Mühlhausen, Thuringia, following the Battle of Franken-hausen (1490-1525), at the age of thirty-five, he took his place in the procession. He had lost sight of Saint John of the Cross, and everyone was speaking softly.

At the door to the house, Ana de Jesus kept her hands on her dress and tried to listen to the rustling of the voices   which moved away. Abruptly, the continuation of the river and the boat — the desert, no one knew what it was: desert, that which pertains to the desert, that which has the characteristics of the desert.

Uninhabited, arid place, deserted, abandoned, desolate stopovers; lowlands, inaccessible to the damp winds blowing in from the sea and subjected to a perpetual drought. Resulting in the total absence of trees and other plants and a drift that forms according to the nature of the winds and erosion (rocky dunes and slopes). A climate subject to sudden changes in temperature, absolute solitude, except in the oases and on the fringes of the desert regions.

Place 7 —

Thomas Müntzer stopped below the balcony where Saint John of the Cross was writing, remembering that it was time to leave. Ana de Jesus closed all the doors and windows, except the one where he was, unmoored the boat tied to the tree, ready to drag it by its towline throughout the unknown length of the journey. John of the Cross sketched a gesture of farewell and stood beside Thomas Müntzer. They looked back and also saw him at the window, arranging several precious objects on the table, including the inkwell and Müntzer's head. Müntzer turned around to say goodbye or retrieve his head. He appeared at the threshold of the door, brought by Ana de Peñalosa.

But John, sleeping or in ecstasy, had fallen onto the table, the threshold of the door had become impassible. He made a movement of farewell and the procession departed, lamenting the one who was absent.

Place 8 —

Always on the verge of writing, Saint John of the Cross walked with them for days and days, without having time to sit down on the ground and write. The place they passed through had been taken by a progressive dryness and the light had acquired the quality of
Bluish light, reminiscence. They hadn't even opened the sacks of provisions, fearing the path would become immobile or dissipate. Before long there was nothing to see, they followed only the horse in front of them and within him John's desire
Always on the verge of writing
he was a desert horse,
Pegasus.
Flying over the sand, and the oases, no other living being was there, aside from him; he moved quickly across the vast yellow expanse, he sought its bounds; but his own velocity seemed to create space and he had never put his hooves down where the desert ends. He knew he had hooves, a muzzle, eyes, a tail; but he had also never seen his entire body. In the desert, the rain that fell was immediately absorbed. To survive, he had learned to drink in the air, away from the seeps of water that did not exist and in which he could not see himself.
Nonetheless,
he had often witnessed the violent atmospheric disturbances

storm,

thunderbolt,

roaring,

lightning

always lying down in the same place: close to the dunes, drifts formed according to the nature of erosion and the winds. He was lying on the sand, a persistent order spoke to him about his closed wings:

— Try and keep in mind that even though visions or words brought by the storm may be true, they can, despite everything, deceive.

During the storm, a woman and living being sat down on the sandy ground behind the horse; the whole length of her legs was covered by a long skirt, her bust on a pedestal of black or slate stone. With the first flash of lightning, her skirt opened up into a rose: the petals multiplied, as numerous as the grains of sand in the desert. Man must relinquish power and woman must relinquish man, thought the woman who was cooking on the sand and was a master in the art of thinking; a thought that passed through the head of the horse who impatiently awaited the storm's manifestations.

The smell of the woman's cooking began to spread out through the space to the fringes of the desert. Teas, vegetables, grains, charred meats.

As she cooked on the grill, the master in the art of thinking experienced the feeling of being a rose, of continually opening up into petals and perfumes, of being the lady where the monstrous hunger ends, and of the ability to quickly bear children, take them out from under her skirt, only a moment between making love and producing children.

It is a mirage, was the idea that came into the horse's forehead. But when a thunderclap echoed, as if his hooves were pounding in the distance, the woman continued to disassemble into roses. Made only of petals, her skirt had an impressive color and a desert perfume. The horse, when the lightning bolt that burned the petals struck, called the lady the lady of the roses, the perfume the desert perfume, and the food that the woman prepared everything and nothing.

Giving them these names was a way to traverse the sky.

Wind rose up, which the woman found very aggressive; night was slow to come, the closed darkness she would like to walk in at the horse's side; she had not anticipated what the desert night would be like, if there would be stars, whispers, perfumes, any brightness. Since the sand wasn't fragrant, she imagined the perfumes of Pegasus's body, especially those exuded by his hooves, which surpassed anything she might presume of flowers.

When night fell, the woman walked at the horse's side, Müntzer and Saint John of the Cross were near but invisible. The woman was sweet but tough.

— Think — Pegasus said to the woman. — So that I always know where you are. — The woman lowered her eyes. According to the mirage, the horse was submerged in the water interrogating his hooves and, when he lifted his white muzzle,   He remembered a text written on a yellowed paper according to the mirage. The woman understood that she could see the horse's thoughts, other thoughts, and she lowered her eyes until they closed:

supper
is the end
of the day's
work
and the beginning
of the night's
rest.
Houseless,
Saint John of the Cross
and Thomas Müntzer
ate
in the middle of the desert.
They knew
there was going to be
a battle.
The horse
had already reached
their side.

Full of life, he ran around them. Always surrounding them, he placed
his hooves firmly on the ground, lifted up into the air. Thus flying,
Pegasus slept, his horse's eyes closed.
Saint John of the Cross,
eating what Ana de Jesus had prepared,
looked at his dream in the nearby oasis,
the place of the book. He had nothing to write with, the words moved
in front of his hand (they did not pass to the paper). He made an
impatient movement on the sand, closed his fist. The shadow lowered

over Thomas Müntzer's body

the sleeping horse had become completely immobile in the air. John wrote upon the sand, kneeling, his body facing forward, four hooves and his hand writing

That night,

as was its habit,

the nearest oasis

slowly cooled off; the fire of the book hovered over sand's surface, the hooves of battle horses, brothers to Pegasus, could be heard, if anyone wanted to apply an ear. Pegasus was still sleeping in the dream although he was actually keeping watch over John and Thomas Müntzer and that very secret.

But John of the Cross wrote without hands, without a pen, and without a book, his severed finger touching every flame; the trotting of the horses interrupted Thomas Müntzer's dinner

the shadow of his head meditated

(in the place where she had prepared the food, the woman's face was full of tears; she had seen Pegasus wake up and, suspended at the point where he had risen up to guard the writing of memory; he ate time, finished the dinner Thomas Müntzer had interrupted).

Ana de Jesus had opened her eyes in astonishment.

Pegasus, the horse, buried himself in the sand, waiting for someone who knew how to write to come and watch over him. While he had been suspended and moved through the air he had felt a blow on his neck, on his right side, beneath his mane; he certainly wasn't going to die but he sensed that immobility, contact with the sand, and the book's living flame could, before the following morning, cure him.

The writing
was the voices
in chorus
of thirty thousand peasants
who after abolishing the judges
made their way toward the massacre of Frankenhausen
and whose footprints were lost in the desert

A polar cold had invaded the battlefield; the peasants advanced slowly, their hands frozen on the tools they usually used to work the earth. A rider suddenly appeared among them, announced the defeat and the massacre telling them that, with such cold weather, those sitting in the middle of the horses' blood would win

the text immersed in the horses' blood tells of the adventure in the desert and how it liberated the mind from all spiritual imperfections and all earthly desires. It entered into that inner darkness where sensitive and invisible things can be penetrated through the snow, supported only by the ascent and ascending.

That is why I call it a stairway and secret because its steps and articles are secret, hidden to all sensitivity and understanding. That is why he says he went in disguise   the bear was born from the snow, from a drop of blood that fell from the neck of Pegasus the horse. In the white and blue reflection he walked fearfully, but with apparent calm; it is a voice, nothing more than a voice, but he heard Müntzer preach; he wanted to look for the writing to know exactly what was in his preaching. He ended up writing on the page of the manuscript, the

bear attentive and sitting at his side. Saint John of the Cross's heart
transcended the text, was buried in the fur of the bear
who said
this is the month I most love; it is the last month of the year. I wanted
to write the Rules
there are four yellowed pages
at my side
on a tiny branch
the paper was lying on Saint John of the Cross's open book
the *Living Flame* and I read, in the middle of the page, that union is
predicated on likeness
those who resemble one another come together
like is known by like.
I continue,
looking around
what I just read
and the moment arrives when I say
the fecundity of the gift is the gift's only retribution
it seems to me, before anything else, that the rules should rest on their
own
that is
that is
that they should be able to remain sleeping,
and be taken as a dream.   Watched by
Saint John of the Cross, Heart of the Bear sat down on the ice. He was
only a drop of blood from Pegasus the horse and he became larger than
him, heavier. He was and was not related to him, he who haunted the
polar and desert regions; all the animals stopped walking, a great silence

spread out through the cold areas and invaded their ears. (The battle came, was coming.) He ended up choosing the ice, leaving through the sand to call Pegasus. He hoped to be able to cross the river that had also frozen. But the crowd of indistinct forms assembled in front of him did not move. Much time passed and they were still in the same place; fascinated by the ground that had opened up cracks from which murmurs emerged. He then made a detour and advancing between trees and walls that were also frozen, at a certain point he did not know where he was and he clawed at his forehead to remember.

When he reached the polar regions he lay down on the snow and, the next morning, was born there; he was large, heavy as a heart without a body and soon the hunters and other animals gave him the name Heart of the Bear. Knowing he had to live in the ice and water, he made a tall man of petrified snow and, for the top, chose a scarecrow; he borrowed wholly from his fur and from colors that scarcely existed; but he learned to work with them in such a way that the rainbow and, more than anything, the color green, could be glimpsed within the white.

Thomas Müntzer did not lose sight of him lest the river melt, summer returned; seen from a distance he seemed to be the polar expanse itself; he smiled at everything and everyone and his ferocity only became terrible when he was hungry and his smile hung from his tongue; at that moment he spoke, rose up, swung his tail and paws; a shadow was cast in front of him and he ate it; it could've been a dog, a wolf, the head of Thomas Müntzer who had not lost sight of him lest the river melt, summer returned; he fed, he continued smiling and walking rhythmically. Everywhere he walked, he wrested power which was the temperature rising,

and which was the greatest danger
for the frozen regions.

On the night he was going to eat the shadow of Müntzer's head, he
smiled enigmatically, and howled with hunger all night.

Place 9 —

As the bear intoned the Rules' adumbrations, Ana de Jesus, in his
arms, thought about Pegasus, Copernicus, and Giordano Bruno. She
dreamed: through the half-open door, she had caught Copernicus
meditating. It was the end of the day, the sun had come in through the
window and through the window it had left. "And the Sun lies in the
middle of it all," thought Copernicus. She dreamed; she knew it was
so but, at that moment, she saw it was so; it made itself known to her
tentatively, as if the ideas had slipped inside the house and were the
last light crowning the furniture; she did not take her eyes off the jar
of water sitting on the windowsill; it seemed as if everything revolved
around the Sun, bright open heart; when she came back to herself,
the soup was steaming on the plate and the monks were silent with
their clasped hands resting on the tray.

Place 10 —

She had let herself be taken by sleep, the hot wind of the desert had
put out the fire
the stars rose in flight over the frozen expanse

Ana de Jesus lost herself in Giordano Bruno, and in the infinity of space.

Giordano Bruno, he of prodigious memory, saw his forehead reflected in the fire and remembered all the seconds, all the minutes, all the hours, all the years of his life; even more intensely, he remembered the texts he had read and the authors who had granted him that pleasure; then he sensed a rising flame would split his forehead in two

but in both parts he remembered that the universe is infinite, populated by thousands of systems with their planets and their sun.

Place 11 —

If she dreamed, she dreamed of forests, and houses born from forests; and shaped like forests. The cities had been destroyed or perhaps had never existed. Heart of the Bear became a permanent place of representations, sensations, perceptions, images, icons, and myths; she had become accustomed to reading texts and seeing animals in him. His enormous, fragile paw had eyes and claws when he wrote on the ground or on paper. A great pleasure rose up from the battle and he followed it with his writing, watching.

What he most loved was the death of the peasants whom he buried every night in solitary places; separating the words

mountains

and rivers

and heads

and punishments.

Upon each grave Heart of the Bear placed a stone where John of the

Cross wrote the epitaph:

this is me, and I am him.

Opening the book, seeing the blank page, picking up any instrument that writes is a great consolation. I believe there is snow under the page, and the heat of the desert hovers around, the sand falls in the clepsydra without the end of this day even being visible or predicted from afar; I gather an infinite sadness from the dead, I collect and arrange its members, and gather them. From a distance I see Saint John of the Cross meditating, the Sun of Copernicus striking his eyes and capturing Müntzer's head between its hands. From time to time Saint John of the Cross kisses his mouth with the lips he uses to pray and I sense that one of his words will slide down the throat of Müntzer who, in this battle, became dust.

Place 12 —

As he became dust, Thomas Müntzer heard the trampling of the horses farther and farther away. He had never died before. He was aware that Pegasus was moving away.

Neither John of the Cross nor Ana de Peñalosa stopped him, grasping his white mane. He turned toward Heart of the Bear but Pegasus's longing was so acute that the bear remained what at the beginning he had always been — an animal that had come from the polar regions. John of the Cross, motionless, continued meditating.

He seemed so absent, with his hand fallen onto the sand,

so absent trying to perceive the voices to which he was listening for the book, so absent with his closed eyes open,

so absent with his mouth penetrated by silence
that Müntzer forgot his own name, when he had been born and, worst
of all, the reason he was going to die.

But John of the Cross appeared to be sleeping (he had never been
absent). He began to write the bear, walking around him, and the last
words he said
take him in your paws
let us go into exile.
Ana de Peñalosa and Ana de Jesus did not sleep for a moment that
night. They wore the dresses that best expressed them; they waited
sitting down, facing one another, always seeing what happened in the
same mirror. They had the impression of walking through time, space
was nothing; they left the house, the window, the river, the desert, the
forest, the polar regions, and concentrated on the word.

Heart of the Bear illuminated the way, in front of them, always with
Thomas Müntzer lying across his paws.
Ageless,
Ana de Peñalosa,
grew to be very old.
She was astonished by the dust
that the bear carried
in his arms,
she did not know
which side
his hands,
his arms,
or his head were on;
she wanted

to give birth to
an entire body
and asked her son,
John,
to let her stop.
Her son,
John,
did not wonder
at her request
and,
one night,
Ana de Peñalosa
gathered the dust
of Müntzer's body.

Place 13 —

I do not know, at this moment, why he would be called the Eudes
Star; but, always thinking about Müntzer and the place his head left
behind, I began to see him behind the page (I myself writing and
burdened by the power of writing) with a star on top of his shoulders,
or rather, with a source of divergent light atop the continuation of his
neck. Now he walks with us always and the place where he can be
found changes with the hours of the night, in the procession; strangely,
he shines the most during the day, oscillating his profuse brightness.
He leans over the bear's shoulders and the star's radiance is cast onto
his claws, which hold Müntzer. Ana de Jesus worries because she still

doesn't know how he, with this featureless light, will eat and arrive at a precise point of exile.

(Where, writing the text, he landed, murmured to himself, "ora pro nobis.")

He put the *Living Flame* on the *Dark Night* and the *Dark Night* on the *Spiritual Canticle*; he wrote Müntzer's open letter, Müntzer who the bear, in front of him, carried in his paws; he wrote a new book, *The Book of Communities*, unknown in his Complete Works.

Müntzer praised the bear's hands:

"hand of stone, meditative, you could belong to Saint John of the Cross"

he praised the night:

"it is at night that he makes contact with the light, when sleeping (deeply), he is dead to himself. But, awake and alive, he is in reach of that which dies, when he sleeps deeply. In wakefulness, he makes contact with that which is sleeping."

Ana de Jesus, Ana de Peñalosa, Saint John of the Cross followed the bear; forced to walk upright because of Müntzer who, dead and sleeping, he carried in his paws, he looked at the trees laden with ice, at his height, and did not eat their bright fruit

abandoned text, he often picked it up.

Heart of the Bear now had hands

John of the Cross counted the crystal leaves.

They say this text

They say the bear

They say this text suffers for having been abandoned.

They say this text was not made,

they say this written text is abandoned.

They say it must be seen, it must be seen.

The text was not made, Saint John of the Cross's face came to an end. Saint John of the Cross lifted his other face, sat down where there was room; he began to embroider words with his finger on Müntzer's incomplete body.

Ana de Peñalosa looked at her two sons, read the writing that covered the back of the headless one. Rapid, astonished sounds came from his breathing, the wind that had accompanied them since the desert could be heard.

Ana de Peñalosa lay back, Müntzer's head was born from her legs, adult, the eyes scarcely unclosed. Having been found, the body stood up and said goodbye to the bear who, like a bear, had moved far away. Ana de Peñalosa began to say in a melodic, enamored voice

—They cut off Thomas Müntzer's head. My son, Thomas de Peñalosa. He may have been born in 1488 but I don't remember how he was born. He was the founder of this socio-religious reform. His intellectual training was excellent. He studied the German mystics of the fourteenth century.

He followed Luther and abandoned him.

In Zwickau, where he was a minister, he met enlightened people, who did not acknowledge any differences between inspirations, prophecies, revelations, and the Scripture.

My son was very impressed. He became a good preacher. Peasants and artisans listened to him because the economic conditions had created a deep discontent. When he attacked the opulence of the Church and the rich, they cast him from his parish. He fled to Bohemia, where he published a Manifesto in which he considered himself an instrument to purify the earth and the Church. But they were quick to cast him out of Prague as well. He wandered through central Germany for almost two years.

Then, for several months, he was the parish priest of Allstedt. At that time, he made several liturgical reforms. He wed.

In the winter of 1523-1524, he founded the League of the Elect, to carry out the program of the Prague Manifesto.

His preaching in the presence of Princes John and Frederick of Saxony provoked a tension so unbearable that, feeling himself in danger, he abandoned Allstedt. He returned to wandering for several months. He stopped in Mülhausen in February 1525. My son Thomas then devoted himself, with all his prestige, to the peasant revolt that spread through Thuringia. He drafted the Letter stating their demands.

During the battle of Frankenhausen, on May 15, 1525, the peasants were finally defeated by the Lords. My captured, imprisoned, and tortured son had to declare that he recognized the errors of which they accused him and he was beheaded on May 27, 1525.

The night of the desert ended (but had it really ended?), a long time passed (and even years) before the night of exile began. A period of calm interspersed with unexpectedly painful moments, which were like harbingers and messengers from the future night of the spirit.

Ana de Peñalosa returned to the house with only one room and only one window. Saint John of the Cross and Thomas Müntzer went into the shadows and abandoned her.

Place 14 —

But sometimes, brought by the river, they moored at the small harbor near the courtyard and she came to speak to them from inside the house, which had no interior, nor exterior.

what news of exile?

what atrocious marvels of the journey?

how had his preaching gone in the presence of Princes John and Frederick of Saxony?

how had he been captured, imprisoned, and tortured?

how had he escaped from the prisons of Toledo?

how goes the book?

how goes the battle?

had they staunched the blood of Pegasus the horse?

would Heart of the Bear return?

who will not be sad to have survived?

She laid her head on her arms, John and Thomas Müntzer put the same hand on her shoulder and their voices could be heard entering the house amidst the noise of the water oscillating around the boat.

The window of Ana de Peñalosa's room was still illuminated; they raised their heads; they looked at the lamplight which could be seen, even though the sun was out; as was his habit, John of the Cross meditated that he was going describe it; that stopping, keeping his hand in exile, would be impossible.

He touched the nape of his neck fearfully. Ana de Peñalosa was certain that he, in the nape of his neck, had already guessed a word. He turned his body slightly, put his fingers flat on the page

John's eyes filled   ; where he saw the words: "Good morning, author of the battle," for Müntzer was written: "Good morning, mother."

She wanted to tell them how they had been born, but the afternoon had ended, time stopped on the boat.

Thomas Müntzer lowered his head

John of the Cross unmoored the boat

and she said how did his preaching go in the presence of Lords John and Frederick of Saxony?

Place 15 —

Following those unexpected visits, Ana de Peñalosa began to write a letter she called "Text Submitted to the Sun"; she wrote slowly, with a carefully drawn handwriting that was part of the square of writing. Of the text

       bathed by the sun

          because she dedicated herself to this work regularly, at the same time, in the same place, and in almost the same position, vocables and certain expressions began to stand out, which she questioned with her meditative thinking: "on the abandoned plain," "blindly at the lost skies," "only son." She sounded out the text to herself, her mouth almost closed and, at times, lifted her head to the open window, believing that the beating of words and oars was approaching. She took a sip of water, returned to the vibration of her hushed murmur; and, as she felt an increasingly acute pain from not being able to accompany them into exile, she wrote to her interlocutor: "If I were to die now." Friedrich N. received the letter.

Place 16 —

Zarathustra was the place he inhabited and the cat he possessed. At the edge of the desk he had a book that loosed an anathema upon him, Friedrich N. He opened its pages and submerged his face. He also had Ana de Peñalosa's writing and many more papers, among which it had been

said

that *The Book of Communities*

should include Nietzsche

but I believe that, in the future,

it will become difficult to write

because Nietzsche is a man

of the book. Black mustache,

hair. Those capillary adornments

stop me from proceeding.

I see his eyes smashed between

his mustache and his forehead.

I could only let myself be taken

by his eyes if they were

deep. Lewis Carroll.

I place my hand in his eye sockets.

My hand enters and floats:

it is the river that Saint John of

the Cross and Thomas Müntzer

descend in their boat.

N. calls them and they disappear,

meditative.

N. undresses, is nude, only
hair, mustache, pubic
hair. He receives a robe from
Ana de Peñalosa's hands. He covers
himself with it. In front of the
mirror he submits to a
mustache trim and a haircut, they
pass a blade over his skull which
is now completely bald.
He looks at me and tells me
I may begin to write. I thank him for
his compassion and sit down in
front of him studying the
robe, the white of the book and
the boundless white. I cannot imagine
the tone of his voice, nor the character
of his writing. That stiff body
is impenetrable and it will
ultimately repel me. I walk
around him, I greet him, I hit him in
the face. He takes me by the hand
unangered, unshakeable in his
compassion. He opens one of his
books and the two of us copy what
is written there, as if it were a text
still unwritten. I practice,
the heat of his hand doesn't distract
me from what we're doing. I stare

into his eyes and know I won't be
able to even utter their color. I feel
powerful and, at the same time, sleepy.
I fall asleep on his hand, but in that
sleep I still feel its impetus,
searching for the place where
it is going

a cave with stained glass windows in the depths from which different
sounds emerged and spread out

silence could be heard in contrast with the lapping water, the skeleton
of a bird had landed on the boat's stern and had immediately grown
feathers and become the body of a living bird.

We began to look at him intently and I remembered to call him
Friedrich N. so he wouldn't abandon my sons. He lifted his wings and
I saw his haughty eyes, which occupied his entire head, where there
was no longer forehead. His cat was nearby, fur bristling, and its aureole
of greenery rose into the air toward the cave's entrance. I gazed at the
bird's eyes. I smiled. John leapt into the boat, began rowing with his
hand immersed in the water. The bird took flight and swooped down
over the bow, reuniting us for the birth of exile.

Place 17 —

When Ana de Peñalosa heard that Friedrich N. had received her letter
she thought again about Saint John of the Cross and Thomas Müntzer.
The cat had lain down on her lap for a few moments because,
soon,

the fire of the day

would be consumed.

In the caves where they were living, Saint John of the Cross and Thomas Müntzer had become unaffected by the persecutions: water circulated at the opening and the boat moored to the rock plunged its seasoned hull into the vibrations of thought.

The bird circled around John. He landed on his hand and an intense cold rose in the water, covered it with frozen particles — the thicknesses of the texts were looking at one another.

> It is a glacial day. We haven't given up:
> we are still alive. I must make
> an effort to write. What pleasure
> in our hands; we warm our fingers
> to write.
> This cold day can only be compared
> to one other day.

Place 18 —

I read a text and I cover it with my own text, which I sketch at the top of the page but which casts its written shadow over the entire printed surface. This textual overlap comes from my eyes, it seems to me as though a thin cloth floats between my eyes and my hand and ends up covering like a net, a cloud, what has already been written. My text is completely transparent and I perceive the topography of the first words. I concentrate on Saint John of the Cross when the text speaks of Friedrich N.

he left the prow of the boat; his small body walks here; he pierces them with his bright-sharp eyes; he roams freely in the garden; he settles on the plants that Ana de Peñalosa watered this morning.

They then sat down near each other, a text on their knees, the breeze descended and impelled the words to the next body. Ana de Peñalosa did not have a book, she had thrust the needle into the fabric and contemplated the wandering of the fish

I embroider and think I know how to embroider; I don't know how I made this association but shortly thereafter I reflect. Knowing and seeing. I can choose the colors, I chose the colors of the threads which are reddish-pink and red, and I chose the color of the fabric, brown — which, for me, is the color of the community's reformulation. What I embroider is an insect, I feel the urge to classify it, know its name and I am, for a few moments, sojourning within in the vast animal kingdom. A finger on the thread, I also fasten my eyes upon the fabric; I find that I see an expansive panorama, my eyes fixed on the velvety brown seem to look all around; I lift the needle from the felt, to me the movement seems similar to that of writing, but inverse.

It was not I who traced this design I embroider but, making my way along it with the needle, I reconstruct the birth of the act of drawing; I lose the notion of time slightly as if my embroidery had come from an archive and was about to disappear within it. I situate myself historically alongside other hands that embroidered fabrics from another era. I wonder, when they find it, what meaning they will ascribe to the insect I encountered today. I pass from writing to embroidery, translating as if both were my speech; at times, I even forget I'm embroidering, in such a way that my fingers become dexterous and my thinking, reflected in the embroidery, a thought. With a book is written another book. As a book is vegetal.

When the clock at the entrance fell out of step and the golden box filled with hours and the shudderings of sound, I realize it is time to change colors on the surface where I'm working. My hands close to my eyes, I notice, for the first time, the skin resting on my bones. She asked herself: "Will they come with someone?" "Will they bring someone?" She was then certain that they would bring someone and she arranged her hair for Nietzsche.

Place 19 —

Resting at the edge of the lake, she ended up smiling; someone had passed by like an illusion, in a boat and rowing — a shadow still unmet; I heard the sound of the water and the oars thrusting. She startled, would it be Nietzsche?; the same boat passed by again. She looked forward at the shadow's solidity, particularly his head, where only his hair could be made out. She heard the sound of his voice: "You the semi-living who surround me, and enclose me in a subterranean solitude, in the speechlessness and cold of the tomb; you, who condemn me to lead a life it would be better to call death, you will see me again, one day. After death I shall have my revenge: we know how to return, we, the premature. It is one of our secrets. I shall return alive, more alive than ever."

She moved with him toward the house, through the thick silence that had followed. But it was a child's shadow: — Where do you come

from? From the body. From the place of memories and vibrations. — I
don't know what you mean — I have memories I don't remember:
they are the most beautiful ones; the vicissitudes of ideas and systems
affect me more tragically than the vicissitudes of real life. — They sat
down leaning against one another. Then, Friedrich N. lay down on
Ana de Peñalosa's lap, ready to fall sleep

(I speak to myself and hear my voice resonating like that of a moribund. With you, dear voice, whose breath delivers me the last memories
of any human happiness, with you, let me speak a minute longer. Is it
you I hear, my voice? My future, which I will reach if they give me
enough time…)

for that night.

She did not marvel when she saw the child sputter fire. She left him
to go make dinner. On her way, she lit all the lamps in the great hall.
Leaning out the window, she looked at them in the courtyard. Without
any light, they were still writing: "It is the radiant night. There will not
be many nights like this."

But those nights were repeated until her old age, which began on
that day.

Place 20 —

To keep her company on the long nights when they did not come
to see her, Ana de Peñalosa adopted a red and reddish-pink fish who
retraced different paths in the water, already overcome by the spirit of
dispossession in light of everything capable of disturbing his serenity.
Ana de Peñalosa named him "reddish-pink fish," or Suso. She examined

him carefully during forgotten hours: his scales, the pink and the red. When she had spent a long time observing him and his itinerary, she saw the beginning of a line appear from his tail, like pearls. Like the beginning of a written work, she thought. But writing doesn't let itself be characterized by only one comparison. This was what was written and quickly vanished: when, so many nights ago, I arrived at this house, I found a tomb covered with sage and other plants; here lies the friend of a man. Around the stone was a vast expanse of grass. Eckhart had not met Ana de Peñalosa. But Ana de Peñalosa had met him on the night when, embroidering next to Suso the fish, she had seen his sermons penetrate the water drop by drop, written in the undulations of the aquarium. It had been a cadenced writing, guided by the fish and the evolution of the shells: all living beings are pure nothingness.

Place 21 —

During the gentle time of her old age she had never forgotten
the portrait
of the adult
Friedrich Nietzsche
as a child.
His straight, receding hair was his forehead's place of remembrance. Broad forehead, short, brushed hair, protruding cheekbones. His abundant mustache fallen, the odd cut of his face. His musical voice; his slow speech; his prudent and meditative walk. His intent eyes betrayed the painful work of his thinking. They were, at the same time, the eyes of a fanatic, a keen observer, and a posthumous.

As she was cooking dinner, she meditated that she envisioned a living writing she could take for an encounter. Meditating, she justified her own desire for solitude

solitude is nothing more than the safeguard of writing when the desire arises.

Solitude is the defense of the text.

Sitting solitarily in front of Nietzsche, she observed him, at night: "It is night, the hour when all the welling springs speak more loudly.

It is night: the hour when all the songs of those who love awaken.

But being surrounded by the light is my solitude.

But I live in my own light, I drink the flames that escape from me."

Place 22 —

Looking at the windowpane, she saw herself portrayed in it. Through an optical illusion, the two of them were outside the house; on the opposite side of the river, where there is a large knot of ancient, multicolored trees.

The one in the center stood out, red — amidst them all lay the red; then, sunken in a filigree of green foliage, a white shrub; and farther away, always among the multitonal green, pink and yellow shrubs.

— If you have come to die, come die in my room. — Entering into ecstasy   the delicious mornings   serenaded by the equilibrium of the mornings

it is a young woman's bed
with room for

a single body;
it is the time of darkness:
all day the sun remains
beyond the horizon;
during that time,
the temperature falls
slowly,
without stopping.
If my sons come,
if I hear the beating of oars,
I will go down to the garden
and tell them:
someone is dying,
and doesn't want to see anyone.

He had the habit, on his walks, of burning in a fragment of time. Stroking the tender shrubs — those that haven't yet grown; when the wind blew and it was autumn, the leaves moved quickly, evoking the sound of footsteps, or an eagle. The cold in his hands always astonished him and he stopped to write a few aphorisms, as if he washed them; that morning (just before noon) he would take an unknown path. The sun, that sun, known, went away and came back. Shortsightedly, he was almost out of ink and he had to select and condense his thoughts. He stretched out on the ground, and a shaft of sun scorched him with its subdued brightness. The tops of the trees, always different, filtered the sharpness of the return.

Ana de Peñalosa had not stopped smiling — The Eternal Return — he heard her say without speaking.

But, at midmorning, there was a perfidious animal, with claws; it devoured the insects and the words, which it set down further away, unrecognizable and transformed; its language simulated a page covered with mysterious hieroglyphs constantly shifting sign and meaning. In its shadow, Nietzsche had been invaded by the terror of being another animal and he couldn't get up from the ground, his spine immobilized — by the weight of the rings and the multiplicity of legs that he did not, logically, know how to use. A thick terror closed his eyes and his hand could not even find the remnants of the writing on the surface. The earth and the light decomposed, chewed by steely teeth lacking a face with a name.

— Is that Nietzsche? — The beast lay its head on her chest; their eyes were extremely close.

(Later, Ana de Peñalosa had completely forgotten what she thought she had seen in that gaze and not even the meditative silence of Saint John of the Cross had made her remember it. Vivid and imperceptible letters.)

— What keeps my sons on their islands? It is night. It is night. It is night.

Friedrich Nietzsche lying on my chest frightens me. The wind blows, the moon shines, O my distant, distant sons, why are you not here?

But today, loving Nietzsche so much, there is an obstacle to this evocation. The silence announces immobility and night, it does not obscure; I drift on a rhythm of texts,

my bare arm lying on the page,

dark and full,

still unaged.

Still unwritten is our future; in my arms, Nietzsche pierces our future with his blind eyes; he sees what is.

The fear that I would be unable to be alone, which threaded through all my Easter days and perverted their potential happiness, has disappeared. I feel as if I splinter melodiously in search of my multiple pleasures (the greatest one — that of the body's sensitivity). It always begins in my eyes, which distribute subjects for meditation to the other senses.

As Friedrich Nietzsche dies, Suso the fish winds through my aquarium, the aquarium was uninhabited; half full of water; our thinking blew across the surface

my dear, distant sons, do not return while Friedrich Nietzsche does not die

Your mother, who also writes,

Ana de Peñalosa

I disappear from this place. My desires lead me to the new territory, to the house whose entrances have no doors, and the windows not even a pane of glass. A distinct brightness suffuses the entire space — in the most distant corner, shadow is still light.

I am merely a body disrobed. I turn to the aquarium where Suso the fish is

and where water, earth, fire, air cannot be distinguished.

(At the beginning of the fourteenth century a famous Dominican by the name of Suso lived in Suabia. He had a subtle intelligence like his Meister Eckhart of Cologne.)

I lower my eyes over Nietzsche's mouth, which is still lying on my chest

it is the fish's grave,

the fish will die at the bottom of the aquarium but the water and fire, dividing themselves, allowed me to see a space full of trees where his fins circulate through beds of leaves, dry branches, deeply marked stones.

He lives with his spirit and his solitude, of which he has not tired for ten years:

always walking, they stumbled upon a deep pit, a kind of amphitheater where young men and women were sitting. Among those who were naked there was a silken body, with gently sloping breasts that reminded him of a harp in full repose. The night, not yet fully ended, was reflected in the hole; gradually, they all undressed — Nietzsche, Saint John of the Cross, Thomas Müntzer, and she herself, Ana de Peñalosa. In their complete immobility, they began to hear the footsteps of those who were approaching. A sudden paralysis took hold of Nietzsche's sex and heads lit up in the treetops. Truthfully, Ana de Peñalosa did not know what awaited her. The text had just been completed and had fallen at the feet of Saint John of the Cross. A drift of pigs advanced into the clearing, the bodies of the naked young women had taken on a precise luminosity. Where there was no longer any need for speech, Nietzsche agonized. Moved, Ana de Peñalosa touched a pig brought him home

to the place where she had slept

if she could be rhythm

she would leave home,

with the house,

tonight.

Tonight, the pig ate F. Nietzsche, contradicting "pearls should not be cast before swine."

When he understood it was time to return, he raised his snout from
Ana de Peñalosa's lap,
over which he meditated
and asked
where to?
Nietzsche leaned over the river that ran incessantly with a vibrant
appearance.
THERE, she answered him. If you dare.
where? repeated Nietzsche
acquainted with rivers, shadows, choirs, texts, courtyards, names, the
geographical and genealogical particularities inhabiting Ana de Peñalosa's house
THERE, repeated the writing that had been imprinted on the water
with the back of a horse,
the paws of a bear,
large scales,
the smell of a pig,
and a delicious beating of oars
She moved all the books, notebooks, and papers to the right. She
had never felt so quietly alone, it was strange that that strange Ana de
Peñalosa had the monk Eckhart — the Pig — in her room. Not a
compilation of the Sermons

> Quasi stella matutina in medio
> nebulae et quasi luna plena in
> diebus suis lucet et quasi sol
> refulgens, sic iste refulsit

not the *Book of Consolation,*
nor the *Treatises,*
but bear, woman, blood, rose
if I concentrate on a fragment of time
not today, or tomorrow
but if I concentrate on a fragment of time,
now,
that fragment will reveal all time.

Place 23 —

This was how Ana de Peñalosa read this writing and she could only
see it through lace, viscera of her body; she had awoken at dawn; at
that dawn's first light she had had the following dream:

> it was dawn, I left an immense unknown place with
> Sister Inés and
> a very young daughter of mine, dressed in black
> (her face also hidden by a veil covered with precious
> stones. The two of us will lead the girl to a place)
> Sister Inés wept and said: This world is ending.
> I tried to console her, saying certainly a new world
> is beginning.
> In that place's silent garden, a crowd of people were
> waiting for alms. I found myself then in the midst of
> those people and, like the poor, a half hour of time
> was doled out to me.

The haloed neck of the pig emerged slowly — a pig of average corpulence gathered the pages of text scattered on the ground and devoured them at the table only when a perennial admiration and the feeling that everything was present became the daily climate in which Ana de Peñalosa lived. He no longer left the garden and every morning he bent his snout toward the river, waiting for the newly arrived: "Why have we no common love," he asked Ana de Peñalosa, "let us have a common love," he seemed to tell Ana de Peñalosa.

Stealthily, the small dog named Maya left for the courtyard, behind the pig. Dawn came to an end and the river ran with the appearance of a stream of clear and unthinkable water. The pig stopped for a few moments reflecting on Maya; in the place from which she had come there were no true cities — the country was not dominated by any urban center and each small community had invented its own desired form of worship; he stopped, his eyes fixed on a small butterfly that was ecru, and dead: a butterfly that had died a natural death.

When she lost all her memory, she never again knew how to make use of her mobility. She reached that state in the aviary; birds landed all over her body and covered her with feathers. She slowly recovered her sight; her pace had become increasingly leaden (or cadenced), such that she was able to move without sensing a single bird. During the moments when she was completely blind and her body lost its sensitivity, she concentrated on the light, which she located with her black and white nose.

this people's decline followed their golden age, almost without transition

they attributed their downfall to epidemics

in the neighboring regions, a rapid

succession of different civilizations sprang up

they attributed their downfall to an invader from the North

or

to popular rebellions against the priests, whose priesthood was oppres-
sive, as well as powerful

to our minds, this decline is incomprehensible. It rained on the small
temples submerged and invaded by the forest. The most beautiful
rainy day had arrived; never, until this day, had she discovered the
rain's latent thinking,

its sonority,

its shadow.

It did not stop raining for a long time. There, it was surprising how the
rain fell, suddenly, or announcing itself with a dense darkening; on the
cemented side of the courtyard, the persistence of all that water caused a
greenish hue to emerge, which did not exist in any part of the temple,

which was peopled with statues

(Saint John of the Cross, Nietzsche, Eckhart, Thomas Müntzer) and
had been erected on the plateau where, every day, they put the beating
heart plucked from a sacrifice

so it could be taken to the god Sun,

so the Sun would rise.   Nietzsche left the room where he had
agonized unendingly; he had forgotten he was moribund when he
heard the grunting, he had gone to the kitchen to eat some of the
leftover food, he had seen the pig turn his back to the river running
rough with wind. He did not feel the rain fall (pour), he only saw
an aura form around the pig's ears — a mane or an incipient solar
corona. Looking up, he encountered an enormous domed vault, and
teeth (when he abandoned the men of a certain appearance he found

a pig; the skin of a small dead mammal had been offered to him at his farewell to show him the future, on the long nights when they did not come to see him).

Place 24 —

The small dog named Maya accompanied the pig in the forest; she was following a few steps behind him when Ana de Peñalosa noticed Friedrich Nietzsche's absence and went to consult the genealogical tree of the Brotherhood of the Principal Emptiness. The blessed Müntzer was who she found just before Saint John of the Cross. I always hear the stream that flows tirelessly even amidst the temple ruins.

Sitting where I am, I do not see the water, I only perceive the continuous noise that ceases at a distance; I change places and, through two trees, the rain begins to fall again among the statues, which are now living in the period of time reserved for mental life and cannot be interrupted by any form of work that is not absolutely indispensable.

We sit down to eat on the right side of the temple; after the morning meal there is another meal; but there aren't any more after the evening meal.

At this hour a gong sounded. Saint John of the Cross, Thomas Müntzer, Eckhart, Nietzsche, Maya the dog left in a procession for the Meditation Room and, each of them carrying their own bowl, they crossed the stream wetting their feet and sat down on the protected side of the temple.

The heat of the damp earth permeated the vegetables and rice; a soft volume of voices intoned the Five Meditations on Food.

I don't remember what those Meditations were; only that the rain fell and that I thought about the Sun, absent for so long, as Maya was filled with the incantation of the water, which produced that noise, which shone, which seemed to us to be moving toward the rising of the Sun; reading Maya's desirous eyes, I now remember that the first Meditation was the Pig; he had come among us with a slow walk and Nietzsche's voice could be heard saying and I who thought my books were so gentle. At that moment, the land darkened even further and the pig began to vomit pieces of earth and a dense mass of texts: Nietzsche's hands passed in front of his mouth and handfuls of pearls rolled toward the stream, wholly supplanting the rain.

The second Meditation was Ana de Peñalosa herself. She had come from the forest where, the evening before, she had gathered more than two hundred floral species; she had put them under a large stone, between pages of text; it was hot and either bright or dark, depending on the clouds. Around her, Nietzsche continued to gather more species, the vegetal species were inexhaustible. She lifted the stone and the pages of text still hadn't acquired a floral stiffness. She stood back from the place where she had just left her feces, the stream rushed over them, flies bluish in the shadow and resplendent in the Sun encircled her, lost.

I remembered, I remembered with great difficulty that the third Meditation focused on a reminiscence from my childhood:

> "I was small, I was playing on the beach, the ocean roared and, lifting its haughty back, shook its white foam toward the serene sky. I said to my mother at this moment:
> — What is stronger than the wind? —

— My mother, smiling, looked toward the sky,
and replied:
— A being we do not see is stronger than the sea
we fear. My child, it is God."

At the end of this Meditation, we all had an immensely enigmatic appearance. The expressions I had forgotten were: "what strange strength, what insane furor."

The fourth Meditation took the appearance of that day. We were still in the temple; a sorrow that could not be spoken blew on the wind that had begun to rise; the figure of the pig had gained mass and surrounded us. On the walls circumscribing that enormous space, John's voices vibrated over Nietzsche's mouth: — Arm yourself with your waves and the energy of the elements. Afterward, rest next to an animal: the tiger. — When she heard her son speaking to his lover, Ana de Peñalosa began to embroider a tiger, and decided to give it life.

I then was the fifth Meditation. I did not know where I was amidst the Sun, receiving my meal with you; it rained suddenly, the wind picked up, I moved toward the Sun, it was cool and hot at the same time.

I write, then I read what I write as if I hadn't written it:
It is no longer a river; it is a stream; it no longer runs in an open field but amidst lush vegetation. So many shades of green over the course of the water, John's boat can no longer travel there, there isn't even room for the oars; Maya the dog floats in the water, swims, howls to the Sun with her whole open throat. That same noise remains. I stand up to look because the stream flows below, in a ravine; Maya continues to glide, I finally capture the green when her body is hidden.

Nietzsche and I should not have named the little dog Maya. She is, among us, a vanished civilization.

Place 25 —

For days and days, the same shadowed and calm weather. Neither leaves, nor horses, nor tidings. In her imagination, the house fell into ruin and at the doors were, standing the absent figures. Ana de Peñalosa thought she had aged, but it was actually the obsessive thought of leaving that nature, in that way, made present. She no longer wrote and her hands, in front of the mirror, seemed long and preposterous. She wanted to concentrate passionately on Saint John of the Cross, but only the feeling of tedium kept them all together.
But
if there were only five days when the sun shone,
when the routine of the open gate was broken, when Müntzer's head, taken from the enraged crowd, fell onto her lap,
when the river emptied and showed the footsteps of the irretrievably lost fish,
when she herself knew that, man or woman, or one of them, she was someone
when,
when,
when
as a kind of house that belonged to her and its surroundings, she had slept, she became bored and prepared for the true death.

Place 26 —

Her garden and river had become a place full of houses, with the air of a city, for an afternoon. She observed it behind the windowpane, preferring to look at the sky abruptly occupied with roofs. The river beaten by the oars of Saint John of the Cross's boat had been transformed into that sky. The myth of the Eternal Return. Her memory ebbed away as if she were old. Or as if she were about to begin another life with new memories forming. The knowledge she had laboriously learned in adolescence and childhood abandoned her quietly, leaving no trace. She was not sorry, nor did she feel the need for it. She then decided she should write, a skill she still remembered, what she thought. The same or a different one. She died, but metamorphosed, taking an absurd transitory form, stitched together by her new memory. I understood that no meditation, no text, would serve me aside from my own writing. Much time had passed. On the dresser in my room, a metallic Buddha and a river-borne stone had filled with dust, which was accumulating in them with different characteristics. I also understood, around this time, that Nietzsche had come looking for me to go outside his texts, take a long walk along their margins. I was willing, that night, to talk with him, using his own terms to qualify what signified a destruction and an accumulation of centuries. I said what I thought about the sex of the books and Nietzsche asked me: — And John? — I sat down on the edge of the bed and fell asleep peacefully, not knowing which bodies we abandoned. We were already very used to the pleasure of contemplation. But, that night, the pleasure exceeded anything imaginable; there we conceived another child, or object, or plant, or animal, which took the place of Maya, the lost dog; with what pleasure he cut his hair and entered into the phase of autumnal silence, where the river had been there was a vast expanse of trees, shades of red predominated, fleeting, until the next few days an expanse lying upon a stone (light stone) pulled by the earth to the place where her sons fought; she looked at each tree slowly, so she would always be able to recognize it. That new being was at her side, composed of the profundity of names and she became lost in thought when she saw its hair was that of her own head when she was young. When she looked at that being's right hand, she saw John of the Cross spelling in a book, reading the first rhythm of his words; when she looked up at one of its multiple foreheads, she saw Müntzer's head on horseback, in an unstable equilibrium, but always remaining upright, miraculously; her opened and closed eyelids lay Nietzsche down upon her lap. Following the horse, a trail of blood heralded a torrential downpour.

Ana de Peñalosa, startled by the contrast of these images, roused herself. In her left hand, all that had taken place flowed. With abundant tenderness, she ran her palm along its back, solemnly kissing its tail. In its raised claws she saw an unfamiliar presence, it must have been the florid fear of the journey. Having spent a short while in her company, its mouth transformed: it wanted to eat the small birds perched on the grass

because a flock of feathers and colors flew until their bodies were left bare.

She calmed herself, thinking "time floats over us and abandons its spirit to us. During my absence, Thomas Müntzer's forehead asked me for my room, so he could write and escape. It is the house's impenetrable place, with seasons permanently flowing above our heads."

(The new being was also not a book. Ana de Peñalosa did not love books; she loved how they became a visible source of energy when she discovered images and images in a succession of descriptions and concepts).

She said to the new being, as she caressed it:

— I worked from the age of thirty-eight until I was forty-three; but I must now recreate a new place of rest intended only for knowledge, as in adolescence and childhood.

Before was the time for learning what they taught me, now is the time for understanding what, during all these years, was said to me. Valuable preparation for the final stage of adulthood, a serene and initiatory abandonment of the labyrinth. — She tired of looking at the place full of columns, buildings, triumphal arches, stadiums, observatories, private homes, gigantic temples and pyramids, sanctums. But, in its still-raised claws, she discovered the evolutions of Suso the fish, the impression that she did not exist on her own, that she was a transitory condition of time and space:

"Beneath your florid claws, I shall dance."

It was the end of the text, but a provisional end.

The next morning the dialogue with the new being began again, a silent dialogue of glances, caresses, absences, thoughts, smiles, and fear.

Maredret Abbey, November 2, 1974

THE REMAINING LIFE

To Isabel
To Jorge and Ana

THE MONTHS OF BATTLE

November —

the new being was a monster; they aspersed themselves with perfume. This perfume penetrated their bodies, it was transformed into
another fish, brother to Suso; it broke a mirror but hastened to piece
it back together, to be soothed by its own image. It talked to itself
in the dense atmosphere of brightness of which it could not foresee
the consequences. Thomas Müntzer had not forgotten he had been
beheaded, he remembered what had happened to him on the many
walls of the room. So he oscillated with his head and his immense
shadow stretched up to the ceiling, beyond the ogival windows. He
whistled like an adolescent; he then saw Ana de Peñalosa come in and
caught the train of her dress.

They walked around the room for a short while to celebrate the
moment they were in. Ana de Peñalosa had a book in her hand, a
kind of book with magic. She made a thick garment with its pages.
She used the last one to wrap Müntzer's head and constantly kissed
the wound on his neck
which said:

— Tell Saint John of the Cross how peaceful the drapes are in this
room, always in shadow and doubly autumnal because I am here and

I am preparing myself to speak inextinguishably, although we are nearing the end I foresee on the faces of the people who visit me. They knock on the door and do not know whether they should enter, the incantation will not change the direction of their steps at the hour of the return. An eternal sound falls, a brumous eternal, but it is, at the same time, bracing and premature. Malebranche, *Vision in God* is the name of the book I have on the table, but it is the name that should be given to a stone.

This belongs to us and disappears alongside us without anyone being afraid or feeling guilty. My vocation is to speak eternally.

Also tell Saint John of the Cross, and don't forget Nietzsche, that the pig was still under the table. He snuck in fascinated by those of us who were eating (and not dancing, do you remember?) at the exact hour of our feast. We had the feeling that we had quickly left a place and that a kind of somnolence invaded our gathering. Maya, the dog lost from always looking for us, came and played with shells in the middle of the room and ran a great distance away from us when we left. I write in full possession of my faculties of reading.

As I rewrite my last will and testament, I invite Saint John of the Cross and Friedrich Nietzsche to abandon your house and the river, for some while.

In the new life I'm going to live, which I would like to live

with you

in open spaces

on ever moving horses,

I have thought about becoming a hunter and a warrior.

Today is November 10. I ask you to choose my most beloved objects, to bury them in your garden.

Once they have been interred, they will have found their final resting place. And much time will pass, however fleeting it is.

Before I go any further, I tell you that, blind, you could not write. Writing is born when you lower your eyes to the paper, lettered or blank; the moment the chorus resumes and the voices gain amplitude, the coercive movement of the words uttered by me, Müntzer, rises up the hand you kept over your lips.

— When it is already late in the evening in terms of desire and I forget all the messages for which you've made me messenger, I also don't remember that the sun will rise again tomorrow; I don't understand why we have to move toward the necessity of your death: it is time that passes with your beheading at its end.

The end of November —

On those nights, it was unclear what decision she should make. She felt, without a shadow of a doubt, drawn to the return; but that unknown place had begun, with Müntzer's help, to become so concave and deep that it seemed she could not abandon it.

She had started, in that large quiet room, reciting the text. Ana de Peñalosa sensed John's presence, though she did not see him. She perfumed her hands before writing, sitting on the floor next to the lit candle and Thomas Müntzer who   eternally being beheaded. Although she had been entrusted with a message, she wondered if she should leave or if she could, some time later still, find a messenger.

The last day of November —

she still slept; but waking was not part of the dream:
she was at the entrance to the house, on the first day she had arrived
to inhabit it; she remembered the upper floor, the long hallway in the
shadows
which led to the rooms of her lovers
part of the message was that, for a year, John of the Cross, Nietzsche,
Müntzer himself, and the unknown Eckhart would come and live
with her, in that house;
the presence of Pegasus, Suso the fish, the bear, and even the pig had
been confirmed, in privileged places, the door open to the garden
that was serene,
and immense with cobbled stones;
the river, exiled, would come to dwell with them,
would follow its course beyond the wall,
and only in the afternoons could it be seen,
although the noise of the lapping water and writing permeates all
the doors and makes the closed windows relinquish their sedimented
secrets.

But the fear of so many beloved silhouettes asked the same question:
if waking was not part of the dream,
I must awaken.
The nightmare continued eternally, the long half-light persisted over
the river, compelled to appear at that hour. An entire moving mass,
netting or lace — peasants, lords, and princes of the Church — had
been divided between the plain, the battlefield, and the headwaters.
Only Suso the fish, among other fishes,

had been told that he should descend to the house flying within the water. Kneeling, Ana de Peñalosa had been able to stop him, had shown him the liquefied volume of the house, and the confined space of the aquarium. Suso spoke to her hands and said to her: "I knew Jonas once."

Enthroned in the aquarium, the water and the fins should liberate the house of the Father, Son, and Holy Spirit, the Virgin Mary, and all the Angels.

Waking was not part of the dream.

Ana de Peñalosa passed through the entrance, for each leaf of odiferous plants burned, others lying on the censer perfumed with their smoke. The nightmare came from not knowing whether that house would be the exact one and whether John of the Cross, Nietzsche, Müntzer himself,

the unknown Eckhart

would want to make the same last request.

The beginning of December —

the house had appeared abruptly, two steps from the river. A not-seen house, evoked by the whisper of the writing that was a salutation. Closing her eyes, she imagined herself blind to better hear the footfalls of those who would come. When she opened them she realized that, scattered across the ground born long ago, Müntzer, John of the Cross, the light, and the animals they had brought behind them, were waiting for her to invite them in; but the house existed only invisibly, Ana de Peñalosa startled and asked the silent books and the plants to guide them. The immobility and appearance of nothing persisted. The animal that had taken the form of a horse ran into the bounded space, and lay down; the noise of the crowd that had awakened looking for Müntzer could be heard,

it was written

that the dreamed house could not serve as a shelter,

neither bed,

nor table,

but battlefield.

Müntzer touched the head still on his shoulders and moved toward the whinnying of the horse; the house wove itself from stones, the windows appeared embedded in the walls, the door opened to admit those who had dared come to the garden.

When he sat down in the anteroom, in front of Suso the fish who was swimming in the aquarium, John of the Cross withdrew into himself and asked: "Where am I going?"

The river passed beneath the house, a constant undulation could be heard. They rested their foreheads on their knees, and the sources ran in a sudden flow, so many thoughts occurred to Ana de Peñalosa, and so intensely, that she believed either the moment of her death, or death, was approaching. But the horse told her it was the middle of the journey, that beyond the house was the end of everything else.

A spider of plurifaceted splendor climbed the wall; and the plants invaded the house discreetly, took their places in the windows, and in the middle of the rooms, where the seeds had fallen: — "O my sons — said Ana de Peñalosa — what is this house for you? Who are you for this house?" — She saw a beautiful animal with the shape of a son, John's soft fur, Müntzer's raised claws, the horse's fleeting eyes, the fish's traveling tail, Nietzsche's lolling tongue.

— I am Eckhart — said the animal — and I have come from far away to tell you that I will soon be with you.

— If I do not recognize you... — It seemed to everyone that the house was uninhabited. The book had been left on the ground, and the two loved one another strangely, exchanging pages, creatures, thoughts, the voice that would birth the text, and the body that would contain the earth.

December —

When Ana de Peñalosa returned to her body, she found Eckhart in the garden. She recognized him by the profusion of greenery in the place where he was sitting.

—You have passed beyond the silence of dusk — she said. She let herself fall backward, meditating.

A December night —

Without the shutters opening, the house does not exist. It can be seen on the horizon and asserts years to live; inhabited by writing, a hand moves in every room, expressing the futurables that the eyes see, prows extending forward. Where is childhood? Where is old age? Where is adulthood? Where is my imaginary Second Person, where is the Third Person of the Holy Trinity that John says he inhabits?

— John — asked Ana de Peñalosa — why did you want such a large house?

— O You Who Sees, did you not have the same desire? It takes courage to conclude your body. If you knew how many shadows will remain living among us, emerging from your maternal body, how many shadows will be reduced to nothing, at night and along the walls, and in the morning will come and lie in your arms, at the moment you confide your dreams to me...

— John, why did you want such a large garden?

— O You Who Sees, could it be you don't know that the river must pass through the garden and that, among our companions, there are still many unknown boats?

At night, nothing existed but the flame. Over the water, the river's fatuous fire. Although no one was there, Ana de Peñalosa's certainty had become so intense that thousands of oars beat, a long time ago. She closed her eyes to be possessed by the flame. It was from the candle wick that her children were born, on stormy or clear nights, she always gave birth to them in different places, now on the beach, now in blood, now in the innermost part of the house. They grew quickly with different shapes, voices, statures. And they left home discreetly, without her knowing. That was how John had been born in the place of Fontiveros, upon the land and upon the river, in one place and in another, now and forever. In one time and in another had he been born and always he had dialogued with his mother, along the sharp edge of words. The page invented, he marked out the boundaries of a territory for the brothers of his immense phratry: pig, horse, bear, fish.

January —

They, the animals, would come. But if no one came, if she could look at the places where the animals would be, if they came. If her sons remained alive forever, not in her memory but through their absence confronting the space of the house. How to explain that this was how she wanted to live with Eckhart; to detect, as she draws back a curtain, the plausible sound of his voice, to see on the white wall not even his shadow; then having closed the door, to come across the *Sermons*, rest her hand atop it as on an abandoned coffer of clairvoyant thoughts; remain lying there accompanied by the light until Nietzsche came and Müntzer explained in her ear the duration of the message that was ambiguous, but so timely. It must be conveyed on the night she was waiting for her sons;

they probably wouldn't come;

who would come saying sweetly at her side: "We are absent." Each of them always communicated with the next room; she spent an hour with her forehead leaning against the growing shadows, for it had been a long time since night arrived without her beginning to reread

that, in secret, they seldom visited her

she let herself remain in the same place,

uttered by the book.

Although she also embarked

for her lands in Spain

which was a land beyond Portugal

where none of her sons, nor even herself, had yet gone.

She was chasing a noise, she realized it was

the noise of a millstone moved by water.

She found herself with one hand on the door

knocker, associating the constant knocking

with the beating of oars, and meditation.

A January morning —

When she went in, it reminded her of a tower. She climbed the steps and saw the wheat flour where the round movement of the millstone was unfurling the concavity of its escape. Invaded by somnolence, she gathered a few sacks and began looking at the beams of the ceiling and their spiders, and their webs: there was a presence in that place, it lived within the solitude; the mass of lightweight spiderwebs lined the ceiling, marked a space possessed forever and the presence oscillated to the left and to the right, imperceptible. It was then that she stilled her gaze: it was the presence of Eckhart and this the place where he had continued to exist, but where? Just beyond there was a spiderweb eternally reflecting, long transparent and abandoned; in the smallest and most diaphanously woven corner, there was a tiny figure who appeared to her with perfect clarity and no illusion. Eckhart, alone. So small, free in his web, unimprisonedly remembering his long life, and the sweet excommunications he had suffered. Suddenly, he became so insignificant and slight that Ana de Peñalosa could no longer see him; but she knew he oscillated, radiant, above her head. She heard distinctly:
— "I am here. Tell Müntzer…"
His voice went out.
Ever since that day, she knew she was supposed to convey not only the message from Müntzer but Eckhart's message for Müntzer. In perfect ignorance she returned to the house, to consult her expectation and solitude. She thought that if she set Suso the fish down in the river,

something might happen; she put one hand in the aquarium, placed the other on the glass; she went to the garden with Suso the fish against her belly; at the river, she opened up the water with a hand and there let fall Suso who returned to the sources, or rather, to that voracious point, which was, once again, in the mill.

The spiderwebs were identical, similarly arranged.

She heard the voice:

    — "Tell Eckhart that..." — Then silence, or the pounding of the millstone.

Still January —

"Today I gathered another word." She then heard the intonation
of the voracious-point, and stopped to listen to it unawares,
motionless,
keeping the objects company,
more specifically all the paintings
which she had placed on the floor against the wall
of her room;
none depicted more than three figures;
as she listened to the fifth Symphony Beethoven was playing,
her white cat
settled against her chest,
facing the paintings.
Ana de Peñalosa
looked at the images,
from the beloved figure

of Lorenzo de Medici
holding the money
he had used to buy the house for
Nietzsche, Eckhart, Saint John of the Cross,
Suso, the horse, the bear,
and the pig,
to the image of a young Flemish woman from the sixteenth century
and an engraving of a peasant
couple
buying a cradle
for their first child.
She stared
into the cat's eyes
and into the chaos born from Beethoven;
her cat's paw rested
on her hand
and throughout the house
the murmuring of spoken words
and her throat could be heard.
She delighted in these objects,
all were known
and had come from far away,
particularly the cradle
for the child.
It was Beethoven's cradle,
it could have been; at that moment
his father paid a secondhand merchant
for his crib

and

Beethoven had driven Nietzsche mad; Nietzsche's mouth had taken on a singular aspect, it emitted the power that composed *Zarathustra*, and the book was unraveling to the margins; it articulated the silence, and the mask of fear permeated the polar zone of the bear's mouth. Between the contraction of Nietzsche and the ears of Beethoven, Ana de Peñalosa had let herself be abandoned   at that moment she understood the shape of her brightness, which had once been called perfect love, and the peasant woman from the painting entered into it, smiling abashedly and coveting the money Lorenzo de Medici had left on the table.

"I think about you; I want to go to your gathering and, at the same time, welcome you in this house that has always desired you. You are alive, and I do not expect to receive illusory persons. Some days ago they sought me out, left their names in the anteroom, near the roses, or the place eternally with diamonds. I read their names, and saw that, among them, Eckhart had come, the one you found in the mill, swinging in a spiderweb, but I have not yet memorized his request, nor his face. He must have some resemblance to you, for me to already love him. He left his imperceptible mark on the table with his name; it was a breath of sand in the middle of a drop of wax. Tomorrow I will look for him again in the noise of the mill, but there are so many webs that I won't see him, if he doesn't make himself known."

— O Medici, always the same dilemma — she uttered, in a loud, clear voice with the peasant woman, in the same nightmare. — My friends, especially Müntzer, tell me I should keep writing.

But this writing doesn't turn into money. It requires time,

contemplation, a scene.

I look at your portrait hanging on the wall a bit like a prostitute.
I am in love with your hand holding money and silver, with your fur
coat, and I show him my writing as if I showed him a body
that he might love or desire.
High Medici, Patron of the Arts, dead in your tomb and in this portrait,
buy me the time I need.

February —

She wrote, some time later, that her land had been invaded by the sea.
Having forgotten, since then, the message delivered by Müntzer, she
sat down on the beach to study the waves, looking for the place where
her sons would gather; but it was an expanse far too vast in width and
depth. In the nightmare, she traveled in the arms of the fantastic being,
which listens to the tenuous noises, a phoenix reborn from its own
ashes which had always been enticing. Müntzer's head also dreamed.
In the house, in the deepness of the window, a light went on, the
monster's single eye. Voices erupted
from the jaws of the
animal that spilled fire and an insistent language,
a true language belonging to Müntzer's past; and dawn did not come,
to the contrary; once again the meridian hours of the night drew near.

A February night —

on the night when, for the first time, she was alone in the house, with
all of time in front of her, the vast space fragmented by reminiscences
and pieces of furniture, she began to feel flowing, beneath the tiled
floor in her room, John's stream;
she had not yet combed her hair and half of it swallowed the page,
her face turned toward the wall behind which the stream was flowing;
and there
place,
moment,
she heard the roar of an animal with a human resonance that might
have dragged itself down to the river and with the river confused its
abyssal paws, and the melopoeia of its blood
though she suspected
she would never be able to determine
what genus of animal
it was
and it was better that way
because insects, images of animals, drawings of animals, bones of animals, classifications of animals,
frogs,
worms,
also existed,
and that animal,
either man,
or amphibian,
had come to lie down in John's river.

She knew then, at that very
moment, that the river had scales
and that between the pages
which composed the body of
Suso the fish
the text traveled
with a libidinal name.

March —

And, traveling, adolescent John went into the house to rest in the
stream
                         next to his mother's ears.
In his room there was a multitude of objects that Ana de Peñalosa had
bought to share her life.

   Salvaged from the water, a small stone lay on the windowsill; John
picked it up and, nomadic, began his meditation with it; enclosed in
the room, he became even more adolescent; his fair hair fell down to
his shoulders and in the only bed, at night, he rested eternally.

Still March —

When his mother went up to see him, she undressed to once again
birth his naked body.

Mother of objects, I deliberately
left the other side of the page
blank; today I awoke dreaming
that I did not live alone in this
house but with my husband,
father to Thomas and John; and
that Hadewijch was loved by him,
and loved us; and, at the beginning of the afternoon, which
was burning and timeless, she
had come to visit us, opening
the books I wrote; she seemed
to have led a group of faithful
women, probably a community of
beguines; I told her my husband
desired her and asked for her con-
sent to bare her body, first from
the waist down, because I considered that part less important, then
from the waist up, the shoulders
and breasts that are the privileged places of the sources and
mouth. Hadewijch looked at me
without uttering a word, her face
illuminated by a grave assent that
seemed to me to be the end of
a long wait. I called my husband
and we went into the room I had

prepared, nearly naked and veiled.
Hadewijch was motionless. In the
near darkness, I lit a candle close
to her feet, and freed her from
what she was wearing; following
the brightness I looked up, and
took one of her garments in my
hands, and in the shadow of the
candle she showed who she was.
At that moment, her legs bent
with weight and nostalgia; I took
off her robe to show my husband
where her breasts were. Hadewijch fell to her knees saying, "I love
you both, I love you both."
I left slowly, cautiously, at the
center of a chaotic mixture of
happiness and suffering, which I
tried to sort out so I could begin
writing:

April —

Much time had passed since the dogs, and the children, with their
wolfish side, sensed the War; the dogs drank water from the wells and
barked; the boys ran through rooms hitherto closed and with shouts
and long fingernails killed the spiders and destroyed their webs; taking

advantage of the dust they made arabesques of spears, sword handles, bows and arrows in the mirrors; when night fell they did not rest, they whispered among themselves like trees in the wind.

In that insomnia, Nietzsche did not sleep; "Another war," he said ironically to himself, with a certain indifference because he had already died and been prepared to die any number of times; but he thought about the other members of the Community, all the events and images the Community had created, which he would like to see endure on the crest of the centuries, although he knew, with his joyful knowing, that it was laughable; he prepared himself, then, to go and speak with Saint John of the Cross, which he had never done. He had a premonition that he would be, at that moment, with the pack of boys, organizing the war's defense; "I am slowly going mad," he noted calmly. "Why do these unthinkable ideas occur to me?"

But, no illusion, John of the Cross was organizing the pack.

He had transformed into the dog closest to a wolf, with clenched teeth and a light step. His desire to write had been lifted up on his strong tail and with his own human eyes he studied the signs of war beyond the window. As he was sniffing all the corners,

metamorphosed into a monster,

which he had accepted because it was a dark night,

he let out a piercing howl, calling for Müntzer.

April—

The first peasant, fleeing from the Princes, had arrived at the gate to the house and Hadewijch, only barely awakened from making love, drew the bolt:

— The Princes are coming to attack us.

After the piercing appeal to Müntzer, for him not to lose the battle this time, Saint John of the Cross, still transformed into a dog, led the peasant woman to his book, and learned that her name was Beatrice. In that room, Ana de Peñalosa, more serene, prayed unceasingly, cursing the Princes of the Church and the Princes.

While preparations were being made for the battle — defense and attack — Hadewijch had gone up to the smallest room in the house; lying on the uncarpeted floor, she had lost her Spirit: suddenly her body had appeared naked to Nietzsche, just as it was, an incarnation of perfumes with a perpetual softness and brightness; although her body was naked, hovering at the window and inciting the battle, one by one, the members of the Community to which she belonged;

came to undress her and pass each weapon over her skin;

when it was Saint John of the Cross's turn he left his quill on her navel; and Nietzsche, with his own hands, crumpled up paper on her breasts, glimpsing through the window the rebirth of the world that was approaching; Hadewijch was born in her bed covered and touched by so many improvised weapons;

when she recovered her Spirit, the house seemed to sway and collapse amidst the battle clashes; she was still naked, covered by the luminous dust of her skin;

her rebellious sex had firm new waves; she moved toward the door, but her hips were held back by the light, and by Beatrice who implored:

— "Hadewijch, help me gather the sources, the fish, and the horses."

The end of April —

As Hadewijch disappeared, the noise and fear of the battle came through the windows and reached the entire house, even the foundations, and the bakehouse; lining the walls, prepared to be mistaken for the ground, the pages and texts brought by the pack had found precarious shelter. Repellant and sweet phrases, written voices, agreed to remain confined in expectation. The rhy(th)m(e), in an accumulation of caution, was covered in horse dung and a nauseating odor would spread out over anyone who dared unseal the bakehouse door:

"A girl and a child, I was taken from the home of my parents to distant lands; as for why I was taken away, I was young and knew not."

May —

When Ana de Peñalosa conveyed Müntzer's opinion to Nietzsche (that once again their defense seemed impractical and defeat, at dusk, would likely be certain), Nietzsche replied: — Let us see where writing takes us. — Faced with the smile of all the dogs in the pack, Nietzsche himself among them, the enemies retreated one hundred paces. Their spears had no equal, save for the raised arms of the community's members, which numbered thousands of wolf claws, bear paws, gigantic bird wings, sea monster fins. Among them, the peasants moved in perfect safety and, gradually, transformed into enormous butterflies that flew over the two battlefields; clad in these powers, Müntzer had modified the meaning of his appreciation and delivered to Hadewijch, as a reminder of the past, his decapitated head; by chance, in a pink hydrangea that Hadewijch had left in the window, a spider had spun its threads and connected several petals with a dome; Ana de Peñalosa turned her aged face toward it
had gone room to room,
meditating on the calamity of the battle,
but, in fact, she did not read, nor pray,

she advanced solitarily among the enemy.

Hands aflame, she threw fire at the chariots, but the stones of the catapults already reached the bakehouse where the community had gathered. In the anteroom, when Hadewijch reappeared among the clouds that were accumulating, the spiderweb took on gigantic proportions and Eckhart reappeared in his full-size body; in her meditation, Ana de Peñalosa wondered whether she should make the web last or liberate the flower; with this swiftly attained gift of ubiquity she walked amidst the din that was being produced in the distance.

But the members of the community, standing against the bakehouse walls, regained their strength, and rested. They were confronted with the pestilential odor of their own texts.

But,

love songs, ballads, and romances of peasants and glass artisans, which Nietzsche, Saint John of the Cross, Thomas Müntzer had already heard and never written, accumulated on the walls like a layer of glaze

breath, glass, images:

"Reginaldo, Reginaldo,
Page to the much belovèd King
You could very well, Reginaldo,
Spend the night with me.

—You taunt me, dear Lady,
for I'm captive to beguiling.
— But how can I taunt you,
when it's truth I am telling.
— And when do you wish, dear Lady,
to keep this promised meeting?

—When night has fallen,

and the King is sleeping." Where we begin to address the dark night of the spirit, and say when it begins. Adults are only accepted into the Community after a long Catechesis. But what can I say? There has never been a Church Father who knew how to say or show what the true Baptism is.

"—The punishment I give you,

for being my belovèd page,

is to take her as your wife

and be her husband all your days"; "no axe shall cut the roots of thought. I died, I was buried, and now I am here. Nor could the earth cover me, before I bid farewell to thee"; in which we begin to address the first cause of this Night, which is a loss of appetite for all things, and the reason why it is called a Night.

Then Nietzsche read (or deciphered) to himself: "You compel all things to come to you and into you, that they may flow back from your fountain as gifts of your love.

Truly, such a bestowing love must become a thief of all values: but I call this selfishness healthy and holy. Truly, I advise you: go away from me and defend yourselves against Zarathustra.

Perhaps he has deceived you.

Any master who wants you to remain his disciple forever is no master"; "as Dona Infantinha was sitting in her garden, running a comb of gold through her hair, she saw the sails of a great armada moving closer to the land; with it came a captain who had the navigation well in hand: there is no learnèd person who can state my intentions."

A May day —

She sat pleasantly run through with cold, waiting to be able to order the events in time, in front of the bakehouse door, not remembering that the Lords and Princes drew nearer, and the drums already echoed in the distance proclaiming victory: a hideous man wielding a sword and clad in armor had appeared standing in front of "guard your horse, which was difficult for you to train,"
without anyone knowing how he had entered; and right there, with tenfold strength, he was preparing to behead Müntzer
who, at the gates of the house and garden, had not left his horse forgotten, and was preparing to guard his head.

Glassworkers had come, with their tools and working materials, and they blew colored bottles and orbs that circled dizzyingly around the executioner
and collided, shattering, with his sword.
Their multiple pieces invaded the text,
and a dense mass of glass and words
advanced toward the center of the bakehouse
where the newcomer loomed with his weapon. He had become a gigantic figure,
with a heavy, bitter voice:
"I am that vast hidden cape,
I am called Adamastor"
and tried to sway the foundations of the bakehouse with his colossal limbs.
But, the dense mass had surrounded his feet, and the suddenly deadly glass and words uttered threats and, always crawling

being, light, crest, and, utterances, windowpanes, bottles, opinions
they had stolen the light from his eyes   nothing had been
left to chance, every room had its fate; a battle would be waged in every
one, and it would either leave the victor, or with torn decorations and
furniture;

in the dining room, on top of the table where the felled tree could still
be seen, the Prince sat down with his escort and footmen, his syco-
phants and leisure animals, from the jester to the large sighthound. His
stupid questions shone in his eyes and the meal he had just finished
spoke on his lips. Even so, he was handsome and Hadewijch could, in
a moment of truth, covet his bed in order to kill him. Nothing more
atrocious than the music that could be heard in the horses' hooves.
Funereal, triumphal music,
full of deceit and excruciating dilemmas,
the widow of Müntzer
(not yet dead)
pregnant and outraged,
had been dragged to the center of the table, and it was on her bowed
head that the powerful Prince fixed his gaze

"I implore with all humility that Your Princely Grace deign to lower
your eyes to my great misery and poverty."

They then saw approaching them, drawn by the Princes, the incendiary
machine of desire; with deep dread they made out armed primates and
golden-haired dogs on the upper floor, catapulting miasmas of plague
through the small openings; a spate of beggars and the sick erupted
ceaselessly within the bakehouse and penetrated the dense mass of
texts and glass; the feet of the colossus began to be crushed, and Ana de

Peñalosa contemplated his ever more prominent and terror-filled eyes; multiple texts intoned his writing and the peasants, Müntzer among them, ate them off the walls and shouted at the enemy; but the texts were not consumed, they could be seen in the transparent bodies, and one had gone to lie down in Hadewijch's lap, and another barked in Saint John of the Cross's mouth, and another had bristled in Nietzsche's hair.

Faced with this unexpected resistance, the colossus, the dense mass affixed to the whole of his body, began to emit a lullaby in an attempt to soothe the battle; but an unrecognizable tumult could be heard, if one were to listen: every voice, every sound could be clearly perceived, and the lament of Hadewijch:

O Ana de Peñalosa, tonight I have scarcely slept — I was so distraught, first because I stayed with Nietzsche in the kitchen and also because, yesterday morning, you had told me that we were going to pray later that afternoon and I had the sense of having failed to keep a promise, although I was somewhat frightened by the idea of praying because I don't really know how it works — but last night the moon was so beautiful, and in the play of light and shadow I saw a strange little man appear, made of branches and dry leaves; I rubbed my eyes (I had wept a great deal) but he was still there and, suddenly, I realized he had the shape of a cross; and I remembered the book I had taken yesterday afternoon and left open on the page you had shown me; the strange little man made of branches was just above the book; then, instead of laughing, I picked up the book and began to read

there must be a room there, a room
with a link to escape, and the sea

roared in its emptiness; nothing had
ever been there, aside from a wall
run through with glances enthroned
on a carpet, which
took the form of spirals of
seemingly undefined colors.
In other times, she had gained
entrance to them but later on, in the
time of forgetfulness, her memory
unceasingly worked to
murmur fragments until the
moment arrived when,
after the enormous explosion, she
herself became part of the carpet in
some dark place.

The last days of May —

Hadewijch died; she fell to the tile floor during the battle, but it was a natural death. She wrote sitting down with the page on her knees as was her habit, drawing the words with the pen as she wrote them; it was during an interrupted moment in the fighting, at the point when the dogs, in large buckets of water, slaked their thirst, and the tearful women intoned melopoeia to their future dead. Suddenly, she was thirsty and trailing her skirts her beautiful mouth transformed into a dog's mouth with a lolling tongue, plunged into the bucket; surrounded by the pack of dogs barking satedly, she continued writing

with her hand on her dress; and, all at once, as if she could no longer
see, she found her tongue alone in her mouth and her hand undu-
lating over the
paper empty of writing
death, death, death,
she said three times,
letting the paper, her eyes, and her head fall.

June —

The pack of dogs let out a howl and their portraits of wolves become
enormous on the bakehouse walls;
in a state of reflecting on what would come to pass, on an afternoon
when she was sitting in front of the door
when night fell she hadn't left all day; she waited patiently and only
to surprise her in the darkness.
    Hadewijch had written: I lost my memory; you are my memory
and you illuminate me; so I step outside myself to walk in the veiled
darkness where there are large trees and large figures on either side:
only one of the dogs from the pack did not become a wolf; he was a dog
that listened to music and lived in his brown fur always close to joy and
death because he is the melody of his invented owner; the dog was called
Hadewijch and he lay down on pillows in one of the house's rooms,
in the dining room,
a privileged place in the house,
where no one ever ate
and, primarily,

at the head of the table;

she did not yet want to die;

she had gone to put a bottle of wine in the cupboard for the visitors who would come in the next few days

when she felt a desire to sit down at the one end of the table, looking into the depths of the next room. It was neither a very full nor an empty place, she immediately realized that, with her, other beings from who knows where had sat down, waiting; her cat and image had not entered, had remained in the kitchen, on the armchair where it slept; one of the beings emitted music, another, at a distance, had closed its eyes; Thomas Müntzer, present and dead, invited her to enter and look into his death.

September and October —

Around that time, the days for Hadewijch, who by virtue of deep love had become Ana de Peñalosa, were as hard as stones; she felt memoryless, deprived of her thirst for learning, betrayed; a kind of unearthly old age anticipated her old age; Nietzsche rose up gently in her books, at the peak of the text; and every day she waited for his thirst for knowledge, for Nietzsche's love to exceed the text, and come near to her; she also hated her gender, she wanted it to be timeless, and lacking a form her friend Hadewijch did not come to see her, taken by an adolescent crisis

but the being sitting covertly in the chair emitted music, and the eternally loved Thomas Müntzer spoke of the passage of death

"You know," he said voicelessly

articulating silence,

articulated in silence,

"You know you will exist for all time"; taken by an extraordinary impulse, she felt like getting up, putting water in the bucket, and washing the floor until it shone; and her thirst for knowledge came to her with her visions, a continuance of fear and opening up to fear, visions without images, utterly dark and enticing,

sometimes mottled with shadows and words. An enormous force arose, dressed as a man and a woman, and with a single eye. For a long time it shook in convulsions with the intention of unifying the bodies, and its desire did not reach an end. It then turned against itself and made love, putting its eye in its mouth, and its hands at the edge of thought. It seemed to be unable to exist before death, and dead it seemed to relentlessly cling and come back to life. There was no human form in it, and everything was night and vague. "The time it spent in my house made me forget myself. I mated with it: face with hand."

She tried to read the words but they exploded, and rolled beyond Nietzsche and Müntzer in no particular direction.

Had she prayed?

Aged?

Liberated her body?

Tomorrow another day began, and news of madness and war would come from everywhere; strange men seized power, and they were imitated. Those sitting with her there at the table would eventually leave; and she would have to return to the privileged room to be able to accept her breasts, one of her body's aberrant places; but Müntzer, when he spoke to her indirectly, said: "Do you know you will exist for all time? In every form?" She saw the horror of the faces seep through the stained glass, and the faces were horrible, and all of them bowed toward her; the colors pierced the faces with a thousand holes, and her body had just at that moment found a place for her hands; she then found other hands with very long nails, and skin with an unknown texture; she withdrew into that vision and went into her room, half asleep with sorrow and love. She was on the threshold of the voracious point, she had just taken possession of your memory, O monstrous face passing through the stained glass. She recognized the dogs disfigured by the fighting and the bodies of Nietzsche, and John of the Cross, and Thomas Müntzer meticulously dismembered. My sorrowful horror began to sing with a sweet voice coming out of my mouth, followed them faithfully as if they were dead and would be buried. I could not nourish myself with anything other than sorrow, and my sighs awoke Eckhart who had just written in the depths of his web could nothing at all be done to make them come back to life.

When the dog from the pack heard the signal for battle he stretched out, as always, to sleep, his ears drooping with pages; his open eyes remembered that he had once been Hadewijch, and that he had become a dog; his peers were transformed into wolves and sharpened their teeth, but Hadewijch resisted his metamorphosis before the mirror
sleeping.

       This is how she would be found after the battle,
far away,
forgotten between the pages of an old
book
written
by Eckhart.

THE CHAPTERS OF WAITING

Chapter I —

One afternoon, when the yellowness of autumn suffused all the windows and Nietzsche, in one of his rooms, conceptually intoned the words before writing them, she feared that the expressive power of language, from an excess of abundance, would abandon her; day of all souls, day of any year, in any time, she formulated questions upon questions, wanted to go down to the first floor, open the door upon the meditation of Nietzsche who wrote, sitting at the table; she constantly heard a horse advancing through the house, and noticed that all the men and women she had known, during her lifetime, were equal. Her time finished

she wondered what to do with the disappeared time

while Nietzsche, always facing toward and away from the writing, did not hear her come in

because none of the people who inhabited the house, or visited her, spoke to one another. Place of a concentration of gestures, water fell constantly in the most distant corner of the courtyard, and animals and plants could not be distinguished from those men.

Thus were long days filled, and it quickly became autumn, Nietzsche, John's heir, always thinking; Ana de Peñalosa lived perpetually enamored, and aging; she asked herself questions that began: "What meaning, what meaning..." "Is it just or unjust?" "What exactly, in space, is the place of this house?" "Will the rule of silence be beneficent?"

At that moment, Nietzsche slept on the page, and Prunus Triloba, her shrub in the garden, yellowed amidst the brightness; in an inhospitable remnant of the courtyard, Hadewijch lived in retreat (she had sealed her mouth with a flower); when the flower wilted, she pointed the tip of her tongue toward the room where Ana de Peñalosa lived and, with her sharp fingers, picked another flower.

The nape of Nietzsche's neck gleamed in the early afternoon more   pages   kept   falling; Ana de Penãlosa wanted to remember a single phrase by Nietzsche, but her memory refused anything that was needed. A vast twilight inundated the writing, and all the facts and knowledge were part of a context of utmost originality;

they were overthrown,

crushed,

neither front nor reverse existed.

Although Nietzsche wasn't sleeping, because of the rule of silence it was as if he slept, she could not speak to him; but the rule of silence guarded the ardently desired visions, in the house the beings met without recognizing each other, or passed by one another fascinated; and thus was woven a consistent fabric, where space and time left neither wrinkles, nor traces; no one was mad, or famous, or poor, or ignorant, or old, or young, and Jade the dog himself sat at the table and, with such sweet eyes, began speaking

and Forsythia and Spirea remained green and damp with the autumnal sun, deprived of water

Chapter II —

when passions intervened, it was another form of war; at first no one
knew the plot of what was going to transpire, only Ana de Peñalosa,
unclosing the door to her room, saw that many mouths had shut
(smiling) or opened (shouting);
but,
in this vision,

there are no passions; as long as I open myself up here to the space
created by the house, left in me by the garden, which hovers in the air
like an insect full of metamorphoses, war and pain are unthinkable. Or
perhaps only present themselves in the form of nostalgia or peaceful
disquiet: how long will this peace last? When will it end? Surely, it will
not end now, but soon it will have menacing faces of war. If we were
to live that way, simply to question   then she gathered the pages
that had fallen yesterday
she noticed how suddenly, around four o'clock, it was clear the afternoon was ending   she knows what species (vegetal) this
night is   it was a bitter pleasure to cut the last dahlias
toppled by the frost
    She would come to feel love for those who are silent, she would
like to receive them here.

Chapter III (much later, still and always war) —

During the war, Ana de Peñalosa went down to the river, a river that passed beneath the eastern part of the house; she took Prunus Triloba, Spirea from the ground and put them in the boat in front of her, like human beings. Wintertime, the branches were bare, and the roots damp; the battle continued and, by the lost shouts coming from the bakehouse, one might imagine that victory was no longer undecided. She struggled to see through the dust, but was determined to go to the cemeteries to ask for help from all the dead peasants.

The figure of Nietzsche, his forehead stone, hung from the shrubs;

Saint John of the Cross, impotent of words, had stripped naked amidst the cold

thin cries of women passed by on the waves

because a kind of fury and parallel slumbers led to the river; Prunus Triloba and Spirea had fashioned oars, and the meditation room became more vast,

moved, glinting in the water's depths,

and continued along the path

with objects, windows, and domes adrift,

the censer, the candles,

the large carpet in the center,

the dog,

and the lone bowl of fruit: I think about the dispersion of the objects; the culpability their accumulation provokes. They represent money, power, an investment of an energy that is power, they form the retinue of the dead, take the place of the dead and, unexpectedly, go beyond the present and morbid conclusions drawn from usefulness. I must try everything to explain their origins.

NIETZSCHE
was a singular man,
a much tormented man,
full of compassion,
very unpleasant
in the eyes of others,
and in his own
eyes.
He suffered from a fixed
idea:
"There are extraordinary things that cause me to think."

Then I feel a gentle, powerful, serene, and enveloping flow of energy that passes through Hadewijch. That I feel it, is a fact. That I am not at all opposed to this, is another fact. That this fluid runs through me and I send it on to Ana, is likewise a fact.

I feel an unbroken current of a flow that has the highest quality. That quality obviously depends on my past experiences.

I thus want this current to remain, be magnified, increase in quality. An ontological quality, or rather, that it not only makes the senses vibrate, but nourishes the being and, most likely, has beneficial and transformative effects at the cerebral level.

They set out on the path once again without knowing where they were going, guided by a source that moved through the air; Ana de Peñalosa, always at Nietzsche's side, could barely see him; a flurry of snow spread out through the air, and their faces, though near, seemed invisible because of their tears; it was a land of harsh experiences and so many metamorphoses that the path itself now appeared to be a thickness, and the snow, dust. John of the Cross, his voice melodious with words, pulled away from himself and his text and, at times, his hands pointing toward the horse, reminded her of Nietzsche and his anticipatory forehead. But the greatest torment, for Ana de Peñalosa, was glimpsing the figure of Hadewijch ahead, the burden of Nietzsche on her shoulders. Their fatigue grew in a spiral, and everything seemed full of sarcasm. The dog howled desperately, and Ana de Peñalosa's heart could not be distinguished from Nietzsche's pursued love for Hadewijch

and at every moment she abandoned the lead.

The others then saw her disappear from among them, and at that moment Nietzsche, or Ana de Peñalosa, said, leaving Hadewijch's long neck:

I had the feeling you wanted to talk to me,

really and truly; that, in the absence of contemporary companions, you had come to my bedside reflected in the water; you were also reflected in your book as if your mouth read what you wrote. Then I felt love for you, more and less than passion, a kind of modification of the feelings of love. You helped me write, I was one of your most beloved necessities. I conform to the way you live, I perform an act of acceptance. I want you just as you are, separate pages and pages of human love. I have nothing to do, but I can spend money, and think of you tirelessly until your sex for writing becomes alive. Is it true you love me? Creating new loves is a daunting task and carries a mortal danger

but the figure of Ana de Peñalosa was already taking shape beyond, at the same instant they heard the thunder of the horses' hooves. A fire without sparks swept the field, and time had not yet reached the

Temple. At that moment, Hadewijch fled from Nietzsche. "Out of mercy," he said, "we will camp here. I want to write *Zarathustra*." But it was the first words of the *Spiritual Canticle* that came out of his mouth as his lost love wandered in the distance; and cast into a great anguish, they called out to one another, and to themselves: Nietzsche, John, Ana, Hadewijch, horse, bear, fish, Eckhart. They remembered all the other names they might have borne, while Medici, counting the money intended for his works

looked at them with compassion.

Ana de Peñalosa then saw one of her fingers on Hadewijch's hand, and Nietzsche's soul in her chest; asking herself about the meaning of death, and giving up on finding it, she turned her head. She wanted to come across a door, pass through it, and wander the world utterly alone. But Nietzsche's head was fastened to her body

who could conceive it without contentment?

She wanted to sleep in the meditation room,

rest here before the passing of time;

the window is the most beautiful

that I have ever seen and conceived,

she sleeps outside this light,

and this house

but watching over it.

And if we had no compassion?

Nietzsche is close to Ana

without life, or death,

he himself

neither perishable,
nor eternal.
The snake that cannot
shed its skin dies,
this text is secondary
like rainwater in a vast sea;
tonight I will remain awake,
I will sleep in a different place,
so that even our dreams,
during the night
will follow this current.

Chapter IV —

Taken by the current, we passed through a country full of contradictions; we prepared ourselves to return to the tasks of work; we reached
the sea in a few days, on the promontory; we had always followed the
river in its multiple aspects; the peasants had succumbed, swept away
by the perpetually bright sky. To arrive there, it is necessary for fate
to have patience,
and for nothing to seem to change.
We traveled calmly,
we traversed this country lost in all countries, with Hadewijch, who
joined us. Other feminine beings joined us but I don't know who they
are, I feel more companionship among my sons, and mystics
who bring
books,

visions,
and swords
and are determined
to return to the war,
the peaceful war,
where we will lose our blood
and if necessary,
our passions for ourselves
for plants
and for animals.
Beatrice,
the peasant woman,
who is not
exactly
like us,
already spoke
to Lorenzo de Medici,
at the bottom of the stairs.
We sat down around her,
and heard her imprecations,
and grievances.
John left ashes
on her head.
We reached this day
still alive.
Lorenzo de Medici
took two steps forward,
and fastened diamonds

to our eyes
so we would not see
the incandescence of the text.
Hadewijch gathered
our spoils
and together we intoned
our provisional
death
while
millions of peasants
and solitary lands
flowed side by side
like a river.
There was then a great sorrow, a great fear, a great hatred, on the path,
with them. Looking into each other's eyes the intimate light of their
eyes fled and the bloody war on the great battlefields
manifested itself in the words they uttered
or scarcely uttered.
They tried to write letters on the stones when they stopped,
but at that moment they did not know how to write,
neither Nietzsche, nor John,
and night fell,
suffused with jealousy
and theologies. Sewing the text, Ana de Peñalosa was terrified, and
only Hadewijch had managed the grace
of evaporating in fear
as the fighting passed through her body, and through the silence,
always invisible. Night fallen completely, the trees murmured, the sea

murmured, and the stars shone, navigatory and forgotten.

There the earth ended and the sea began, with multiple aspects of the journey to other lands, on the same land.

The river had gone out, Nietzsche wanted to throw a body into the water, even his own body, and slowly, contradictorily, between the waves and columns of anger, of envy, that had taken Eckhart, the peasant woman, Ana de Peñalosa, John and Nietzsche, and Hadewijch returned to her gender, before the metamorphosis,
trod the tenebrous sea of the West.

There was bread on the water,
and an immensity of signs
but no one was outside, and they had arrived at the house, in the center of the war. The peace they felt was the usual peace, Beatrice was dressed in purple and had sat down in the place of Ana de Peñalosa who floated;
thus they recovered the serenity of writing and could live together for some years more, although that day Beatrice taught them to speak her language and keep a vigil over her body;
because at one o'clock in the morning it was as if she were dead and she lay down on the large table in the dining room, among all the quills; looking at her and knowing the battle would begin again the next morning, they fell into a great meditation
which perfumed the room with all of Beatrice's limbs and her exciting desires:
one by one the peasants came in and took their designated seats; lacking a circumscribed body, they let themselves fall into a single body, dead in the center of the table. A breath moved through the air, putting out the brightness and replacing it with candles; time receded

and, at a certain point, the dead woman was resurrected as young as she had been.

From her open gaze,

came weapons,

shouts,

dogs,

horses,

snakes,

and raised fists of men, without stigmas of writing. Ana de Peñalosa had opened her mouth, and Hadewijch had taken her hand above time and her children loosed from their texts

> having forgotten how to write
> they still wrote
> because a drop of blood
> spread across the page and con-
> cluded the words and the culmi-
> nation of Frankenhausen which
> made itself known.

If they hated her writing, she remained among the fabrics and plants. As the echoes of wild events reached her from afar, her passion for fabrics and plants became so gently violent that she learned to make bread in front of the bakehouse

while, at the same time, she heard the call of the threads and fabrics,

secret,

nervous,

intensely written with drawings.

Weavers and bakers came to see her when she was sitting there, gaze intent, and putting their hands familiarly on their knees, they spoke of their children, pleasures, and suffering.

At that contact, Ana de Peñalosa wept her writing, and gave her slumbering and uncovered hands to all the tasks.

Until one day, her writing appeared to her at the entrance to the bakehouse,

in the shape of a man and a woman, and perpetual ashes and flames.

Night fell and, sitting in a circle, listening to the wind that had no relation to time, they thought about how they would fight, and where their lives would be buried,

> they needed this anonymity where writing is produced, or rather, its links with all things, their destruction and rebirth; they wrote without a place, looking at each other on the path along the margins as if they were on the path of their footsteps. They looked at the entire world, and no one. They knew the entire world, and no one. They repeated: "These morning hours are words and letters." "And since I immerse myself in them, I surround myself with true fabrics, and objects from the time to come."
>
> There are moments in the future when nothing else is desired any longer. I aspire to the time when, with you, I will become part of time. If I am already part of space, that trace had only been left when I came near to you; for loving you so

my dear son, my dear lover, my dear sons, my dear
lovers,
I aged prematurely but always surrounded by this truth — the truth
needs to be powerful; Nietzsche confides in me that, with time, we
are outraged to see, now and forever, how cruelly those with so few
personal virtues make those who happen to be born with none suffer
for not having them;

John leans against my chest, and I always feel the babbling of his
words which do not belong to me, but him. And Müntzer, my most
intimate and most unhappy lover, makes love to me at the hour of his
broken spear and weary horse. On the walls of my room, I always look
at his shadow which grows impatient because his time to die ultimately
does not arrive; once again we are on the eve of a new battle, and I
am afraid of John's babbling; Hadewijch comes to keep us company so
rarely that, despite her youth, she will end up disappearing: among us,
no one is eternal. You know all this, but without ever having lived it,

I am writing to you speaking about myself when I
become lost at the beginning of this battle, in the
middle of this river traversed with illusions. Nietzsche
still speaks to me: "Ah, the most radical cure for love is
that old radical remedy — shared love." If Hadewijch
comes to participate in the battle and if I, unafraid,
still know how to write her name, we will travel far in
the water on horseback until we find Müntzer. I think
of him night and day without forgetting the others
who are so many and innumerable, like tigers, inter-
dicts, lions, jealousy and arrows, peasants, and loaves
of bread. If he died, and where he died. I wanted to

pilgrimage there to the peak of his ashes, and with them make a son for Hadewijch.

Eyes full of tears, I abandon my body where there is hunger and spirit, and peacefully envy her forever. Threatened by these spears, I first met Müntzer in his time,

in his eternal,

and hasty time,

where John

waited

because he had seen.

Chapter V —

Swiftly, time passed alongside time; Hadewijch was invisible there

or rather,

or rather

that she would exist forever. In the bakehouse there was a table of singular beauty with an embroidered white tablecloth, from my mother's house and my house

where the white held everything, what had been done, what hadn't been done, and what still remained to be done; I had left the sharp, agile pen there on top of Hadewijch and the tablecloth; a fire-colored cloth was on the right side, and I thought in the darkness left by the candle that the following thought would contain something of Hadewijch even more ineffable; she herself had created the contents of the bakehouse, much better than anything other beings

would have done, Eckhart had told her when, as a child, she delighted
in talking about angels
and other invisible figures
and materialities.
In the courtyard, the snow had just melted; she wanted to disappear
sitting on the ground, or on that chair beside the light
as if the long series of meditations and the events of the war had given
her, at last, a soul. Finally, Eckhart, as expected, had just come in. They
raised their heads, greeted him with their hands, but Hadewijch let
one tear fall and closed the book. The cactus that had been exposed
to the February frost had ultimately succumbed. The voices began to
reverberate, my voice and the voices, the voices
(Beatrice, Hadewijch, Nietzsche, Müntzer, me, John, Ana):
Tell me, I beg you, tell me
If you are ready to live the eternal cycle.
They had always imagined him lying in his bed, shut away in his room
but he was standing, eyes half-closed, smelling a camellia
        (the moment I was an immortal, at certain hours of the
day lost from time, I had no knowledge, not even vaguely, of your
memory)
and yet the memory of the temporal sequences distanced from my
solitude,   suddenly appeared at the door and I loved you, at
first sight,
but most of the time, at that hour,
I knew to find you in the house of Hadewijch
who I will call Hadewijch
because it pleases me.
In any event, today I came into contact with duration, the serene and

delicate objectives of duration

During the night, by the window, homicidal memories accompanied the dawn. It was harsh, suddenly bright. I could dream about myself lying on the ground, trying to fly using my hand

every day was special. But on a day particularly touched by an animal monster which he called numen because he had never seen it before, in his visions or lucid dreams, its name, apart from the first letter — an n — was felt, or found, or thought, on a piece of land inhabited by a house where there were no longer people but living beings, each one belonging to a space, or a century.

The fleeting moment had arrived when every resident of the house, if they were female, chose their man   animal object to make love to with body and intelligence. During the year, each member of the Community passed through the room in the tower that carpeted the entire house on the top floor. It had been the last space to be conceived, with walled-up windows and imperceptible silences. Their women   animals   feminine objects entered in a procession and greeted the monster filling the wall which was also an equal and living being. Sitting motionless, they knew they would never again have children because time had undergone a conceptual change, in addition to everything.

How to proceed? So certain were those colorful, multiple beings, that the forms of making love flowed from a thousand sources, gestures and words, gazes on objects. An unimpoverished universal language was written in the room beneath the monster's feet. The tiniest being approached it, flexible and smiling. In the mouth of the monster there was brightness and darkness, its fur was black. Its name began with an N, of the being that advanced along the ground, it knew nothing. At that moment, an immense roar passed through the house, with a color that had never before been seen preceding it fearfully.

Chapter VI —

My body and spirit underwent so many mutations   that I felt suspended on the edge of an abyss, simultaneously rotation, rising, and falling; possessing two languages, among many others that were less persistent and visible, I began to live almost entirely on the first floor, the war and Müntzer's decapitated head forgotten. Among threads, colors, passion and temperance, Easter eggs I'd decorated with Nietzsche by my side, the perpetual movement of objects and furniture, I read new books and practiced new writings on the ironing board. I gradually liquefied, became current, phrase, plant, small plant, and stone, and I saw myself tiny amidst them all with the vast dome and vast architecture above my head. Different images of myself
Ana de Peñalosa,
returned,
went around the world,
and found me in the same place waiting for my sons. Hadewijch had become subtle and loved, always absent, and her bare and florid room above me restored hope to my senses.

washing, sewing, ironing our garments of eternal shadows, embroidering bones of my sons, I plunged into the night thoughtless and sleepless, beside the lamp of wakefulness. I heard the war from a distance, I contemplated the interior and exterior, and the lightness of the footsteps; when she opened the door, the foreign travelers did not surprise her, she let them enter silently and showed them to their rooms, knowing the answer was suspended over the house; her favorite fabric was a black fabric that had once been blue; dusted with stars it had come from Spain and she would make an apron with it

if she knew how to sew; between her fingers she rubbed the fabric's structure, its imaginable color. Most remarkable were the wrinkles she smoothed, elucidating the cloth as if it no longer thought; then the conceptions, the preconceptions,

and the transitory mental representations came undone. Neither Hadewijch, nor Nietzsche, nor Saint John of the Cross, nor Eckhart, nor Beatrice, nor Lorenzo de Medici, nor Müntzer were present but they could not be distinguished from celebrated words and real tenderness. Those who passed from one room to another and sought to confirm the direction of their face knew that good/evil had been broken and that pervasive loves covered everything. Her husband had become tangible and full of metamorphoses. One afternoon old and wise, another afternoon as young as he had been, always thinking about Hadewijch and always destroying thought. That room was a place of leisure and work, of a barely perceptible delicious order; Al-Hallaj was still a stranger

enveloped in woven books and circles

He had spilled out everywhere, or in a corner,

such that looking for him quietly occupied Ana de Peñalosa day and night in the decline of her life.

Day and night,

without rest but deliberately,

she awaited Al-Hallaj's revelation. She had been told that the first shoot emerging from her body would lead her to the peaceful place where Al-Hallaj bloomed faceless

as Müntzer had bloomed headless. What happened filled her with understanding, she had put aside all her work except the sewing, lest Al-Hallaj moving past surprise her unawares. Placing herself outside any morality, any system of principles,

she again found Lorenzo de Medici as she had seen him in the quadrangular portrait (half-length)

the sun had gone, although it was not yet four o'clock in the afternoon, the garden had lost the radiance that had created it,

the powerful hierarchies produced

by the different shades of light. The garden seemed to her to be a peninsula occupied by a vast desert. She went to the gate because she sensed the nearness of Lorenzo de Medici, the linear legs of his horses. "It won't be Al-Hallaj, it is Lorenzo de Medici," she said to herself rolling up her dress

and penetrating the penumbra of other thoughts. On the façade of the house, Lorenzo de Medici's silhouette had appeared between the verandas,

and she herself felt a great comfort,

a barely explicit desire

to return to the past,

and her royal family,

parents, grandparents, siblings,

friends and servants,

dogs, money, collections,

titles, tapestries, and silks. So she went over to where Lorenzo de

Medici was silhouetted, becoming intoxicated with reseda and the perfect luminosity of the sun which had returned intense and lower in the sky. She had closed her eyes to everything, following the hand of Medici who fled into the shadows letting his memories fall soundlessly. Without knowing where he led her, she surreptitiously watched the ground and his feet, his long hand gloved to the wrist and adorned with a non-circular ring but which, in a paradox, followed the rounded shape of his finger. Al-Hallaj had vanished among the opulent crowd in the garden, had left without making himself known, neither to leave nor to enter had he opened the closed gate. Always following Medici, his hand and mink sleeve, full of memories and stigmas, she moved through the shadowed house, and when she sat down on a chair with a vast seat, she imagined herself in a book, the book where he had cast her.

Evening fell on the dining room windows   glasses, cups, jars, and bowls. In the middle of the table, Medici's hand lay on a floral centerpiece. Ana de Peñalosa put her forehead on his fingers, he imprinted the pressure of his square ring onto her forehead, and when she raised her eyes she noticed a tall cup made of crystal and gold into which Al-Hallaj's thought had plunged which Medici had given her as a present. In the eternal return, Ana de Peñalosa saw

> Nietzsche coming out of the dark-
> ness and
> suffused with language
> descending the river,
> the river of the idea.

in secret maturation
he navigated with a
dense book of water.

1   everywhere, and everywhere else, Hadewijch could be seen spreading out her body and her lands, as light as a fish is alive.

2   she had made love to herself
at the bottom of the boat
and all her beloved
thoughts were with her

plants,
cats,
dogs,
and beings of immortal originalities.

3   the boat rocked amidst the writing of Saint John of the Cross who
continued toward his decline.

4   ancestors and descendants, lands of Portugal and Spain, Flanders
and Brabant descended the river, current of water and Hadewijch's
mind.

5   and Müntzer meditated on the undestroyed state that would be
abandoned.

6   with this idea he lay down at the bottom of the boat, between

Ana de Peñalosa and Hadewijch, and all the remaining impossible things of time.

7   his unbeheaded erection had sought refuge in the water that circulated dizzyingly:

8   let us be singular and entirely irrelevant.

Prunus Triloba was tall and green, was a name, a desire, and a representation; it had been planted an arm's distance from the house last spring with much hope for inspiring texts, and no anticipation of the future; the person who had planted it ascribed it kinship with something and it grew with a green tip that was always more prominent than the others and, above the roots, immaculately clean soil; its pink flowers bloomed and withered within a few days, its first year of living and inspiring texts it had remained unknown to everyone and to me; yet it resembled something; when it bloomed in spring you might say that it bloomed with reminiscences, wanting to take me to the air of the garden and a new time. It certainly understood me deeply and had an ineffable patience with me, always behind or in front of my body, without disturbing me in my own light; the sun it saw was not the same, an unexplored amalgamation of energy and sayings where I, a separate body, had not yet arrived.

For that reason, early every morning, around the time I began to go down to the garden before the sun rose, I sat down on the mat as a humble figure and asked it as if I asked a book bereft of text, and read by another writing: "Tell me, Prunus Triloba..."

9   We reached this territory after a long journey, without children, with companions and animals. We still carried the paper with the writing; Ana de Peñalosa, always present among us, sat down in the position in which she wanted to spend the rest of her life.

Her glory was already gone, but she had left us the territory that was our meditation. We sat down on it as if we were leaning back against it.

Territory of meditation. We always thought it desirable and put it across our chest.

Chapter VII —

What was being meditated upon was happening on the lower level of the courtyard; it was growing dark though it was still late afternoon, giving food to a white cat that had found refuge under a car; everything was bluish light on stones; one cat here, another there, the bewildered dog did not know whether to run, bark, or remain silent. But the thin shy cat, fusiform, had climbed up to the balustrade with Fokouli, our white cat, where they kept a certain distance. I watched from below; lying on the ground on top of the mat I felt myself a daughter of the night, I wanted to live with them and among them, I no longer wanted to be named by men. Every last one of them desired me. Especially my caresses, even before the meat was cut into pieces, and perhaps more than anything to hear their name, and the intrusion of a time where men, if they continue on like this, will have disappeared.

I had the impression of hearing voices, that my cat and the shy cat told me: "disappear with us. Long is the night, let yourself be taken from your home, which is no longer that of your parents, to our lands."

We thought to light a candle because this constellation of cats and territory obsessed our spirits; always meditating, we concluded that the time of fire in candles had come to an end, everything that could be seen had its own light

it was a star of vast grandeur.

Chapter VIII —

This morning we spoke with someone who emerges from this penumbra but who, living in the city, has no territory. Müntzer's head, which we always brought with us even though it is heavy and seeps blood, constantly repeats to Beatrice: "The mystery of the world is not in the ambition of the powerful but in the willingness of the poor to be enslaved." Ana de Peñalosa speaks unceasingly, is not a man, nor a woman, runs among us in the form of a filthy pig:

"O much belovèd Müntzer,

I recapitulate these days that weigh upon me as an indivisible block of time. Only in the morning, in the usual climate, did we become lyrical and, somewhat freed by the possession of this new territory, we always thought of you, disguised in shadows of writing." The anxiety was less intense, the river of Hadewijch had come. Even if it was a mirage, the page was full, I wrote because I had visions

even now, when the lands of Portugal seem to be an impasse, I know that multiple journeys into the territory would be enough

to fall into amnesia every morning

lose any possibility of identifying myself

and having a name,

the common places of culture forgotten. Beings with an anonymous provenance contemplate each other in silence and at the margins. The state is cast into our immense sea,

an abyss where it will remain enchanted forever.

Pledging communion with the eternal, Ana de Peñalosa gave Müntzer a hair from her body:

— Let us leave the provisional to everyone else. For the two of us, what is eternal. — The days are different in different places. When Beatrice, Nietzsche, Hadewijch, Müntzer, the cat, or John come, they are not distinct, nor many. They are a part of me

as I am a part of them.

Chapter IX —

Night is going to fall. I will see the windowpanes darken and the light come on inside the house; I become aware, although without being able to describe it, that there is a recondite life of enigmas, incompatible with a gathering of people subject to common law. I want to hold on to the thread of this feeling but, all at once, nothing can be understood.

Walking, I'm afraid because I'm not a coward and next time I will still try to see in this enigmatic brightness; we moved naked within the house smiling at one another without speaking. I learned to see each body's own thickness;

thus I went along the path where Saint John of the Cross is usually found; it is the only place on earth where as soon as I arrive I can no longer evoke his figure and his footsteps, although I see him; amidst so many requests, so many doubly secret enigmas, my face fragmented and scattered by time stills, I envision the new departure. Naked without his long robe he beckons me with his fingers, and I bow my head over his advancing feet:

— You were slow to arrive. — Ask me about you, about Prunus Triloba the mad tree,

about the nomads.   (In fact, I need to return. It is difficult to return, or not return,

but for us the absence of movement is impossible.)

There,

nothing belongs to the same context of the old days any longer. We are the fruit of an experience of exile, and we have our own language and freedom. We practiced it during endless years in an open and closed house. We moved with all the spirits.

In that country I glimpse an absence of vague borders and terrain.

John,

I begin to remember drawings of sea, shells, hesitations, and very salty thoughts

John,

this path is always your country.

Your house and landscape without my knowing why.

Recapitulating what I wrote,

it is as if I said:

Following my solitude,

I went with you...

John,

the history of the Princes is a succession of intrigues, conflicts of powers, subtle and violent deaths.

Scholars know history to satiety and, nonetheless,

they want to experience it,

without assuming the fatal consequences of what they know.

THE LESSONS

Lesson I —

Ana de Peñalosa reached the end of her life. That it was the end is irrelevant to her, has little meaning. Once again she thinks about using the writing
that always served her
as laboratory
and alchemy.

Reflecting,
she said to herself:
It will not be a demonstrative art.

The writing,
seeing it being written lucidly,
is the foundation of this reality.

Lesson II —

We had come to a place inhabited by a horse. It was a true place, amidst a tangle of greenery, with an acrid, disturbing odor.

Prunus Triloba was at the door to the stable, planted in the soil and casting a faint shadow on the Prince's horse. Thomas Müntzer conversed with the Prince, Henry, the eighth of that name on the throne of England before rising to power.

— As I was saying — said the Prince — I would like to die on a battlefield, on the back of this horse.

— As I was saying — said Thomas Müntzer, resuming his previous speech — this is a brief encounter. It was only by chance that we have the same horse, and passion for Prunus Triloba, the same tree.

When we leave this place, I won't even try to find you to congratulate you on the birth of your children, nor will you send anyone out to look for me to save me from any kind of death.

— Any kind of death — repeated the Prince, meditative.

It was dusk. The Prince's horse slept, but his body cast a shadow of that same horse walking, trotting, galloping, carrying a rider on his back.

— Observe — said the Prince to Thomas Müntzer. — There is a rider on the horse, and bloody intrigues and execrable defeats everywhere.

— All times are equal.

— These bloody voices — continued the Prince — I devour them like a piece of game. But what is Prunus Triloba doing here? Is it a woman?

— I don't know — replied Müntzer. — It is a mad tree that has accompanied me throughout my life, that sits down when I sit down, that gets up when I get up. It is a dog.

— An obedient dog — said the Prince. — No. It is a still-young tree because it is a shrub, meant to indicate time.

— So be it — said Thomas Müntzer. — Who will take Pegasus? You or I?

— He is still sleeping — replied the Prince. — We will wake him so he can keep us company.

— This horse will sleep forever — was Müntzer's prophecy.

Lesson III —

We noticed that, twenty times using the measure, she took flour from the sack, leaning over the opening; she saw the flour running through her fingers like a sandstorm; she was very young, with slow thoughts and a precise smile; it's been a long time since she heard a crash similar to a voice grappling; it passed through the high windows and the walls of the abandoned chapel with the same intensity; and bread rose in the deep kneading trough. The next moment, when she came out of the torpor in which she was trying to recognize the nature of the voices, a seemingly poor man crossed the threshold of the door and, before remaining silent for long moments,

said

it had been a mad attempt and a catastrophe.

So we witnessed the wailing of an unknown poor man:

it is a place outside the house, where I'll be able to stay if it isn't too cold. I crossed the entire forest to find a place to rest. In the village, in all the places, there was someone or a trace.

I returned, therefore, here, to my place of work which, without any activity, suggests a double silence, a silence that is doubled as certain dense pains are doubled.

My father also used to return to his place of work, on Calle de las Espadas, in Toledo, when night fell and, I think, because it was night.

From a distance, I hear the last cries of the children, glad to see them leave. It is the hour of the wind which, today, stirs the treetops incessantly. I think about my poverty, about how to continue it. I need to know what will happen precisely and patiently, that is, meticulously. Then I will begin to write.

But the wind never ceases, it will unfortunately be a windy night, I left the windows of my house in ruins where I put food for the cats on one of the windowsills.

Here there are all the utensils needed to make bread. The spatula. The flour. The peasants. The poor. Here once again is Müntzer in the despair of losing the battle. So humiliated before a Judge who, nonetheless, is not a Lord of the human species. — He turned inward: — Sacrificed to the arbitrary decisions of the Count, my father ended his days at the gallows.

— Curious coincidence — Müntzer whispered nearly voiceless. — My father as well.

— And my mother — continued the poor man — they beat her repeatedly for nothing.

— My mother was also beaten repeatedly. She did not die old, nor young. Curious coincidence.

— I am the son of nothingness.

— I as well.

Lesson IV —

Consolation for Müntzer:

— Here I bring you the *Missa Solemnis* that Beethoven will write
after only three centuries have passed; for the time being it is nothingness, nothingness I offer you; soon you will also suffer your death,
you will also be nothingness; may this gift of gathered unborn voices
console you; past and future, Müntzer, are nothing alone.
Just like the present.
I meditated many years of my life on the emptiness; waiting, I ceased
to exist
but I have the sacred power to offer you this *Missa Solemnis*, born of
my blood before the birth of Beethoven's deafness.
Your father is speaking to you, or the father of your ignorant father,
dead at the gallows.
The emptiness does not pass by without anyone knowing.
Müntzer of my name,
or rather,
Müntzer, son of nothingness.
As Beethoven, deaf, wrote this music,
you, losing it, had a vision of the battle.
A while longer, and the final pain will come,
and the following moment.
My words are ignorant,
but you knew the lost peak of the battle.

I brought you, then, the *Missa Solemnis*,

still unknown,

so that you can rest your Spirit in it.

Lesson V —

Müntzer was dead,

his head rested on his arm and his desire to exist had passed without excessive pain or passion.

As a fish plunges its head into the water, the poor man accumulated words, sparingly and lucidly. His serene spirit had survived Müntzer's test, and he began to consider that poverty made sense.

In the place of Prunus Triloba, with Henry VIII, he did not covet the power of money, power over women, or the power of weaving hierarchies and rising to the top of them. He reconstructed the vast nothingness, which during the hours of the day   he did not open his eyes, nor smile through the mouths of the powerful figures that surrounded him, with cloaks and the most different signs of royalty.

He wrote in darkness, with clairvoyance and ignorance. His only light shining upon a tree trunk, it illuminated a fragile, retractable thickness. A faint incantation uttered his name, which was Poor. Who would believe that out of the clamor of peasants that filled the whole of Germany for years and years, Frederick Nietzsche would be born, son and brother. Son and brother, whisper and attempt, waterfall and spiritfall. A refusal that shook the spacious lands of Germany, inconsolable from the loss of their most perfect children: this peasant mob which, losing in Frankenhausen, lost the Europe that has drowsed, ever since, in hibernation, in Müntzer's head.

as a child, he remembered a day such as this, the wind and
clouds: "a succession of days in the same year of my life. At
the beginning of autumn, daylight faded slowly, waiting for
the chanting of the wind.

He plunged, in front of my house, into the movement of the
leaves that sliced, with a cadence, through the air. I dreamed
about the summit of the night, its highest point. What finally
happened to me later would follow from that day when there
were very few incidents. I then had this, my last thought:

My wife would be in the garden. It would be a fleeting
moment in the afternoon, the oval of her face emerging from
the fabric

so that her sorrow could be concisely revealed."

Lesson VI —

All this is typically feminine — my love for Hadewijch and Müntzer;
I have sewn unceasingly for days, worried about all the events; I make
dresses that adorn the walls of the house, the walls of the world, because
I eventually imagine them on horses that leave
and take them away.

They are multiple presents for Hadewijch
who like me,
plumbs history;
it is so mysterious that everything ends with our death,
that I think

about Müntzer's life,

whether I work, eat, or write, or love.

I love John of the Cross, as everyone knows, and his light, protracted footsteps. But I also love what is far from here in space and time, the nearness of my dog and our animals,

flowers and plants

advancing through the autumn. It is the first time I've read the Prince, although I myself have longed to be one of the greats of this world, vagina or phallus. Gradually, my glory changed places, nourishment and not only writing, voice low or silent. Ah! the Princes, ah! the kings, ah! the state, ah! the immense cities. I, Müntzer's wife, was his last thought on the mild afternoon, in the cage where they put him on display; from that point on I disguised myself in a thousand shadows until I was born with Ana de Peñalosa on an autumn November day. Hadewijch was a child then and wrote ballads and poems, our kin. Someone, with our face, cannot walk peacefully through the streets.

So I became the Poor. I call my dog Lord, which is another mockery. I have no Lord, nor anyone who is my slave. I am poor. These are strange days. Even in the afternoons that seem calmest, chaos teems.

— Come here, Lord, come to my feet. — I sat down at the door as I spoke, the night is lunar and deep. The moon passes dimly beneath the clouds and the dogs, Lord's friends and enemies, bark. It is a canine murmur, with words and music: — I live poorly at this moment, I am hungry and my ears hurt. — That woman, Müntzer's wife, arrives and asks him:

— Are you the Lord? Tell him not to bark. — I reply that days when

I don't have to go out and beg are rare.

— I do not walk on the paths today.

— I do. If Müntzer were alive, we would be the same age.

Lesson VII —

The Poor gradually became Hadewijch during the night that was white. We did not sleep, not because we had decided
not to sleep,
but why did not we sleep?
Still Poor and during the last moments of his
transfiguration
into Hadewijch
he said
that until she was six years old she had always lived at her grandmother's house interspersed with some moments of presence in the
house of her mother, also called Hadewijch. The first place was dark
and illuminated   sleep and lucidity   the second
had a permanent brightness, with enormous prudence and less reality
As Hadewijch's face was taking shape
she said
with an infinitely poor voice: — I was the girlhood
of my grandmother, always sitting in the corner, whose blue eyes
gave me, with deep precision, to you.

    — To whom? Our voice? — inquired the Poor who, momentarily,
remained himself.

    — There were many traces of you all over the house, and in our way of living. Old people do not always have an old sensibility. After two generations there was me, and my girlhood. Once I had been born, I lived with a child's spirit. My first memory is of light and shadow, and being within the circle that brightens toward the edges. There is a deep sorrow attached to the carriage compartment. We were close to harrowing moments, I must be about three years old. I am alone on the bench, there may be a crowd of people around me, even beloved people like a maidservant, but the loss is irreparable: they just separated me from my mother.

A summer must have followed, in the house of relatives. It was an extraordinary place for a city child, and one such as me. There was a house with an abundance of old wood, an expansive veranda overlooking a garden/yard where animals, vegetables, flowers, a pond edged in stone, and a well with a pulley lived side by side in the peace of the land, and the curiosity of my spirit. Beyond the yard was a large space with trees and plants that was accessed through a gate. But you couldn't always go in, you had to be invited by the neighbor. I liked, among a multitude of things desired, to climb up to the edge of the pond and dream, through the movement of my arms, and the haughtiness of my forehead, that I drew water from the well. I remember that a thin vegetation covered me in shadow, and that I looked at it cast against the stone, feeling high up. My uncle's hunting dogs, Scheldt and Tagus, which are rivers, ran freely in the yard, everywhere. In a darker place, in the shape of a triangle, chickens paced interminably. My aunt, a country lady and woman who raised them and ordered them to be killed with the same love, gave advice, distributed a hot drink and moments of rest to those who had walked a great distance. Most of them brought her gifts, chicken and olive oil crackers. There was always an old woman sitting in the kitchen praying a third of the Rosary for our intentions, and for our dead who were to come. Even with the windows open, a Church religiosity hung in the house. Beyond the windows, a pagan religiosity, my extraordinary love for the tree trunks, and the penetration of any light.

Although the house had its own light, I especially loved the flame of the candles, and the oil lamps; they were for me the day of night, the place where my eyes had one final awakening before slumber. My bed was old and had been restored by my father, with a crucified Christ I still have today, and was one of my first presents, hanging at its head. They always left me a lighted lamp, another flame, and I don't remember if the maidservant slept in the same room, or in the adjoining one. She certainly did not sleep with the other two maidservants, as she had a special place in the family; she was the goddaughter of my grandmother, to whom she was directly connected by love and strict obedience, although she was an intelligent and fearless woman. She would sometimes speak to me of other realities, later on.

At that time, she often saw things with my spirit, the two of us studied, in silent complicity, the luminous depths of the cave.

I assume we must have taken any number of walks, as was the case later on, whenever we were in the countryside. She did not know much about the uses or names of plants, but she could recognize them, and told stories about the beings that went beyond their reality.

Lesson VIII —

At that time in my life, my father, who sent me curious messages every week from far away, kept a coffer of memories. He had come to spend a week with us and looking out the sash window, saw a beggar in the square. He sent for the barber to come to the house to shave him and cut his hair. He sent someone to look for a white shirt and clothing, he ordered dinner be given to him.

When I look at my face in one of those memories, I am reminded of my present face reflected in the mirror. Superimposed, but nearer, I contemplate my aged face, my long hair falling over my shoulders like a feather, not dark brown: already white. In the depths of my present face and my aged face is my face as a child. And they are all the same face with my eyes looking out.

Lesson IX —

The Poor had not yet left Hadewijch as she spoke. Hands on his knees he contemplated his own bones, and the memory of speaking. He had an attentive ear. Hearing and seeing all the way to the great scene of the closed manuscript room, open only to me and my father; hearing and seeing all the way to the windows and the door was the specific vocation of the house, with a hallway and bedrooms, and rooms that shone with cleanliness, profusion, and tranquility. There, my seemingly fabulist monster and my later visions traced out their fate:

> in the house,
> which Ana de
> Peñalosa passed through,
today, rain and wind replace the sun,

which is equally bright in my spirit. Besides being the man
who makes our money,

Medici,

who else will you be?

As a child, I shed my blood in every room, in a difficult struggle without truce; at every threshold a question about who they were with so
many years, and so many irreparable deaths; the ability to illuminate
that I had; over this family of mine hung the desire to buy the past, to
suddenly be born with vast family memories,

or did that past already exist as its belonging,

and had been interrupted at an unforeseen hour?   This kind
of enigma of purity was a heavy burden, so much so that my father, my
maidservant, and the blue eyes of my grandmother Hadewijch seemed
to coexist with a refinement of principles and habits that involved
a certain continuity of education and time. Ana de Peñalosa would
have a past of domains,

powerful beauty or dark night

Mesus, neighbor to Medecisa, was immensely wealthy; he was a sun
worshiper in the objects and luxury with which he dressed and treated
his slaves; the opulence of his speech and writing was unmatched, and
all the kingdoms and sciences of the earth had collections and precise
concepts; his late father, who had a clouded spirit, had gone mad
contemplating the brightness; but Mesus, all-powerful and fearless,
lived among fragrant furs, and they said he would eventually go blind
among the luminous waters of his garden

or was she a larva deposited in the present, in the absence of time and

thickness? Often, opening doors and pausing angrily between the rooms, I wanted to surprise this secret. Often, looking through the illuminations, or sitting on the furs, I wanted to surprise the spirit of those who had read the manuscripts,
and closed the windows with such exactness.
Now I lean toward the version that a certain ancientness must have existed, but one that was absolutely original and unexpected. Not aristocratic or with an orderly family tree
but

Lesson X —

The Lord said to the servant:
— The time is beginning to come when the light will reveal all the corners of the house. Have you cleaned all the dirt, all the dust?
— Not yet — said the servant. — I have been meditating on cleanliness, and the dirty pig. A great confusion has descended upon my dark spirit. Isn't what we call dust nothing more than matter from our mouths tracing its vibrations on the walls and floor? Isn't what we call dirt only the darker layer between the brightness and the sun?
— If you know more than I, then I dismiss you from my service.
— Let me accumulate all the dirt and dust in a sack and leave it, at the exact same moment, in all the corners of the house that the sun reveals.
— If you speak to me in riddles, I will dismiss you with no gold coins, and no sandals.
— My florid feet are already moving toward the door,

I will serve,

whoever awaits me.

— May you be confused in their house, which is a labyrinth.

— In my sack I carry the handkerchief with seven knots: "when all the knots of the heart come undone, then right here, in this human birth, the mortal becomes immortal."

Lesson XI —

If Müntzer, and those that in Hadewjich's house had found a form and manifested themselves, traveled far with her, really far, as far as the rising of the sun, perhaps we would find the continuation of the journey:

but this time, following her gaze, Ana de Peñalosa left the house. Without traveling down any path she found herself in the city, at night, surrounded by incarnations, pathways, details; it was a nocturnal overflight, an anticipation of her future state, no thought, nor the contexture of the writing itself, had left with her. Far off in the distance, she knew she was still somewhere

but it was another image of her body

which had begun to work the land with Prunus Triloba Plena in front of her and, at her side, Beatrice, who could not bear the silence

her spirit always rising

she looked at her double image sowing the seeds.

The desire to leave lifted her up.

Lesson XII —

She gradually entered a realm where plants and animals spoke without a sharp voice or accusing silence. She had passed to the next moment and had remained in front of the open door like someone who stops, and escapes. Dawn broke in the place of darkness and, behind her, her objects lined up prepared for the anguish of exodus. Prunus Triloba, which she was going to leave behind, bloomed enchantingly and guarded the visions that remained buried in the ground knowing that the world is vast and limited. Without a single tear, Ana de Peñalosa turned and released the objects into a large pit she had made within the house. As a murmur went up from their mouths she looked at them questioningly, and lit the last lights. They looked intently at one another ready to bid farewell, and not a single one had asked her hand to pick them up, since they were heavy and, presumably, mortal. The houseless cat passed beyond the silence and, this one in particular, was unwilling to accompany her, because Ana de Penãlosa, through the colors of her dress, had become immersed in the green in such a way that she was now only vegetation and water.

Lesson XIII —

The objects fell silent reflecting on time and the nostalgia that was to come, but a faithful figure had leaned over them and cast an uncontrollable space suffused with air and the chants of anonymous sailors. The house disappeared behind her and she spoke unceasingly with a word for every being. — It is an abduction — she said to the gate when it closed. — But without violence — she said to the first stone — I would be unable to leave.

Lesson XIV —

After Ana de Peñalosa's departure, different types of thought invaded the house. Several autonomous intelligences traced their fate on the books they made and which were secondary, primal was the documentation of a thinking vibration in a place. The long narrative that was going to begin did not come from the interpreted description of their lives, but from the evolution of their interior transitions, which might come to converge, at some points, with the universal adventure, their experimentation and flight. She had reached the end of a deep melancholy, for she had never stopped wanting to know more about Hadewijch and her companions. Nearby, Hadewijch had sent her a message   for you, for your birthday. Adding up time, what time, what time remained, what was time?

Lesson XV —

What verb was meant for her?
What was time?

The purple flowers that tumbled from the shrubs belonged to a marvelous era. They are now only flowers, as they lack the presence of Hadewijch, to whom they were connected; near the gate, in June, the cherry blossoms and lilacs rose up. An untrod ground led to the door of the house. A perfume of multiple scents traveled through the air, collected by an enormous pond of water. I get up to work unwillingly, always thinking about pleasure (that it alone awakens my spirit). Hadewijch, whom I was cultivating, no longer passes beyond the door. So I wonder whether the flowers are still the same, or whether Hadewijch, as well as being an image and a place of enchantment, is not yet a person and a spirit.

(In the primitive egg, neither the representation nor the idea roared. Jealousy slept with its mouth closed.)

Lesson XVI —

She is somewhere, and night falls, almost no light is reflected in the window curtain. What is she doing? Who is she speaking to? Is she silent? Nearby is a child who was born during the last few days, mother and daughter are connected by a lapse of time. There are more people in the house but the figure and her child are thinking about another space and another era. With a sovereign air she approaches the cradle and examines the features of the child who still has no face. This child, her daughter, liberates her from having children. She meditates on this, with the profound hope of recovering time
in every sense,
and walking freely,
without dust
or
moments

of unbearable sorrow.

From that face, in the cradle,

appears a furtive bird,

enveloping her in a heavy

green light — the black light is torn apart, and an orchard can be seen

full of fruit,

and birds as agile as they are migratory.

Lesson XVII —

I looked behind me and saw that I was being followed. The path of my desire is inexorable; I must travel it; those I encounter demand it.

After planting the sunflowers I went up, depressed, to my room. I picked a peony although I rarely pick flowers. I put it in the glass inlaid with silver on the windowsill.

The fly buzzes and, suddenly, silence falls, the peony with its pleated corolla often draws my gaze. A sumptuous crimson red.

The furniture in the room, the coarse curtains have a sandy whiteness, my eyes use the light to become fixed upon a point; and then, rising up from my womb, I'm certain that I am going to encounter myself, a child contorted with feelings on a day during her fifth year. I am doubly present, I am a double person or image, and the shadow of these faint moments is red, like the carpet where I'm sitting in front of the book; I return to the pages and come across a castle   a castle, and come across a frog   a frog; water flows nearby like the round skirt of women, ladies, and protected servants.

Throughout the room,

in this one and in the other,

there is a climate of nascent love,

it is the moment of my conscious birth. I bow my head to the crimson figure, her voluptuous and infantile arms. "Crimson," I repeat several times, bound to the curling pages of the book. Crimson touches me laughing with a thoughtful air, from a thinking childhood. Unfurled into several people lost in times, I lose my voice. My hand moves toward the place where I can see her,

and I give my hand to Crimson,

lifting her up. Her undefined beauty has no end, she rests her feet on the ground, on the air, she bobs promising she will exist forever, which I believe. She was until now hidden to my senses (as if behind a cliff), although she had visited any number of beings that welcomed her indifferently. So she returned to the family home, after looking for me unsuccessfully in different lands, including the land where we are born for the last time, which is now abandoned to cemeteries and insipid battles. Crimson lays her face on me, and surrenders to the pleasure of seeing me stretched out, ready to unendingly give birth to her,

and keep her alive.

Lesson XVIII —

From amidst the glass windowpanes that unceasingly dispersed the light; from amidst the perfumes that were your vegetal voices; from amidst the body of Hadewijch that now had the shape of a perfect little bird; from amidst the barking dogs that call us,   the welcoming of the figure had been born.

His name was John, and he was old,
although he was poorly dressed,
you could tell he had been an aristocrat in some other world.
I moved
to his side
to speak to him,
his hesitant eyes closed.

— Are you John or Müntzer — I asked him, always bound to the
distant perfume that guided me.

— Are you Ana de Peñalosa, or Hadewijch, or Crimson? — he
asked me in the language of gradual perfumes
which I had discovered since that morning.

Lesson XIX —

I return to his room and find myself, a subtle form with a hanging
head, a space of blue in my arms
and the astral scent of hours. A deep feeling finds refuge in this
my body,
and at that moment John of the Cross speaks in gestures that I understand as if I were clothed in them,
or lay down with them; the blue is triangular and true stars were falling
into it; stars upon stars, stars from all the ages, stars maternal and old
like John at the beginning of light. From this blue form is born
someone whose name I do not know, who demands my silence,
always silence. (From this moment on, I will always wear the blackest
black dresses,

lakes with small signs, these nocturnal colors are the extreme intensity of light,

what am I saying?)

John looks at me complacently, knowing that I am following my path, which is dark,

a dark night. — Look at how everything behind you is lost — he tells me — it is the past passing by. Look at how everything ahead of you is lost — it is the future of the present.

Lesson XX —

They spoke to me about the quality of what I wrote, and now I write hesitantly throwing the papers to the ground; the blue comes with me; our writing gradually became so fragile that it was on the verge of perishing. I dream that, in the place where I lay my head, I had been born a stone. Hadewijch, always with me, wants to introduce me to someone I already know from a portrait. She is a woman in whom the sexes are the most predominant part of the body, and she confronts me describing the quality of my writing

of my living

and dying. Hadewijch tells me: "Put your hand on her." Hadewijch tells me: "Go and fetch the open coffer where the landscape is resting delicately." When she comes in, I first go through her books, and the closed part of her life; we look at one another with no apparent expectation; a cloud from Portugal passes by, and our eyes lift up and open; we sleep all night, with dreams and incalculable hours of wakefulness, and the day became an intense gale. Hadewijch serves us in silence and without stooping, among cacti and other plants that break through the room's earthen floor and lose themselves in the window. Side by side, that woman and I contemplate Hadewijch; she wears blue sandals which produce a murmur of flowers that appear to have fallen into the water as her feet move; a smaller cactus leaf emerges from the largest leaf and guides the green over the windowpane. Still seemingly inert, we progress unceasingly in a written thought; Hadewijch now intones a melopoeia whose meaning remains a secret and falls over our hidden texts like a veil; other cacti with numerous leaves hold on to our voices

because

the two of us sit down to receive instruction on the princes and mysteries.   But what drew our gaze was the departure of the caravel.

Lesson XXI —

Our vocation was to create institutions and books, and we murmured like an echo resounding in the vaulted room:

for my volition to be volition,

no other can exist,

shadow without measure,

grandeur and shadow. She and I, through the open window, we began to imagine the barren king in the wake of the river. We immersed ourselves in the imaginalia mundi, and left our life there to go on living. We wrote while he spoke, not what he said, but the echo his words made; we wrote, by chance, on notepaper erratic world, lost continent; achieved by will, cunning, or a balanced budget. Achieved by will and cunning, liberation from the yoke.

We raised our voices in our writing: Its power was a representation of other powers over it, a capacity for creation sustained by a coup of power, the power wasn't its power, it depended on a powerlessness that wasn't its own.

Lesson XXII —

We confessed to one another: — How sad the dispossession of time makes me.

Embarking on the caravel, we said to fear: — I shall see. — At the port, the caravel was docked in the night that opposed the day of the year; black seagulls bordered the sails,

and stars had taken root in the houses along the port

because the river is celestial

and mutual death may find us along the way.

Lesson XXIII —

The narrative begins in the exaltation at the end of lunch, game and history. Which book will it be? Which annunciation will it be? Which figure will it be? I do not know, truly I know nothing about this sequence; I am sitting to the left of the window

on the carpet of tile that extends all the way to the door,

it is early afternoon

and the young woman writes

to the one she loves

about what she loves

The shadow is so unobtrusive that it covers her feet with a thin oblivion; sweeping her gaze across the light there is nothing that displeases her; the wave of her hair perpetually covers her ear, and her voice moves toward her fingertips; time constantly recedes, and surprise stills her gaze on a spot of green, which is still an unknown color; her throat becomes suffocated as if she were overly perfumed; a constellation of enigmas forms under the name mauve; she deciphers the remote green in the square of the window; she lies back down, remembering being taken by the river,

and her head covers Müntzer's

which has just lost history,

or its body.

Lesson XXIV —

The caravel   built for high speed and sea routes close to the wind   sailed through the waves at an angle; the whole of the sea plunged into her head, and the green — an unknown gaze — interrupted the possibility of her expressing herself.

Pan had called the sea a perverse green force, and sitting up in her bed

bed of sleep,

bed of death,

she clamored for the final corruption of the world; her foot hanging off the bed was muscular and firm at the tip; if someone wanted to read her gender in it, they would have to raise their eyes in the darkness up to her face, sweetly incomprehensible according to our moral experience of facial features; she opened the window that looked out over the sea and her hand, or right wing, became an escaped fish.

Unspeakable monster, it was unable to distinguish between these last few days because there is a strange aspect to time: the slow pace of life; the noise that disturbed it, without causing it fear, accumulated, alone, at the bottom of the caravel.

Ana de Peñalosa was in the house of July and August awaiting the approach of that sea:

her guests, rare presences, would come.

Jodoigne, August 6, 1977

TEXT FOR THE REMAINING LIFE

"A man learns his own name very slowly."

William of Ockham

This image is false.

In the great peasant revolts, and in the attempts at urban autonomy, it was not the bourgeoisie who was successful but the Princes who were affirmed.

This was said in a book.

In a book it will be recanted.

Let us see.

All wars have been a single battle, of kings wanting to keep and expand their reality, of bourgeoisie desiring free cities, of peasants propelling themselves furiously toward the place where all this comes to an end and theirs begins, of clergy and soldiers distributing words and weapons for fame, money, and the kingdom of God that is coming.

Of men, not even a shadow. They are many, numerous, mutually denying this name, which belonged to all of them.

The illusion of only one man, the purpose of a human universal, is rightful expression close to the voracious point, where pulling out eyes is the most important thing, because a defeated living being is an unconscionable visual sign. A sign there was no Golden Age, there isn't one now, and not even he himself — the survivor — knows when it will come.

Here, the survivor is named Poor. It is impossible to even say that he is a poor man. There is no man, the Poor is an image of the lost part of the battle. An image that in this text is a Figure, or rather, a remnant and archetype. What remnant was left to us, what remnant will we inherit?

A continuously lost battle (the most generic definition of time), for the benefit of the princes and, when they are dead and obsolete, for the benefit of their powerful successors. What was left to us was a conception of reality, a shadow, an empty space and a virtuality.

The series of successes, our defeat, affirmed the princes in their endeavor: they only wanted one reality, we ended up thinking there was only one reality. Even dead, three dead centuries ago, this reflection remains: reality is social, there is only one reality, and it isn't our own, unless, because of wealth, cunning, or merit, we believe ourselves to be princes. And, as such, we continue the battle. Why isn't it surprising that this one (what other name could be given to him?) is called powerful, he who took us for parts of his unhappy ghost and could use us as he wanted openly, and can take root in us clandestinely, as a subservient means of his enchantment? Why isn't it tragic, this idea that the world is social and also the rectangular landscape where the images of power are found? What else is history if not the place where the powerful incarnate their ghosts, achievements that are counted in lives, which the text will fatally call pre-human, in endless human lives, when only one was enough for it to be an irredeemable scandal? Why wait to express nostalgia for the moment when images of power will no longer be free to roam, unpredictable, hungry, and tyrannical?

This text contradicts those others that nullified this remnant, this immense remnant; contradicts the idea that in order to silence this millenarian scandal, they conceived the relationships between pre-human bodies as an exchange of mutually beneficial services, for lord and slave, for prince and peasant, for captain and soldiers, for clergy and faithful. Some of them gave protection and a name to those others who, in exchange, gave their menial bodies.

This text says that if there is no memory of being human, it is better to remember the remnant, all the remnants, the remaining life. This text says we were not left with only one idea of reality, it also says that a shadow remains in the remnant: one of vengeance upon the remnants.

It is clear, from the limpidity of the pebble polished by immemorial streams of water, that vengeance does not change, nor inaugurate, but gives unpredictable successors to dead masters; unity is the strength of the new master, as disunity was the fate of the old master.

The same waves of battle left this place empty.

This one? Yes, the social place, an attractive estuary for our gaze. It was said in a book that man is a social animal. Will we have read correctly, if the social is the evidence that this animal was never able to be a man? If animal wounds the ear, let's say pre-human bodies that had never accepted anything except the the different names they had in the battle.

And why are the Lord and the slave called men, a reality that exists only in language, that this is the imposture where our hope might sleep?

Because the Poor (another imposture where a hope of ours might sleep) is not only the remnant, it is an archetype.

The text immediately nullifies this imposture: the Poor is not the proletariat. It is a name whose singular character will not reside in vengeance upon the master, nor in redemption for others, the other pre-humans. It is its own mutation, undergone at its own risk. And that is a signal. It will not be an agent to preserve what exists, nor an instigator — an emblem of the revolution to come.

Why choose it then?

Why choose this pre-human image, preferred over all the others? Why identify this text with the image of the survivor?

Because it is the only one that allows us to go beyond the Prince. Everything has abandoned it. It is therefore the first in which (and not in whom) the ability to create from within can be fully exercised, since in the outside, in the social space considered to be the only reality, it is no one, a thing of nothingness. Renouncing everything is the rule for opening up to this transformation.

The text does not give reasons.

It only writes the landscape it looks at and, like an ambushed observer, it sees that it was out of this thing we call a human body, more precisely out of its different names (only these names exist because the human is still a theozoological fact, although not social or, even less, introspective) that, three centuries ago, the nostalgia of being man was born. The nostalgia that, contrary to what is believed, does not reach the past, but is a "delectable" act of futurity, which cannot be dismissed as coming for much longer, in the hope that the Absent is not the Monster, as always, although not this time.

It thus takes shape: not a founding myth, but a final myth.
Man will be.
Everything that has the body of a person may be human.
Everything human will be socially insignificant, or nearly.
In the intimate place within every man, the insignificant will shield the

different images (prince, bourgeois, poor, peasant, priest, soldier, et alii) from the enemy metamorphoses that guide their historical development.

All the poor images, lacking man, entangled in that final archetype, as if the intimate were not only past sedimentations, but also a cove for capturing future cosmogonies.

It is in exile, in the outside of the outside, that the network of figures, like Ana de Peñalosa, Nietzsche, Saint John of the Cross, Eckhart, Müntzer, Hadewijch, and others, takes root in order to receive the myth of the remaining life, and wonders whether there will be a place in the human body, among their bodies, where fantastic cosmogonic changes correspond to incredibly slow social mutations.

Since no life can ever be lost.

The text is, then, ambitious in what it inscribes, because of the demands arising from the final myth: extending the theological dignity of souls to the entire zoologically human body. The idea that immortal souls accompany hierarchical bodies will be inconceivable there.

Soul and body will not exist separately, nor will they be two, because the body will be with itself, assuming access to itself and all its own cosmogonies through feeling, in such a way that no body may naturally construct alien images of power. The purposes of the human will thus be the exclusive responsibility of the pre-human species.

A. Borges.
Lisbon, September 28, 1982

IN THE HOUSE OF JULY AND AUGUST

PROLOGUE

From what the Great Lady tells me, I lost you in the abrupt whorls
and interruptions of my letters. It is your unanimous feeling.
I move away from it because, if you still insist on reading me, I will be
able to inhabit it from within.
It is clear I'm not telling the story of your lives.
("You don't know how to tell the story of our breath," you say),
nor indeed am I telling much about them.
I know you by name, Marguerite, Eleanor, Martha, Beatrice, and You.
I know where you are. You tell me what you do. And I construct a
perspective.

No one who reads me will be able to imagine what your lives were,
but they will know, or so I hope, the finality you are becoming.
They came, they existed, and they left.
Only what you left behind interests me and I train my spirit to understand what remains. The abandoned and buddhic fire in the places
where you stayed. The growing life of your deaths, homes.

So I describe what we are given by death, the figure following the
metamorphosis that moves you.

Let me enter you: spark my light in the intimate brightness you cultivate. I come with the perspective of death, not the death that strikes
fear in you, but the death you cast off, as you grow in your existence.

You are the precious raw material of the nudity that triumphed over innocence and exalts virginity.

I am writing incredibly intimate things here, which I place in the intimacy that belongs only to you. If they stay and are able to sleep in quiet slumber, you will see that they look at you. A perspective that lets you rest and, dreaming, announces the figure following your luminous virginity.

You did not give birth to Nothingness.

You will not have nursed the Being

and its terrible Weft.

Your body did not perpetuate, utterly singular, it left berms.   You go on becoming,

and they ask you how many you have, if it was difficult to have them, if they have a father and a recognizable name, or if having had them you do not let them be seen because you're ashamed of their illegitimacy.

If there is a flower, the flower isn't in the vase, nor hidden. So many have asked you whether the tree is fertile, how young and experienced you are.   They will insistently ask you to account for the absent fruit, as if your being should stand still, astonished, in a deathly kind of constant autumn.

If you did not come to nurture, what did you come to do? they demand of you.

You surely notice that I leap, from sentence to sentence, trying not to surrender any meaning to their misunderstood fate. It seems I'm trying to leave unfinished the images I use to dwell within your feelings. There are even sounds that don't go together and I write them along the edge of dissonance.

It is true.

I write as if you are a finality.   A movement that abandons fruit and flower, along the berm where you are staying, a sovereign force between being and not being the woman they expected to bear fruit.

What I am saying is let those who know it's important to see do anything they want.

My perspective, why not say it to the end?, is the amatory form of my knowledge which, if you so desire, I will place in the intimate luminosity of your still-incomplete sovereignty.

Do not be anxious about the abrupt whorls and interruptions of your lives, my correspondence between us, because the fire, Link, is not a story we can tell.

(Luis M.'s third letter to the Ladies of Complete Love)

1st part
RIVER-TAGUS

(1)

In the house of July and August,

for many months, years, implanted,

with the entire range of spirits. When I sweep my gaze along its façade
in the place with the mass of nettles, I penetrate its walls, I am inside
its navigation, which is unusual for such a thick and heavy house.
Through the last window in the far corner,

which now remains until the half-open night falls completely, I watch
the descent from the cross, the end of all glory.   The seated man,
always attentive and absent in his presence, seems to have been there
his entire life, on an unknown path. His occasional and eternal wife was
a phenomenon strictly associated with distance: she often wondered
about the quality of her memory. When she thought about Brabant,
where she was, about the places and time she had left behind, the
emotion she felt now seemed much deeper and, in certain aspects,
more real and akin to reality. She remembered it as it had been but
with a certain inconsistency of energy, or module, which gave the
slightest detail a singular acuity and amplification of meaning. In the
large cobbled courtyard, harmful and extravagant weeds, whose names
she only knew in a foreign language   polygala   epervière
          tussilage   laitue des murs   were drying out to
be uprooted; cobwebs, spun in splendor and free from the domestic

associations of ideas, hung forgotten against the walls; because she spoke about the man when it was from man and gender that she was going to be liberated, she slowly climbed the stairs and saw him sitting at the table:

> without circumnavigation there is no land, only an idea of land.

(II)

After the departure of John, Müntzer, Nietzsche, Suso, Hadewijch, Eckhart, Medici, Ibn Arabi, and Al-Hallaj, different types of thought invaded the house. She had finished reading "To the Ladies of Complete Love," and any number of people were sitting at the table, A. Borges, he himself — Luis M., and the remaining figures who, with their visions, finally made the monotonous feeling of life in the house disappear. Any number of autonomous intelligences traced their fate on the books she made and which were secondary, primal was the documentation of a thinking vibration reflected in a perfectly unknown place and material. Her effectiveness did not depend on memory, but on knowledge. Looking at the writers sitting around the table, she found that this term was empty, and that their images were defined, more than anything, by the position of their gaze, and their abandonment of the old way of reading and writing. Meditating on their fates she saw that nothingness was approaching, but it was powerless. The long narrative that was going to take place did not come from the interpreted description of their lives, but from the evolution of their interior transitions, which might come to converge, at some points, with the universal adventure, their experimentation and flight.

(III)

Among them were Jasmine, Martha, and Mary. Jasmine is the being of difference. It introduced itself to me with a smile because it finds everything that beings different from it do to be natural. It has an adolescent quality, and roots in the best age of life. One might say that it knows the emptiness of the Palaeozoic and has a sense of what six hundred million years is. It has contemplated dinosaurs, pelycosaurs, giant tortoises, and what was inscribed before nothingness. It spoke to me using silence and smile. We were, Luis M. and I, on the night that was a lasting dawn, sitting at the table of water and medicinal plants, in front of the low flame of the candle and two images, the brown fabric of the tablecloth, and the pink of the teacups.

— It is time to leave history and go and live in the world of six hundred million years — it told us without using any figure of speech. It was surrounded by a large number of species, it itself was a rare species; it lived alone with those multiple species, in a house opening onto a garden, in a garden opening onto a house. There was no more than one of every species, and their differences had the same weight as the barest indication.

(IV)

Luis M., third lover chosen, had come twelve years ago, but had remained invisible as if he were unborn. Now that he had arrived there, he was the murmur of silence, and his concentration reminded her of John of the Cross, Eckhart. As for Ana de Peñalosa, her youth elapsed (in another four years she would be fifty) although she kept childhood in her face. Martha and Mary also lived with them. Martha made a drawing of Mary. Or exactly, ten drawings. Women who changed in Mary's vision, transcribed very lightly.

Curious things then took place which were intended to prevent the normal course of the new annunciation.

(v)

in that distant house where she was usually happy and imagined to be well, there were vacant hours filled with a great sorrow; the days mounted in a vast hierarchy to master; the fleas abandoned the body of Stone the dog and invaded the rooms where they slept; they felt them bite their legs as they wrote and once again (as in the year before), the July holidays tried to show them that they are a place of illusion. The housework appeared to her to be invincible, one after another the dust motes accumulated and demanded her mental effort to eradicate them; the garden, with an indescribable exuberance she'd never before seen, had surrounded Prunus Triloba until it nearly toppled over; and not only this had come to burden her, but also, suddenly, the disruption of her financial life; when she went down to the kitchen, the newly born cats, which she had brought home in order to rescue them, along with their mother, she either loved them or hated them. For their sake she had unfurnished the anteroom, and her reference and resting places had disappeared in the half-light she opened to the beginning of the History of Portugal as if she had some kinship with it: "deep and damp valleys favor isolation," as time walks toward the place where Luis M. had been born.

(VI)

At lunch they had said that this narrative will also be a meditation on roots: uncultivated land, a wooded landscape, bare fields of grain lying fallow,

vineyard, olive grove,

all this had been seen in the visions of Brabant which was a different quality of land; that's why she was confused, and her monster appeared at every stage of her life

she spotted the discovery in the middle of an unirrigated parcel of land where the act of telling was as vague as a breath.

(VII)

Mary and Martha occupied an expansive room with three windows: Martha needed all the light, Mary needed some shadow; with their hands lying fallow they remained there during the day, although they were free to look and fear; Mary had changed her dress when she came in from the back room where the luminous wall crushed her with the falling night. Martha knew what this was all about, guided the preciousness of the lines.

Luis M. gave himself over to work
with no illusion,
and Ana de Peñalosa wrote
finally weary of writing
"in the figure hanging on the wall, and on a very cold July day..."

(VIII)

It was necessary to make an inventory, the list of goods left behind.
One after another
the days sink like stones. The stars are the light, glimmering they do
not die. But she is not a star. She knelt beside the box where she
kept the valuables, sat on her heels forgetting the varicose veins that
were beginning to cross her legs. What came out of her mouth was
"year"; several times she uttered this name as a kind of second name
for the coffer; several times she had already tried to put some order to
it, but the time contained in it made her fearful, with so many dark
faces. The diary begun in February was interrupted in July, continued
a year later, the year Plantin Moretus had begun publishing Ortelius's
atlas. January, March, April, May 6, in the afternoon: "the beginning
of the decline is plenitude." The following year: "Insensitivity is, on
an emotional level, the equivalent of stupidity." March 15: "my pain is
the nostalgia of being between two paradises: the earthly one, which
I have already lost, and the divine one, which I have never known";
April 27: "because this ash I inhabit is human"; April 29: "I was born
to destroy myself at night, and conquer myself in the morning"; May
25 (Thursday): "you were born for absolute love. Accordingly, do not

agonize when, on earth, you love everything that can be glimpsed or an image of my absolute love"; May 26 (Sunday): "My daughter so alone that I, God, torment and surprise myself"; July 6 (Wednesday): "here you will not have a submissive mouth, or knees forever kneeling. Here you will only be eternally intensely loved." The afternoon of August 9: "Arm me for life with a knife in my mouth." One of those years she was covered in a perpetual desire for sleep: "give me the grace to go to sleep"; November 28 (Thursday): Grandmother's death. At the age of thirty-three: "Let us not make our human suffering useless out of despair." Undated: "just before nine o'clock in the morning I am on my way to the library. Through the carriage windows I see the detritus of the city piled up against the walls. If not for the stench, the garbage would be beautiful." November 27: "There are demonic periods in my life."

(IX)

And nothing had been lost; the still-small climbing plant had been sacred. She had carried it with her thread, and put her wedding ring on top of it; afterward, looking at the light behind her, she felt she belonged to an invisible species from the sea crying out for help. Oceanic was the whole of the window, with the climbing plant in the vision of whiteness and maritime fates; even the houses were transitory places of the sea, when it came to land.

On the periphery of dawn, she rose from her bed, with a deep longing for Luis M.'s fate. She came very near to him without speaking or making noise and soon, for no apparent reason, they were talking

about narratives, boat keels. Luis M. said "exile has led us to speak the language on the inside, and look at it from the outside." At the far end of the room the plant climbed around a column where the desire for nomadism was always present; in front of the darkness. It was a column of silent waters turned toward different places and also Portugal,
a tower studded with olive groves,
cork trees,
episodes, decades, pilgrimages,
pleasant stories and sojourns that had visually disappeared. Writing, painting, storing away melodies.
Creating eternal forms.
In the scent of the vast open bed, in the brightness for reading, she imagined herself, or truly was, in a place where the shadow of the cork tree was cast onto the ground like candent clay; later, reflecting, she told me I had discovered my reality of Man;
yet this discovery received not only a formulation but, more than that, an abstract formulation;
the discovery was the lifting of a veil:
the body offered is a body of feelings; the offering of the body is the gift of the heart;
it was the heart that intruded into my perceptual field.
It was the empty and itinerant kingdom of toys, the door open to the height of the storm.

The garden that grows, and looks for a new geometry of masses, and scattered flowers, is covered with a dampness that emphasizes it because it has rained without any water collecting, and disturbing the Nordic atmosphere of summer; I acutely recall the presence, another constant morning in July:

— ...we love each other. We only practice acts of violence and survival. Lovers we are not. I am loved. — Martha and Mary had come. They work on an egg that contains the seeds of the future, whose multiple potential is indicated by a series of openings, and the five triangles that are the organs of understanding; they lean against the window trying to look outside but they are mindful of our deep melancholy and Mary tells us, "I am loved by a stranger."

If only those who have already fulfilled their destiny are able to love, I will accept my absence from the room and hide down at the pond where the rainwater fell to the ground without a final form. But I still hear that we only have the experience of loving infinitely with a shudder.

(X)

there was also the unsolvable problem raised by the mother and four cats I had brought home
after the twins
had killed the fifth.   Which cats do I keep? Do I keep Cisca, and send away Bergamote, Marguerite, and Estelle? Do I keep Bergamote and send away Cisca, Estelle, and Marguerite? Do I keep Estelle, and send away Bergamote, Marguerite, and Cisca? Do I keep Marguerite and send away Bergamote, Estelle, and Cisca? It wasn't a Byzantine question because Bergamote was connected, in fact and in her spirit, with knowledge and the voyaging rupture of writing; because Estelle was a luminous vessel, although darkness murmured in her movement and permanence; because within Marguerite a solid battlefield

had been created and the available knowledge had generated a desire for power; because Cisca, for nights on end, was an egg in a valley of strange cold and breeze.

(XI)

Throughout this long journey time passed — a few days — Monday, Tuesday, Wednesday, in precise terms; at certain moments, the house and its grounds, its garden that evolved in perpetual combustion, seemed peopled with men and women, cats, their ancestors and descendants, dogs from the Middle Ages in large numbers. Hanging from the gate was a wreath of flowers which spilled out a perfume equal to that of the honeysuckle in the beguinages   which couldn't be canonically religious. These beings, without being religious, had their own statutes and led a sacred life. Young women like Martha and Mary were there, although they weren't looking for spiritual guidance or the protection of men; the possible departure of a cat filled their minds and hearts with disquiet; as if at night, opening up the large gate, the men had left their wives in solitude; although no one had been killed or taken prisoner in the war, or the Crusades; although those women had no precise religious vocation, nor did they seek support from the clerics, or a secluded life that would allow them to give meaning to their existence; although there also was no ideal of purity, nor poverty.

(XII)

the first feminine being to appear would thus be the first to leave. A night of sun and fog fell quickly, the sunflowers that hold the green against the wall maintained, according to my intentions, their watchfulness. From the windows everyone noticed that there were sharp stones everywhere, and that the cats hid themselves behind them gleaming equally; their lithe bodies reminded us of waterfalls.

Marguerite stood up, then, and looked at us, by chance, always walking; everything is fleeting,

or rather,

time only seems to pass; but, after her departure, Martha encountered Marguerite's beauty in the mirror; her eyes blue, or without reference, resplendent; her cat face did not seem fantastical to us.

Nieuport,

that place

had a sea

with low waves

as cannot be seen along the coast of Portugal; she was behind the windowpane, in front of Luis M., who had absented himself into the territorial landscape of the book; so with no one to keep her company she abandoned herself to the pleasure of being alone, thinking intensely about the beguines lost or found behind the small windows that looked out onto the trunks of ancient trees,

and who came from different families, fortunes, and generations; she herself, Marguerite, had surrendered to the freedom of abandoning the hermitage for months on end, although it's believed she had been forced to leave; but when she was with Luis M. in the gardened enclosure looking at the line of ants winding across the ground, unable to still her cat instinct and make it innocent, he, with his hands tracing the air, told her that there were many emotional conflicts among the beguines and that the circle of their companionship spanned the distancing and the journey; without any mystery, Marguerite vacated the space in her room, opened the closet and unmade the bed, folded the sheets. A placid dampness took hold of her feet and her eyes coveted for their keen vision

or repellent feminine beauty

which the Cathars hated, and Luis M. always advised her not to hide.

(XIII)

Dressed in black, hood white, what is a fabric?

Luis M. says it is a landscape, as he also says it's important for me and the beguines to make bread and do other tasks, burdensome for their monotony and the presence of people so different from us. Luis M. says, "of another species."

I have to leave and it isn't easy, how I love this orderly crowd of houses, and the quiet presence of the beguines; our conflicts are transitory and timeless, and we will never shed real blood. Eleanor, Martha, Mary, Blanche, they told me about their lives fearfully but plainly, and I hope not to have wounded them with my attentive listening; it isn't easy being a woman with knowledge, and who can protect themselves from not loving, in this world? If it is difficult for me to leave you (the living beings) it is no less difficult for me to leave the trees. Only Luis M. do I have the impression of not leaving, because his hand fated for

writing accompanies me and makes it possible for me to have a future lover; today is August 6, the Transfiguration of Christ; they also accuse us of heresy, and perhaps that is also why I'm leaving; I told Eleanor that I will only let myself be guided by my journey,
and she rising from her knees replied
      higher than the sky is the mountain
in which I humbly recognize that the teachings of Luis M.
bound to the natural nobility of our spirits
liberate us;
nor do we neglect our duty,
which is the light in the house,
and I told Blanche to keep the wide chest of lace closed until the prices at the market are reasonable.

   I drew closer to knowledge with them   who appear in rapids of water that enter through the windows and ornament them with drapes that seem to repel reason, even in the watchful dream I usually have; the voice of this man who sings, who sang all last night, has become more attractive than I might imagine, and I don't know
why he sings,
where he sings,
or how his singing reaches my room, and thus my desk for writing, doing nothing, or making lace. It comes from Blanche's room at the end of the hallway, which she inhabits with me,
and I believe it is Blanche's clear voice that has taken on this trouba-dourean aspect, because knowledge can be anything but unexpected; here, in the house, the voice says that there are no heresies, and
   I wasn't even surprised that I wanted to leave with so many obvious reasons to stay; I let my hands hang out the open window where the

honeysuckle reaches up.

I recognize that Alfonso, the Wise, has great wisdom, and that these melodies are being brought here because we aspire to successive migrations; we are not sedentary, nor wayfarers
but I aspire to traverse the darkness.

(XIV)

It rains serenely and we are in summer, it is a time of testing for the beguines; I don't want the night to advance any further without writing you, Eleanor, but I am completely bereft of images and narrative; nonetheless, I wanted to warn you, although you shouldn't give it much importance, that the time will come when the brothers of the free spirit will be persecuted by the hierarchies and that we, the beguines, will hide them in the fabric of an extensive underground network.

this afternoon, when I was sewing on the black, which has often happened to me without my ascribing it any influence, I began to consider the nature of our garments; now, my preferred way of working is to read and sew together and, between the two durations, I write; such that there are three activities, the sewing, the text, and the book,
without forgetting the lit candle, the windowsill and, behind the windowpane, the honeysuckle I have already spoken about, which cannot be distinguished from my experience; in my secular life, when I still believed in singular relationships of love, I had immense beneficient disappointments; and today, when I went to open Luis M.'s Book of contemplation, as he allows me to do so we can all be filled with

multiple perspectives and no less dreams and contradictions, I saw he was sending a letter to someone — Hadewijch — who in insurrection-ary times had contributed to Ana de Peñalosa's knowledge of sorrow; it is a high Saracen or invading letter; "you are not a memory, you are a landscape"; "at some point in your suffering, you sent me a landscape that is a dune facing the sea; a landscape that smells of the sea, where I rest my spirit in order to see time"; "no companionate being lives there, but I see it, and it seems to me that the dune shouldn't always be deserted"; "we are sitting on the sand and we marvel at the beauty emerging from our emptiness; I cannot assuage the pain, but on the sand of the dune, amidst a few trees, is the joy that was recognized as fragile and precious";

(XV)

Yesterday I was dropped off on the street, in the center of Antwerp; wandering is my fate and on this square,
sitting at the table,
I dare to leave the high walled house,
I go back in,
and here I wait for the day to forget itself,
so I can leave.   I walked several hours from the spot where the horses left me, the place where I'm supposed to spend the night doesn't even belong to a community of beguines; the city is dispersed, flowing along different pathways to the Cathedral, and the market that rests with no shouting because I don't hear it; in no other association would they let a woman go out into the streets, but no one bothers me and

I begin to believe that my presence, from my dress to my fingers, has become invisible; I will not speak for years and years or perhaps the time of this short visit to Antwerp, except to Hadewijch, and the consolation she sends me; I am in the Index with this shadowed ability to create beings that are not exactly humans but are beings, and abandoned until now; our passion is mutual and we have survived every day without encouragement or any conclusive reason; our bodies came to rejoin the city, on the Vrijdagmarkt, and I begin my conversation with Hadewijch, incomprehensible to this people's ears or instruments.

Luis M. moves away and does not hide the multiple directions of his anger. We talk and talk over what we are drinking, lights come on in the perpetual dampness between shadows and laughter; but there is still daylight, and on the ground, around us, on cloths, there are signs of an immense movement toward the Cathedral

Luis M. hands me a letter addressed to a friend,

which I take with me when I leave

after learning its contents.   I must spend the night at the house of Plantin, the printer, so that for the years and years of my short stay in Antwerp, I will know, as I know my fingers and lace, everything that relates to the Book, including the manuscript works: I was alone in my room and I felt the arched entrance shudder, and an indistinct voice call out for me. Unable to pull myself away from this writing I did not dare to open it and later I regretted my failing. I found Plantin in the proofreaders' room and when I told him my host of sins he said that it was time to go in. I was perplexed by the austerity of the first room and he told me that over the course of thirty-four years they had published more than twelve hundred works before his death in Antwerp on July 1, 1589.

(XVI)

It began because several women shared the same house, which belonged to the wealthiest of them; we reduced our needs and exchanged the means of satisfying them; we opened our doors and formed nine small dwellings with one, two, three beguines. I live with Eleanor, Blanche, Martha, Mary, Hadewijch. It is a large number but we are all silent and I, with them and without them, structure my life. We all have a common love — the aspiration to the candle flame; we all have a common difference — the true difference; when they suspected who we were, we hardly spoke, although our Great Lady defended us; I do not envy our Great Lady — Ana de Peñalosa — because we are all great. Luis M., as always befalls innovators, was much discussed and maligned in his own time; Odile joined us and, now seven, we rounded out the number of the house. We also have a common aspiration to succor plants, and I distinguish myself through my compulsion for writing, the preferred light,

which led me to the Plantin-Moretus printing house,

although the immediate reasons were subtle and multiple like our ideas, I mean, affections.

Plantin told me that, although I was a woman, I could write in a room next to the workshops, because for him, books are more important than gender, and books make gender invisible; he introduced me to his daughter Marguerite, he spoke to me of Marguerite Porete, a Cathar burned alive and we, three Marguerites, became silent, and absented ourselves in the depths of the house with small windows, where we exchanged motivations, and I explained that I had not taken my final vows,

that I can, at any time, release myself from my word like I can leave my house, and come here; Marguerite told me not to be blind to the books that surrounded me: — Marguerite, do not be blind to the books that surround you — and her speaking captivates me, like the expansive harmony of the house built around a rectangular garden profuse with tall climbing vines, which I inadvertently compare to windowpanes. The aspiration to the candle flame, Marguerite, is real and not an image. Around five o'clock in the afternoon, a kind of premonition invades us, and we go down to the common room where the first to arrive lights the candle. Fascinated, we look at it as if we were alone, and today, in your house, that is the moment I most miss
although I have a premonition that the candle is being lit, and Eleanor who lit it today surrenders her spirit

I don't mean to say "like someone dying," but in her smile it rises up; she is the youngest and, with no contradiction, the oldest,
and when the compulsion for writing comes upon me,
she often does my work
as if she wrote, and the writing falls at our feet, so secondary.
Plantin is moved by how much of myself I reveal; but his discretion casts night over the secret.

(XVII)

It is an intensely veiled night
as if Antwerp had disappeared; I sleep in a room in the middle of the house, and after writing the last lines to Luis M., I open a door captivated by the tranquility of the water; it is a basement, and I have to

walk down several steps; even though I'm almost asleep, a veil is lifted:
I bend down to pick up a ring that I believe is on the ground — a
crystalline floor like nothing I've ever seen — and I plunge my hand
into the water because the ring is merely a reflection of the reliefs
on the vaulted ceiling. I then think that if Luis M. had been here, or
Martha, or Mary, perhaps they could have made a drawing because
anyone who wants to depict what exists using only words leaves the
task undone.

(XVIII)

I had to return to the house of the beguines because I received word
that the rain hadn't stopped falling; I was reading the *Liber Contra Man-
icheos* when I was transported to the center of the flood — Eleanor's
simple room; a stream passed beneath the ground there and, because
the volume of water had increased abnormally, a torrent of mud came
through the wall beside her bed and spread out, in the image of blood
that cannot be staunched; we sensed that an impending death would
follow and, although it was almost five o'clock, no one went down to
light the candle. We then witnessed the following phenomenon, which
I will transcribe, as I want to recount it faithfully to Luis M., and print
it accurately at the Plantin-Moretus house. Blanche, who finds it difficult to consider herself someone's sister, stood at the window in the
common room, erect as a column; Eleanor and Hadewijch came and
stood behind her; the mud spread through the walled grounds, and
the flowers around the single large tree turned the same color; Odile,
at the entrance, tried to divert the swampy course of the water; but,

as she continued the work, her feet became covered in silt; the last in line, behind Hadewijch, was Marguerite, I myself; Martha and Mary were on the ground, eyes closed to the tumult; the cupboards where we store the provisions and usually eat, one at a time, had opened up, and the broken dishes and loaves of bread followed, with a crash, the current of water; Eleanor climbed up to the center of the table, kicked the candleholder (later, during the evaluation of the facts, someone stated that she had only given it a sharp tap with the tip of her foot) and we thought we saw her transformed into the large tree, with multiple breasts and rare fruits; the water did not stop spreading and we saw the reflection of a face angrily enduring the nearest power, which was the vast lineage of our hierarchical superiors. If, with false modesty, we turned our heads toward the garden, it was to be able to return to the reality of the house, which we cleaned for days and days amidst murmurings, sighs, and concentrated moments of silence; we were so tired that our thoughts seemed to depend on our eyes and our smallest impressions; I spoke to Eleanor who envied me continuously with sagacity, but who was possessed by a great vibration, which manifested itself primarily in her walks in front of the tree, which was growing, and her troubled eloquence. I asked the Great Lady to allow me to return with Eleanor to Plantin's house; which she finally allowed, because the rule of obedience is increasingly losing its meaning among us.

On the journey to Antwerp, Eleanor told me that she was a Cathar and that it was very difficult for her to speak to me because she lacked a means of expression. I smiled, provoking an intense attack of anger which translated into a torrent of words that contradicted her and confirmed my smile.

— The candle — she said — was for me a demonstration; in the same place, I always followed it, never ceasing to recreate Perfection like a frog in its metamorphoses; once, Marguerite, I saw your face/ soul in it, and a thousand powers that encouraged me because, if I were a snake, I would want to die coiled up in your secret.

During the flood, Plantin would say "au fil de l'eau," our cats perished, and my face must have transformed because, at times, I fell back upon a certain physiognomic immobility, from not wanting to weep. Eleanor, in front of me, trembles with the vagaries of the carriage, and searches for the meaning of my spirit, always with her eyes lowered; the animals, in their silence at the level of the word, in their bizarre corporeal form, move me like no man.

She asks: — Even the snakes? — and I hide my face in my hands and cry,

which joined her to me forever.

(XIX)

What she was thinking became clear to me: "now that the common wall behind the house has fallen down, I will be able to contemplate the verdant confines of the next garden at length; in the bower, far back in the depths and in the shadow of many leaves, there are also statues where the green no longer seems to be a deposit of time that flows, but a surface that mirrors; the old beguine comes to speak to me, offer me parsley and roses that survived the catastrophe; we talk and talk and she says that, in order for us to know each other a little better, it was necessary for the wall to fall down; I never even thought about this deluge. If what I can conceive is not infinite, then I do not yet know the limits of my knowledge."

(xx)

Intently watching Marguerite's hands, I read, without difficulty, the following writing: "Luis,
let me describe the art of intelligence and love, and the height of my anger... Do you remember when, on the grounds of the house, a cat that is completely foreign to us because we have no obligation toward her, had her kittens, and Ana de Peñalosa herself brought her milk and scraps? I knew Yolande had killed the kittens and, before I spoke to her, I wanted to see if it was true; then the cat looked at me in the empty place. I went to find Yolande and asked her why she had come to kill on our doorstep, and she responded
that they were only cats,
destined for hunger.
I repeated why did you come to our house to kill
and kissed her angrily to not sink into hatred, let me describe my feeling of knowing to you.

I lost the letter in which you suggested that I, some time later on, should attend the Community, with Ana de Peñalosa. The letter had given me a certain power of affiliation. Through no fault but my own, I lost it. And perhaps also because in it you told me
'and unto them it was given to live one of their lives forever.'"

(XXI)

Plantin awaited me at the door.

— I would always come.

Eleanor isn't staying with me, but in one of the houses on the same square; the curtains in her windows are linen, and they cover half the windowpanes; I think I see her face behind the window, showing me her room and the place where she is staying, for I will only have direct access to learning in the workshop, and a mindful reading of the books and manuscripts, but I should convey my light to her,

at night on solitary walks,

or at the table in her room where she awaits me.

I consulted treatises on Gnosticism, the Cathars, alchemy, and it seemed to me that the two of us would journey through a future already past; it was night and, at its end, the large tree was lying on the path; Alexandra, another beguine, rapped her knuckles on the door and I understood that it was time to leave and cross the square; of my light, on that night, nothing had been written, she had refused to listen to me, and rocked her body repeating ironically   knowledge knowledge   knowledge;

I told her that few women, in our year, and century, and millennium, had access to science, let alone any power, and she replied that at least the wind tumbled through the darkness,   and, on different doors, the repeated chord of the beguine's knuckles could be heard.

But she was worried about my health,

that I wouldn't catch cold when I left the house and crossed the square,

or look at the candle on the windowsill, which she was going to put out. I turned my head and saw that she was making signs at me, wishing me not a good night, but that I would steal what had been asked of me.

(XXII)

I found Hadewijch with a strange face covered in tears, on my walk around the Vrijdagmarkt; this dispersal among different houses makes her suffer, and is inexplicable. — "I do not think as she does." — "Premature or undesirable?"

(XXIII)

After spending several hours looking at the beginning of the *Mutus Liber*, I closed my eyes with an inevitable somnolence; I was lying in bed with the shutters closed and Marguerite, Plantin's daughter, played an aria in prayer similar to an intrigue half-spun at the moment of discovery;

the strength of my exhaustion overwhelmed me and, in the meantime, dusk fell as if it were winter; that night, I was supposed to go to Eleanor's house, and give her part of my deep feeling; I could not, perhaps, awaken from the slumber where I believed I was being pulled down heavily by a star descending within my body; if I did not wake up to go and visit her at the expected hour, Eleanor would get up from her chair, lay out the precious lace on the table, and stoke the fire with the poker, turning her face toward the darkness where footsteps always grew and disappeared. "It seems she did not have time to finish her work," although she hated this unthinkable argument. She would pace through the room like someone taking flight, persevering in her hope; later, a torrent of insults will come out of her mouth and, breaking the rules, she will open the door wide so the beguine cannot knock with her knuckles; I believe she will eventually put out the candle and all the light, even that of the fireplace; and, in the swift night surrounding her, go alone, angered with her fate, and benign and opposing forces;

I sleep, and always the born star radiates like a hydra over the closed book on top of the quilt; I want to speak, send her a message, but it's already a morning of vague shapes, and I imagine the slumber that breaks me ultimately shines upon her beautiful and almost unknown eyes: may heaven and earth be spared such a devastating encounter.

(XXIV)

When I came in, Eleanor was lying down and her face, without any light in her eyes, had followed the migrations of her ancestors; her immobility and air of death surprised me, but there was no reason to wake her   time had flung an infinite staircase in front of us; the movement of celestial bodies was present in the room, especially in the fire; halfway up the chimney it did not dare go out, preserving the golden age; I myself had dressed even more modestly, and had brought her what she called "stolen." I had laid it down under my cloak, on the windowsill, like a surprise in a place, and an event full of precautions. When the sun rose, progressing through thick hours as I held her lace in my fingers and stoked the fire, she was still mute and, when I touched her arm, she seemed to have cooled and taken on a metal

stiffness; it was the age of Eleanor, her age, I saw the silence of the
room read it in her mouth, twenty years, and no more; I approached
the window, disbelieving the reasons for this immobility. Tormented,
I left to call the beguine who did not sleep,
but I stopped in the hallway because the land of the bed was sacred.
Eleanor had already stood up, and said to me: — "I fell asleep not of
my own decision, but to obey you."

(XXV)

"Luis,   I am uninterested in my own nature, I go out alone not
because I'm weary of company, but because the relentless desire to move
toward Plantin's house invades me during the hours of hard obedience.

The windows closed, the door closed, I protect myself from looking
ahead, or to the side, passing my extensive memory over the most
telling moments of my life; Marguerite moves further away every day
even when she is coming; I dwell on the pearl in her chest
contemplating the nakedness of my intelligence, and warding off the
shock of the noise.

I returned to the material in the book, but then I know that Antwerp is overly fraught with symbols, and I imagine Plantin's printing
shop where Marguerite lives, because the material of my daily life is
imaginary. As soon as I enter the workshop I look for my corner and
place, and today, in a recondite spot that I believe to be hidden, I piled
up an armful of plants, and ashes, and I began, with slow monotony, to
want to fabricate paper, thoughts to read to you, and an expansive life;
I mixed an intensely colored pink with the name of my work, which

will be a far-reaching Treatise burned and resurrected."

(XXVI)

In two identical messages, Marguerite and I received Ana de Peñalosa's orders to present ourselves at the Hospice to care for the sick. Such a sudden interruption caused us a deep discontent but we presented ourselves scrupulously to the regents, with one of her letters. The woman who welcomed us did not want to know its contents and murmured, head bowed, into her lace collar: — "Goodwill is enough."

That night we were on duty without seeming to have anything to say: the fire was out in the large common room which, in this case, was an infirmary and a Chapel. Eleanor wanted to light it to make it less secret, so it could participate in the life of my coming which, that day, was aimless; less than routine, obedience, and passively traversing a stretch of night. I wanted to write a caption for the scene, but the scene was interrupted without any actual substance to guide my spirit: two women dressed in black sitting on either side of the credence table resting their feet on the fire represented by bricks that had just been warmed; they were awaiting the work, or the work was awaiting them; many unknown symptoms were lying on the beds   a girl named Alice whose body has an unusual complexion, a rose, an image of the moon in its conjunction with the sun; a lush plant that still held the scent of its extracts and essences,

but covered by a thick cloud that wearied their hands and backs when they lifted her up. — We are a weak spirit — said Eleanor. For hours and hours before the Mass it would still be night, and the craft was learned in relative darkness.

All this was enough for the nuns to come and pester them with silent questions. All it took were glances, moving quickly past the front of the door which, that night, was open letting in a slumbering air. — Give me your blessing — a few of them said, judging them to be sisters with much light; Eleanor turned her face; Marguerite twitched her hand in disgust, and sunk into a wait of inaccessible understanding, unless it were for the descent of a holy dragon. "Above all we must do nothing, except read, reread, and meditate. Until dawn comes, and the regent sisters jealously enter the hospice."

(XXVII)

"Luis,   today I did not care for the sick; I was alone, completely alone, I retreated to the back of Plantin's garden in the space occupied by a mass of sunflowers; I do not know if it is autumn but my body produces an experience of death that may be an indication of the beginning of the work; the wind had severed three tall flowers, those that have a human aspect, whose heads hang like the sun falls upon man; first I picked them up in order to lay them on the ground, my eyes now bleary with tears; then came the tears that speak truth, and I moved away toward our book bringing all of them with me."

(XXVIII)

To reach Eleanor's room I must spend a few seconds looking around the inside of the house where there isn't a single bird, or movement; though there is a constant volume of voices in prayer, and bodies fleeing from me along the walls; there are three beguines of unequal heights who constantly appear, destitute women who came there to vanish; always, before going into Eleanor's room, I see the enormous shadow of a man cast onto the door and, fastened upon him, the fingers of a young beguine who aged long ago; inside, Eleanor, standing, also senses the shadow rising up between us, and moving toward the table with the one who is speaking, she deftly writes about her sanctioned plants; she is in the time of being young, and of presenting herself as young to the world, her cropped hair makes me lower my eyes to the shadow, which goes out; I go into her room and tell her, as an evening lesson, what I just experienced; she writes, and drops the pages into the flames uttering Luis's name; "be quiet," I murmur without leaving the doorway, and because I don't want to identify the shadow. In the hallway, the three sisters complain as they usually do before going to lie down, or pray, as they usually do before going to sleep; we then see our lost sex appear in the ashes with the appearance of a split-open seed that has survived the test of fire; Eleanor moves toward the threshold of the flames, and her undressed shadow teaches Luis M. the profound journey he does not know. I, who should guide and teach her, am overcome with an intimate respect and, eyes closed, I lie down on her work table to be gathered.

(XXIX)

I was scrubbing the immensity of the floor in the room that is both infirmary and Chapel, when the child brought me a letter on which was written, as an address, "immensity of gardens, palaces, churches, old convents, eminences, and towers." This is my pseudonym, which circulates between me, the Great Lady, and Luis M., and so I recognized that the letter was addressed to me. I opened it carefully, after cleaning my hands of the water's dampness and again, as the only text I read "immensity of gardens, palaces, churches, old convents, eminences, and towers." It was an order, or a suggestion of departure, as if I had already been scrubbing the floor in that part of the world for a long time, and I began to try to decipher where I was supposed to go: I always sensed a few symmetrical streets in a future Pombaline structure and I understood that I had to exchange Antwerp for Lisbon.

It was also written, in a second text placed alongside the first, that I must leave Marguerite's knowledge behind as a real presence live in the city of Lisbon in a small humble house to the West of the Portas de Santa Catarina, work for a gardener and his wife, and cultivate the land. Only at night, if my spirit managed to find a lost hour, could I make contact with Marguerite who, herself, remained in Antwerp, in Plantin's house, to learn the art of printing and, more precisely, to gather the alchemists' experience and collect the dualistic doctrine of the Cathars. This difference in fates surprised me in a moment of great wisdom and, after I had folded my flowers and medicinal plants in a cloth, after I had considered that, in any event, I was also going to descend to a subterranean universe, I connected Antwerp to Olissippo where there were, after all, extraordinary names for my cats — Boa-Hora, Graça, Madragoa — because I would find them alive in the house of Alisubbo the gardener.

(xxx)

I am lying on the bed that is my work table, my bench and, very often, the table that sustains me; Alisubbo's forehead and the warm scent of the fruit trees are at the doorstep where the dog stalks the bone without boldness.

In the deep rhythm of fatigue...

here I have my library of herbs; won't Marguerite have an herbarium of books?

at night, in this solitude because I do not know the city, in this solitude because I barely know Alisubbo and his wife, this entire land of fields, barren in part, but already laid out with seeds and gardens, with orchards, vineyards, and olive groves, retreats with interstices of gold until my bed, and in my memory I gather phrases that delight me; yet nothing here is unknown to me, and it is normal, because even though I had been exiled, I wanted to be a Cathar with the Cathars, and dust with the rest of the earth. If it is true, as I teach myself, that every being that incarnates has, in the invisible, its celestial correspondent, the Angel, I have a vague premonition that it is more present here than in Antwerp, and that it may be possible to never end up procreating, like Alisubbo behind his fence.

I am less pleasing to the eye than before because, as a precautionary measure, I loosed my hair, and smudged my face with ashes; when I bring scraps to the pigs, I stay with them longer than I need to, and today I told the pregnant sow: — The embryo is in your womb; it is four weeks old and a few centimeters long; and I still speak.

As for writing, I do not write; Marguerite writes.

(XXXI)

The Faithful of Love approach without hope that might be fleeting; it is suddenly night after my labor which was shaking olive trees and, later on, picking up the olives on blankets; in my corner, Marguerite no longer enters in the same way, neither in memory, nor in miracles, but in a breath of light. On my bed I accumulated several sacks of straw, and it rose up into the air distancing me from Alisubbo and the chickens coming into the house to sleep without fear. Alisubbo calls me, and gets no response. I patch the sheets thinking about the fire, and Alisubbo's wife, named Alice, is still at the threshold of the evening's coolness with the door open. She is half blind, almost elderly, and very kind, behind her I do the housework, picking up countless objects which she drops begging forgiveness: — "Forgive me Lord because it is a punishment that I don't have my old eyes. Forgive me Alisubbo because it is four hours past and..." — My solitude and hers invade this hour of four o'clock in the afternoon.

(XXXII)

She tells me that two nights ago she had a dream. It was a dream I made my own. I ask her to tell it to me, she says that her blindness prevents her from having a good memory but that, in the darkness, someone or something wanted to kill me, but another hideous specter appeared from behind and paralyzed the threat of the first in a fulminating way.

(XXXIII)

Alisubbo is wandering as a soul. He does not stop from sunrise to sunset and, as soon as he sits down, a new task appears, often a nothing that he performs meticulously, saying that the plants have their fate. He also utters enigmatic phrases and I believe it was because of this enthralling side that Luis M. and the Great Lady sent me here. As soon as he finishes watering the garden he goes up to the city in the bloodless dawn, without me knowing which part of Lisbon is his domain; when he returns, he knows more about the land; when he plants potatoes he does it precisely and, at the same time, raises them up in the air and tells them a word before covering them. He naps restlessly getting up a thousand times to look after a tree trunk, divert or kill insects, straighten out green beans, or climbing vines, water a cornstalk that dries up with thirst; not even at night does he finally settle himself down to sleep

he gets up to put out or light the candle, call the dog moving further away outside, split the last piece of firewood he forgot. Alice confided to me that his birth is a shrouded mystery.

— Neither a mortal being, nor an immortal being, but one that exists? — she confessed to me yesterday, in a conversation at my bedside before I went to sleep.

— I will wait for you down there — said Alisubbo because he wanted to speak to me. "Down there" is the golden part of his lands, with flowers that are a salvation in this late September, dahlias and cyclamen of yellow, lilac, white, and colors for which there are still words to learn; there are also sunflowers with us, those that still persist, and those that die. I don't feel that it's Alisubbo's house but rather the garden of the Community, and that Blanche, Martha, Mary, will come here as thoughtful and resplendent enigmas; there are also lemon trees and petunias, and climbing vines that catch fire in my hand when I touch them; yellow bellflowers hang over our heads, which are closed to new thoughts; there are also geraniums, and a multitude of fragrant plants from mint to rosemary, and I don't know why he wants to speak to me.

Alice showed me the land behind the house. And I understood that by the will of our Community I had come there, not only to help gardeners, but to learn the things necessary to the reality of my fate.

That day Alisubbo said nothing to me, and the next morning was foggy, which is rare during this in-between season. I did not know what he wanted to tell me after the long hesitation: "If I could...." Perhaps he could have suddenly become almost mute as his wife was almost blind; all at once he became calm, sitting beneath the olive tree without moving, neither in gestures, nor words; beside each other, Alice and Alisubbo did not speak in the usual way, they let the distance rest between them, which in a certain way was identical to the kind of relationship I wanted to have with Marguerite. Alisubbo's shed was behind the house, as was Alice's pond, surrounded by olive trees, the trees of this country.

(XXXIV)

Marguerite,

I am in the house of a gardener, at the gates of Lisbon, a city I had never seen and must see, they tell me, from the top of one of the hills to be able to see River-Tagus, and the mouth of the sea. Alisubbo will take me there tomorrow and, out of longing, I can hardly sleep or write to you.

(XXXV)

I don't know why, but in Alisubbo's house there are never displays of anger; it's as if a candle always burned above us and captured any other kind of fire; he often stoops down over the soil, and I believe he converses, in all his quiet, with the land that will make him.

On Friday, Alisubbo was the victim of a great fright; he was overwhelmed by a vision and told me that, as much as he wanted to, he couldn't yet guide me

to Lisbon,

to the Largo do Convento da Encarnação,

so early.

(XXXVI)

The water, solidified by the cold, always crystallizes in the same system; November 30, today snow is falling on the inner courtyard, the sundial marking its center is already covered. My days have also been covered by the departure of Eleanor and I haven't dared, with the respect that is due to them, make or consult the books. Time has passed, and it is no longer Plantin who reigns over the House, but his grandson Balthazar who announced to us that his emblem will be a star. No one notices me, not because they're indifferent but because they want to let me live, and I can sit down for as long as I want next to the fountain that has the shape of a chair and rests on the ground with claws. I see such intelligence and labor in Plantin's courtyard that I constantly smile in the winter light, although walking, eyes lowered, my perspective changes: it might seem to be a carceral courtyard liberated by the hermetic procession of the windows and by the sky during three seasons of the year; the sun has now illuminated one of thirty-six glass panes in a window, already counted by me.

Without fire, no combination can be made, not even with water; I keep myself as young as I once was and here they still respect my ability to act and think as a reflection of beauty.

(XXXVII)

Eleanor water,

I imagine you just where you are. What is the country of Portugal? I began to study the language you inhabit with such delight that I can already use it to tell you about my life and very nearly proofread its books. See if what I'm going to tell you is correctly written, for you told me in your last letter that, following the path of childhood wisdom, as soon as you arrived you heard Alisubbo welcoming you, and Alice telling you what you should do and where you should sleep: years ago, on a day similar to this one, it was a morning of grief: two of Plantin's printers had been accused of heresy, and the magistrates had entered this House; I remember that an official was next to the vine, and the vast memory of these books was scrupulously investigated; I was sitting down studying in the proofreaders' room, penetrated by the language I am using to write to you; they looked down at me and and I intimated that I came from another realm and that my origin was the origin of the earth. In that language, I asked them the following questions: — Who are you today? Where are you? Why and how did you end up stopping here where you feel like two strangers? — A servant had come in and placed two new texts in front of me which rose up in a stack that almost reached the height of their heads. — Where were you and who were you when you possessed your true identity? When will you be able to return to this initial condition, and be reborn in your lost entirety? — One of them put his hand on top of the stack, laid his sheet of paper down upon it and I understood he was writing that I was mad and foreign. I continued speaking in Portuguese: — I am serving the Great Lady in the place of my fate; not to be a slave but to be a link. — He questioned me in French, and I did not remain silent in that other language: — I lucidly entered the world of the delirious... — They became calm when they learned I was a beguine and, since they smiled, I smiled.

The only thing they still asked was: — Where is the sister that's supposed to accompany you? — In heaven. — And from there, our meeting closed like a book.

(XXXVIII)

Eleanor earth,

I shouldn't speak to you so much about books because you, naturally, where you are, don't have texts at your disposal, nor any occasion to read them: nonetheless, on my desk, the following works accumulate:

the *Biblia Regia*, or *Polygot Bible* in five languages, the botanical treatises of Dodoneu, L'Ecluse, and Lobel, musical scores, and all I have to do is flip through a few pages for the book to remain latent in me in all the accumulation of its knowledge.

(XXXIX)

Eleanor fire,
it was under the empire of knowledge that you overthrew the candle flame, causing a great scandal; it was such an important moment that I never stop thinking about it, no matter the time of day. Our sisters, the beguines, let out an exclamation, it seemed, Eleanor, that your virginity, or widowhood, had been violated; later on, a wound opened up on your foot, I said that the fire had become embedded burning eternally and
breaking the rule of what is forbidden and sanctioned, I bite your ankle, outside the Community, in the Plantin-Moretus house where nothing, except the knowledge of dreams, guides us.

(XL)

Eleanor dissolving,
Plantin always dressed in black, and black always dressed in Plantin. Plantin is an attribute of black. I found him in the Great Library, beneath the Altar; I raise my eyes up to the Christ with the feeling of not being able to console him about his fate. I sit in a high chair, my

skirts don't brush the ground, he asks me with whom I learned the foreign languages. — I learned. — Behind him follow the Choirboys who will sing the Mass to the Chapel; the shortest one, his face raised in a kind of concentration on the tasks he was going to perform, drew me in such a way that I turned my head discreetly. If this child isn't Luis M.'s son, who,

if not my son,

or your son,

could he be?   At night, with the face of that child no longer present, on the Vrijdagmarkt, and on streets like Kammenstraat and Geeststraat, which surround the house, bands of malicious young men knocked down passersby and, with brass knuckles, knocked on doors that opened up, run through with an enchantment that cannot be described, although their voices said in a chorus: "the alchemists deceive us and promise us what they do not have; they believe themselves, falsely, to be masters of alchemy; they give us, rather than real gold and silver, a metal that deceives us. We order that all these counterfeiters leave Antwerp forever." — I recognized, in these terms, phrases from Pope John XXII's "Spondent Pariter" bull, and since the waxing crescent had already become a full moon, and I did not want to be found, I climbed the stairs to my room, and crept through countless hallways. But the following night, which was imminent, because the day had been short and empty, the same faceless band struck the same streets, at the moment I lay down thinking about why I lived in a house with the motto Labore et Constantia, and the Golden Compass as a symbol. I thought then that heresy covered us; I put on my thickest cloak to raise doubt as to whether I was a man or a woman, and I braved the intensely cold street: "Bands of children running loose in the city are creating havoc, and I am unable to determine what force, or leader, organizes them. In the street, I see a group of these children, and I decide to follow them; a vehicle appears at that moment, and the driver, someone young, head covered and beardless, hastily makes them get in; rather than concealing that I had seen him, I turn my head and stare at him unabashedly. Later on, another person who is also myself concluded that, since I am a terrible witness, that man would try to kill me."

It was for that reason, and on Plantin's advice, that I sought to leave that house, and those places; but I lacked references and friends elsewhere, having ruled out the possibility of reintegrating into our sedentary Community of beguines, or going to meet you.

(XLI)

But I did not even have time to reflect on my departure because before four days had passed, that same man came to see me with the intention of killing me; as soon as he sat down in front of me, at my invitation, I understood that I was prepared to welcome it; and, turning my back to him, I went to the window and leaned out over the Plantin-Moretus garden, which stretched out in a vast brilliance, and where the flowers, with the vine, were changing states.

(XLII)

I wasn't surprised to still be alive, after the man's surreptitious departure;

perhaps I had died, but my love for You had not changed, nor the bitterness of my tears.

(XLIII)

The day after the probable visit of this death, there was a man who wanted to convince us that he was capable of relieving himself in front of us; we placed ourselves, obediently, into two rows, and he passed between us, crouching with his pants in his hand, having produced the outcome he'd proposed; in the end, he formed large balls with his own feces and hurled them suddenly at our faces; I was inconsiderate and, when I opened a door to the House, which Plantin is always careful to lock, I found a vast illuminated room where you, the beguines, sitting at long tables, wrote your lives; the first part belongs to a dream. The second is a vision.

(XLIV)

The bands of young men, when they departed, left behind a calm that presaged a new eruption of violence.

(XLV)

You were with them, and I spoke to you:
— How are you, Eleanor?

— Well. Haven't you read my letters?

— Yes. It seems so.

— What are you writing?

— What you are reading. — There was a moment of silence among them, and Martha said:

— Your vision has deceived you. We are not writing our lives.

— I know. In the shadows, you write books for Plantin-More-tus, which I will proofread later; or, later still, translate into different languages.

— Do you know, Marguerite — Eleanor caught my attention — the man from your dream was not a dream.

— Then who was he?

— He was Alisubbo, with whom I live in Lisbon, and he wanted to show you his body...

— ...let us part ways. That is what Alice's dream meant.

— It was Luis M. — Blanche said innocently. — We had hated him so deeply for being a man that the only thing left for us to do was like him.

(XLVI)

Once again, I set the clock upon its work. Since that desire, very strong, was in me, I looked around to choose a reason to make love. Sunday, and the city is closed. I go to the window, and after the pro-cession of relics has passed by, the afternoon slowly abuts against the evening. Inside the room the flame was lit, a beeswax candle, or oil lamp; I saw nothing, except the brightness sensed in the shadows.

Marguerite, Plantin's daughter, played her stringed instrument in front of the sundial, at the center of the inner courtyard. Without cold and without anguish she had been sitting there since early morning, the servant brought her food, which the dog licked. She waits for her lover, intending for the music being played in the house to die out from not coming into contact with the true air.

Her lover, who arrived in the afternoon, raised his face, and never stopped looking at my window where not even the slightest sign had been lit. I thought I recognized someone, Alisubbo, as you said; Luis M., as Blanche would say. That man remained standing next to the seven columns, retreated, sat down on the wooden bench so solid it's almost stone; laid his hand on the open-mouthed head of the fountain that pours (poured) water at every moment of his life.
Volutes and claws.
I go down to the garden. I walk toward the sundial. I retreat now, and retreat, and retreat always, hearing Plantin's footsteps between the rectangular flowerbeds; Luis M., the possible, has been placed next to the central bust, on the southern side of the courtyard; I raise my eyes to the compass whose aperture determines the diameter of the armillary sphere; all the busts of the Moretus brothers are surrounded by laurels and fruit, the cornucopia of abundance; illuminating the head, the eight-pointed star, between every two points, a ray of fire. From this fire is born the vine on the two sides that receive sun. I pass by Luis M. as he passes by me: in silence and without adoration. Has he decided never to speak to us with his own voice again?

I am the oldest, the one who will succeed the Great Lady: Marguerite. I lean back against the bench, so the stone can touch me. Tonight, Luis M. is a guest in Plantin's house, and he himself is the messenger for his letters which he leaves, surreptitiously, half at my seat at the table, half at my work table. And he has already left.

(XLVII)

I had the impression that death had passed by, that a body subtle in its differences,
had come to demand our bodies,
Eleanor,
an entrance to the closed palace of the king.
On the 25th, at night, there was frost; on the 26th there was a bit of snow, today, the 27th, it was cold. Tomorrow the weather will be milder; on the 29th, it will rain. On the 30th, the weather will be uncertain.

  (You know the importance we all give to the weather. If I speak of it to you, it's because I must speak of it.)

(XLVIII)

The river rises up over Lisbon; all this fog is a shock. We advance through the dampness toward the water, Alisubbo and I, at dawn on the 24th. I do not know the city nor do I know the river. I know certain aspects that pass through the air, in the garden. My task now is to carry buckets to the house, I lean against the dam and wait for the water, thinking I see River-Tagus. Tagus the dog follows behind me, when I am loaded down, in my wake. We call him Tagus to name the river several times a day, and so we can leave.

After so much time, today I looked at my hands. I am dressed without valuing or deviating from the Rules, and a white collar accentuates the inflexibility of my behavior.

I am not telling you about my life so that you will ask yourself questions. I wouldn't trade even one of these affections for books. They are all part of this inclination: people, mountains and valleys, the garden itself and the rising air, you, all the bitterness and hardship, and the buckets.

I received your tidings which told me, word for word: "Childhood stories remain by my side, when I lie down, as the library of the mystics remains. Christmas has a meaning for me — a convergence between beginnings and winter, and the intervening paths of life, which visit me in dreams and wakefulness. Beings reflected in their eternal images — animals, men, and what is beyond them.

If Plantin and his family do not leave, if I cannot shut myself away inside the house for ten days, I will feel pity and a kind of longing. The visitors will remain at the door, they will not dare to enter the inhabited illumination of the House. They, or I, will remain alone. Eleanor asks for this not to happen. I will confide in you all that is going to happen."

Marguerite,

I am leaving on a pilgrimage to Lisbon, which is happening to me for the first time because, beyond my great desire to see River-Tagus, when I spoke of your Christmas vows of solitude to Alisubbo, he told me that a pilgrimage, or a journey, can be more than a prayer. So, to make it possible for you to be alone, I am leaving with Alisubbo for Lisbon. He will be my guide, and his wife isn't jealous. And, if you are able to remain alone in Plantin's house for ten days, we will be some of your visitors in our genuine images.

(il)

Marguerite, I want to make love to a blue bird. When you confided in me that the Vrijdagmarkt had been invaded by a band of young men, the end of the year was approaching; it seems as if no time has passed but another year is already ending and, to celebrate multiple things, I am going, as I told you in my last letter, to Lisbon with Alisubbo. All along the way, after resting, or feeling weary, I want to make love to the blue bird which, with the height of a human being, and open wings, walks steadily at my side, and drowns Alisubbo's presence; Alisubbo respects my remoteness, and has become my guide while I see. My desire binds me, and I fall behind, to see if the blue bird will stay with me. It stops, looks at me with its blue color, and its feathers, and its beak. We look at each other so intensely that we fly over a stone, with which I lift the weight of time:

in Madragoa there are sea folk, and Alisubbo says that here the sea belongs to all folk — fishermen, fishwives, stevedores, noblemen who will disappear, cloistered nuns, and fishmongers. He leads me to the corner of Trinas where there is a hospice of the Senhoras da Índia — Madres de Goa: — The conventual House — indicates Alisubbo. We are in front of a door leading to a walled enclosure: "1651. This house belongs to God." I don't want to go in, although I have considered Alisubbo my guide.

— You will see the one they call River-Tagus — he tells me.

(L)

These women live strictly separated in the fulfillment of a destiny; I see them pass hieratic, something that I, who have some experience, had never before seen; they embody the work they do and those who deal with the clothing, circumspectly, seem to have become fabric; they revel in the starched whiteness, and in their appearance and downcast eyes, they acknowledge the weave they all inhabit. I asked Alisubbo, mournfully, why he left me here, if this was River-Tagus. He remained mute, in his impassible muteness, and traced the waves of the sea with his hand. I made him understand that I would prefer to return to the garden, and Alice's bright secrets: he nodded his head, and communicated that he had somewhere to go without me.

We had passed through the walled enclosure and reached the beginning of the House. In the great room where they received visitors, the nuns passed unceasingly, and I recognized the tasks each one did and even the prayers they prayed in solitary places. They had illustrious gestures, with a noble origin and excessive sharpness; it perpetually smelled of washing; in the next room, the entrance opened onto the laundry, populated by empty wardrobes piled high with sheets made of cotton and, more importantly, linen — simple, edged in lace, or embroidered according to their bloodlines. They brought trousseaux, like brides.

I, soon, although my stay had become long, would be unable to ignore their myths.

(LI)

I knew, then, Marguerite, that I couldn't write to you but I vowed to bury my letters close to the roots of the rose bushes because "by the roots of the rose bushes," according to one of Alice's secrets, "passes the messenger."

(LII)

Those who sew most of the day are the dreamers; if they aren't making habits, for themselves or to bury the dead poor, they embroider on cambric with threads that are almost invisible, almost always white; they get up from their chairs with an unimaginable lightness, and run to the altars to adjust the candle flames and change the flowers; a thread falling to the ground is an imperfection; a fabric becoming wrinkled is a fault; a garment dreamed upon the body is a sin.

Those who garden most of the day bow their heads lower than the others; it can be seen in their disappeared hips, when their large aprons are absent; they look around to make sure that all the flowers are still fresh, and smile happily because they live in contact with the open air.

On Christmas Day, nearly a year after I entered this gathering, I learned from one of those who sing in the choir, who have voices that please the Lord of Hosts and are unable to utter even a single note of the canticle when they are alone, that I was going to meet the man who dwelled in the attics, and who lived as a fugitive in the convent; he should still be in Siam, Cochinchina, Ningbo, or Lampacau, world of the ambitious and insurrectionists from this country of River-Tagus.

I was guided by one of those who care for the sick, almost always old or widowed, and who can confront all the enigmas of bodies.

Since it was dawn, which could already be seen through the window over the river, rather than saying "good morning," I greeted him: — "Good dawn." — He was a merchant, a pirate, a sailor, or a wayfarer. — "Good final hours of the dawn, merchant of China" — Eleanor continued, with cautious respect, still wearing her nun's habit: — "Gold from Japan, silver, silk, objects manufactured in China, spices from the Moluccas. Clove." — "Korea, Manchuria, Mongolia, and Tibet" — I said as I let my head drop and the nun moved away.

Uttering the passwords Alisubbo had taught me, I only had to wait to see what would happen; the man was sitting down, engulfed in white and brown garments from the neck down; the night was fading above the candle flame, which spread a scent of final brightness.

— Before we exchange our knowledge — he said — let us exchange our tenderness for a while. — He took the rosary from my hand, the only sign of affection he had for me during the time it grew brigher.

(LIII)

So I will tell you what he said to me, in his own way:
" — Hodie, puer natus est nobis.
Everything is always a first time.
A time given, all at once, as something special.
Or so the body can memorize it, every time it proves necessary:
A single time,   a single body,   a single form without duration
        without extension   without volume.

Thus the body. Part by part, savored,
or embedded in the intimacy
of a children's game, always new, not yet begun.
In the same way, the Form. Only one, with different possibilities.
  One and one; one and two; two and one; two and three.
  One and one, intimate.
  One with two, sororally.
  Two lovers, in one, loving their openings.
  Two lovers, with three, equal.
Outside the Body, everything can be kept: duration, extension and volume. But in my own, I keep a children's game as something singular, without another Law, without another's gaze, without an unfamiliar gesture."

I came down from the hidden parts of the house without having arranged a new meeting; because it was written that I would find myself in an intensely violent desert; in the desert of my cell, eyes lowered, trying to bury the Christmas memory where the rule of absolute simplicity was sweetened by an unexpected kindness from Blanche, who brought a certain small tree from the forest, which she arranged in the anteroom with its decorations of candles and flowers.

This community in Lisbon is one of true nuns, although not of our truth; other than the canticle, and the voices in prayer, there was nothing. Completely lost, any trace of these women I see moving away down the hallways. But I try to look at our Christmas tree, and lie down in its shadow. Without doing anything. Not even writing. At this year's end the beguines went to sleep, they rest. I feel full of work in a whole and weary body; this walled enclosure, this house, these sisters bending over one another, this writing, this Christmas. Just like

Martha, I opened a few doors and passed through them a few time. I rest on Dante, atop the thickness of his book. He wrote it, I hide it, a boldness I will tell you about later. Below it is a Nietzsche and his Dawn, this birth made itself known to me within a few hundred years, the stack hovers invisible, although consistent with a certain space. I remain in this atmosphere of candles and voices from different origins.

Nonetheless, that man's voice called out to me; perhaps because they seemed to be part of a Gesta recounting the histories of different peoples, that man's thoughts began to be conveyed to me through the singing of a bird, which I identified without knowing it by name; it is one that perches on the linden tree and is pleased to be my intermediary between you, Luis M. and, at times, those who remain. That is how my letters will reach you.

There are those who only take pleasure in the visible world.

(LIV)

On another occasion,
on other pilgrimages I will make with Alisubbo later on, I will approach this Gathering by sea; they are places tangled with multiple paths and there are cemeteries among orange groves that will speak of our passage; we had lost the sense of the dead,
according to other men,
and only saw their works raised among us; this will be an exultant era, whether it rains or the man remains absorbed; the attic dweller will not leave his country of immobility though there is always an ebb and flow of movement within his ambit; eventually, the bird will tell me

he is a statesman expelled from his territory, condemned to disappear because of a conscious assassination perpetrated by the generality of its laws; afterward, his space will be a new seclusion, which you must also try to access by sea;

such a hideous psychic figure, Marguerite imagines, might be River-Tagus, and its sweetness of living; Alisubbo will say little, only showing me landscapes; into these dreams, these doleful daydreams, I fall here most of the time; I gradually become the nun who dreams, the lunatic; I wanted to escape to a hermitage where the first reply to these questions can be found, even if I had to live my entire life alone, with him.

(LV)

At the beginning of January, I write to be able to endure the fear. It is either menstruation, or penetration into a dissolving space, where everything that surrounds me, or hovers over me, threatens to annihilate me; they are the gregarious voices of the Order and the universality of its precepts which, in the asylum where Alisubbo brought me, condemn the statesman to interrupted seclusion in the attic.

I speak of myself in the third person: "The one visiting him is Eleanor on her pilgrimage to River-Tagus, and for several days she will be struck by such a great fear for having seen the monster with reason that she will fall into the most dispersed motes of her feminine dust; the other sisters, recondite in their habits, do not know the origin of her fear; when they saw her chatter her teeth and refuse to open her eyes to any light, they warmed her with thick blankets, burned scents, and put out the candles. She stayed in bed like one newly born."

As I had had a crisis, vision or lucidity, this morning I received a secret and unexpected letter from a sister who had recognized herself in my fear:

"Since you are a lucid woman, tell me who I am; I continually live in fear of countries, the organization of cities, family, the religious community I was accepted by, with the dread that the sensitive form of myself would come undone. Even with so many sisters, there are only two or three in whom love is respected; for the rest of the days of my life I may pass through an invisible crisis. Different silhouettes are more prominent in this delirium so close to truth but I have never found a compatient messenger among us; days ago, when I thought there was Spanish and Portuguese blood in my origins, I spent the night rebuilding an enormous cliff which I carried upon my back, and I remained motionless in this present, only able to rant; what do I have in common with the monster if on its land I am a fleeting shadow, and on its sand the sun that writes? Do I have some kinship with the monster, like the others? I also visited the man in the attic. Our loves were secondary and unviable. More important was seeing, destroying, sleeping, and awaking in sleep. Abducted, my language." She had signed "Alice," the same name as Alisubbo's wife.

When, convalescing, I went on a walk for the first time, I met a very young nun who was sitting at the gate to the garden; her face emerged from a nostalgic cold, like the cold of these Atlantic places. She asked me this delicate question:

— Has your illness cost you?

— I don't know — I replied. — I believe I became ill in order to abandon an even greater illness.

— How so? — And from the intonation of her voice, I saw that she was there as someone who is surrendering themselves to their passing.

— For you to understand you would need to age a bit more.

— I shouldn't have asked you my question; it is the hour for wandering, but always in silence. What I wanted to know is very intimate: why is it that yesterday I seemed mad, and today I seem to be in sound mind? — She got down on her knees in front of me, and she looked like you.

— Was it you who wrote me the letter? So I would love you? — I saw that she was not only young but intelligent and they said that because her father, brothers, and all the men in her family had left for the Discoveries, she had only known women until she left her house, and shadows after that moment.

When I received this letter, and this outpouring, I began to study these women's faces and lives with more attention: they had their own lives, and habits; memories (mostly forbidden); families left behind in the distance although they returned in brief footsteps heard in the locutory. The forbidden books were covered by the diaphanous veil of the sanctioned; the library, almost empty, but which Alice and I visited secretly, so I could imagine living spirits for her, and tell her about works still unwritten, works unknown, works destroyed and burned, which I always retained in my memory; one day, I told Alice that I was an old woman, although I did not look it, that these unforeseen encounters with time came from the parts of me lacking any sense and lucidity.

This was what it had been like when I thought about the concept of dust, and what had happened during the scene in the refectory:

The face of one of the youngest sisters, when I observe it at the table, becomes demented or smiling. The refectory is so spacious and

long that all the doors are far from us; the meals, in which we all
participate, are the best time to contemplate all the heads bowed over
the food which, in winter, is a piece of fruit, whole-wheat bread, and
eggs; from the row of open windows at the top of a wall, a slanted
brightness radiates; Luis M., if he were to enter here, would transform
into a pontiff, or frozen dust; we sit down, on the enormous benches,
one by one; the Superior rises to her feet, and asks: — What is a fire?
— Alice replies: — It is the state of a body that burns, producing
heat, or heat and light. — And another, with a name that is unknown
to me: — The flame destroys regardless of its will. — Despite the
immensity of its space, the refectory is stifling and, when the daylight
ebbs, little light remains; though I remain focused on the concept of
dust, I heard the voice of the Mother Superior still insisting on fire, as
if she feared a blaze; few still listened to her, they were watching the
final light of that ever so abstract day; but then we heard her ask who
wanted to get up; following her order and obeying my desire, I went
to the sideboard and put out the large candle, so total darkness would
close over our starvation; meanwhile, at the head of the table, I saw
the face of Ana de Peñalosa, as if, for a few moments, she had come to
replace the Mother Superior; it was her lesser-known face, subjected
to a fascinating rotational movement, which slowly began to capture
all the gazes of the seated sisters; we then began to eat silently, picking
up the fruit which was an orange, already peeled in the kitchens; the
segments were heavy in our hands and mouths, and we understood that
Ana de Peñalosa had retreated, guiding herself without any need for
light; the first nun, who did not want to resist, stood up to follow her
but the door, situated so far away, began to sputter, although in silence.

Some weeks later, more precisely on a Thursday, when I looked at the nun who had stood up I was absolutely certain that she was pregnant. Not knowing what to do I began by remaining silent; the winter nights had become very dark but it never snowed; nor was there panic when, in the middle of the night, a shout was heard, as it was believed that, at that moment, somewhere in the city, a man had been conceived. It was a belief I did not share although I heard the shouts. In front of the Almighty there was always someone kneeling who helped the new being come into the world. At daybreak they called her "the godmother" and this intercession was the particular vocation of the Convent. These women were more involved than I initially thought in the wandering powers that caused births, abundances, and catastrophes; underneath their apparent candor and ignorance stretched a body of water, on which lay a network of intricate enigmas; each one had a certain type of knowledge that could be discerned from its discretion, if it were carefully observed. I found that I distanced myself from you, Marguerite, to examine other women I did not know. A kind of vertigo had come upon me and these notes, made at night, when I was full of weariness, seemed to me to be an irregular writing within writing.

If I was afraid to stop writing to you, or that writing would have less importance in my eyes, I would have stopped observing these women, and taking note of their behavior. But fear, in me, was always futile.

(LVI)

I did not arrange another meeting with the man in the attic because I believe he circulates among us disguised as a woman, so as not to be imprisoned by his enemies; the women care little about his presence, which intrigues me about the nature of their desires, and true ambitions; at the last Chapter they wanted to elect him Mother Superior but they were afraid to expose him, or expose her, in such a prominent position; he is now the sister responsible for opening and closing the doors and his eyes follow us without bothering us. We are becoming accustomed, progressively, to another fate.

I bared the center of the kitchen, I sat down in that center to write; my motive is to express that there is a life which is not spoken of, and cannot be sensed, although it fills, hiddenly real, the essence of the first life.

A few moments ago someone came in, I thought it was the wheat, or some species

of grass

because today,

the grains,

swaying in the wind,

are always in my field of vision.

The wheat is like Luis M., in certain areas they have a common nature; that is to say, like Luis M., or Eckhart, or one of those beings experienced through their deepest and harshest nature. The sisters allowed me go to a place where I could whisper words to those beings, exchange delicacies and murmurs with them.

The center of this kitchen must be a predestined place; I was able to capture it as one captures a spring of water. A current passes here; here long ago, I am certain, grew wheat, and its splendor hovers in the house, seeking implantation.

—Are you certain, Eleanor? — asked Alice who has a special understanding with the night, and at night. In the vast circle of these women

there is a small circle who do not speak to one another — they understand each other; some note the presence of the cats and the remaining
animals as mysteries with a penetrating significance; they are cultivated
in the art of movements, and of speaking with their lips almost closed.
So delicate begins to become my respect
for you,
that I find your conventual life has a rare singularity. A nostalgia hovers
in your eyes, and I know it is nothing more than the future of the
dead wheat plant,
which now,
only appears to you
invisibly. Alice tells me, silently, that the more I keep quiet, the more
the animal rebels would reveal themselves to me. I will be — she gave
me this hope — allowed among them, in my right mind, if I abandon
the harsh language of these signs; a cat has come to rub against my legs,
and in the place of the wheat she lies down asking that I be drawn to
this lasting image.

(LVII)

I got up to throw out the garbage which already stank. Heloise, the cat
that was killed, during the month of September, by the entire second
litter, was in the sheltered flowerbed, next to her daughter, alike as two
drops of water. After so many months when I thought her vanished or
dead, it seemed natural to see her today. She looked at me for a long
time, but I still spoke to her articulating some of the words I know.

I am now between two luminous sources, always in the state I found myself in when beginning to write.

Marguerite, leave the Plantin-Moretus house, if you are able. Tell Ana de Peñalosa, who believes in your word, and come find in this place an undefinable path
which is neither a deep hole,
nor the high sky.

(LVIII)

I get up at five o'clock in the morning when someone passes by and knocks on the door, though I had already been awake. It isn't hard for me to wake up early, it's as if I move toward both sides of the night; at that intermediate hour, I feel diluted in water, in the transition of light, in the books I will read, in the silence I will exchange with Alice and her beloved nuns, the presence of River-Tagus which for the first time insinuates that we must treat with true opulence the death of Thomas Müntzer who is still going to die. Everyone thinks "who is it?" or about an offering, an accompaniment of incomparable value, and yesterday Alisubbo asked River-Tagus to lead this ceremony, which will have an unparalleled intelligence. I don't mean the mundane magnificence of intelligence, of visible luxuries, but the entire range of qualities that are like the precious stones of space and time. Will he not die beheaded as River-Tagus secretly flows to India, trying to summon, from the methodical and insightful arrangement of the attic, an expansively long Requiem? Here we will hold their funerals and end the battle.

It is night; the convent rests in extreme freedom; all day yesterday I analyzed and cleaned books and rooms, with this thought. The man in the attic, or River-Tagus, intrigued me deeply; in the enormity of the house he walks stooping, speaks unceasingly with Mozart about the Requiem for Thomas Müntzer. They speak noiselessly as if they were possessed by the darkness; the women do not remember them, nor do they forget them; they see them in every corner, at the doors, standing, and, during prayers, kneeling with the music surrounding them; their eyes are drawn to a sleeping vision: the birth, life, and death of Thomas Müntzer; it is forbidden to speak to them, nor do they speak. But their concertation always resonates, powerful, in my ears, their force and understanding pursue me without me, in the current sense of the term, loving them; they are a single being that circulates among us, and I only know that, when it leaves, I'm going to leave with it.

(LIX)

When I go out into the hallway, the candles shine and the air is pure, not yet suffused with low voices or footsteps. I wanted to remain standing on the ship after I crossed the garden where the darkness has changed places. I pause for a moment, seeing my sisters walk past with their features bare; they stop next to Alisubbo, and reflect the end of night, and on the end of night; at times, we hear the cries of Müntzer's wife, confronting her painful fate; some of the shadows dissipate, and we look at one another searching for a succor that will come, and has already been translated into our airy flights of revolt, and letters. Müntzer's burial will be at dawn, and everyone has promised him a silence of fierce battle. The trees are so distinct, the books so different, the hours of the day and the lessons so swift, this burial has such a deep meaning that I'm asking you, Marguerite come soon, for the spirit of Ana de Peñalosa, trained in the state of ubiquity, and other as yet uncommon gifts, is always with us.

River-Tagus is also with us in the room, the door open to the garden. It has revealed to Alisubbo that it is water, subduing our interrogations. We witnessed the battle between water and fire, both equally important to us. We looked for the Requiem, "et lux perpetua luceat eis." We saw the peace made between water and fire, which was hideous; during that dawn, or in the time after it, we were transmuted, and either River-Tagus no longer tempted us, or we were all known by it;

On the day of the funeral, as today, I did not feel I belonged to the human species; even the dead body only appeared to be Müntzer. I must not evince a being from any defined and recognized species, simultaneously it is possible for me to roar and fly, be loved by you, raise myself up on my paws; deliciously write, and write to you, Marguerite, with a hand dexterous in our genealogy of millennia. Remember Heart of the Bear, and how he accompanied us? Also during his last burial rites, the bears stepped in to follow Müntzer; the coffin was pulled by Alice, the youngest woman in the Community. She was alone as befit her metamorphosis because at the turn of the path, leaving the garden, she will be transformed into a singular being, although one perfectly embedded in our way of living the centuries, which is full of banal and hierophantic events. No one knows which species of animal, or plant, Müntzer, beloved body, will remain with, if not the bears which will keep vibrating and disappearing alongside him until the day of his loving idyll with one of us, who will live to be his writing, government, and sword. The place is ideal, open to the shadows, and undisturbed by anodyne footsteps. Someone sent me a short poem by Saint John of the Cross, with his admiration for me, and my horrendous stars that are yours. We have surely gone beyond any usual configuration, tell me whether Luis M. still looks the same, or has already metamorphosed. Around me they are praying, they are the quiet consequence of an as yet controlled clarification. Some see spirits beyond what they are praying, and the end of the Cathars approaching; so many species intertwine that I take on the force of dust. Ask Ana de Peñalosa if I can free myself from the link that bound me to her, and only bear this love without obedience. If I die before the end of the day, which is possible, as it is possible to still live many more years and ultimately become your rebel and fire, ask River-Tagus and Alisubbo about my last days. They will be described in my desk drawer, next to the account of Müntzer's funeral,

who it is difficult to see die without also dying.

Exordium:

No one makes love to me today because a single cry of mine would fell your peace of spirit.

Today, Müntzer's second burial moved me deeply; my hands still tremble, although a bear gave me its paw, and consoled me with its cadence; and, despite this, I also hated Müntzer, although I weep sincerely at his burial, not daring to compare myself to the bears, which guide him through time. Let me be forgiven, for I was one of those who commissioned the Requiem from Mozart and Mozart, corresponding to our request, died shortly thereafter.

I did not recognize myself as only guilty. The specter of the idea that we did not know where we would bury him followed me; we walked around the massive house, I knew that Alisubbo sought to fathom, in that regard, the intention of every tree. River-Tagus had taken the way of its own water and, for a few moments, we believed that Luis M. had joined the procession, which would not happen by chance. He was a small, cold man, eyes voluble, but wounding those upon whom they fixed; if it was him, he was disguised as a furniture maker, with a saw at his side, and wood shavings in his hair.

We tried to find, to no avail, the place where we will leave Müntzer for his resurrection; not at the foot of a tree, not at the foot of the bench, not at the foot of the Church, not under the window to Alice's room, not in the garden of Alisubbo, who was present. Without knowing how, we found ourselves on Travessa das Izabéis, among the passersby, in the early evening. River-Tagus sensed that its safe waters had suddenly seen the path they would travel. The passersby did not notice us, we were a group of women in the rain, with a gardener and a cabinetmaker; some nuns, others secular, we moved toward the sea reveling in our footsteps and our silence. Reaching the beach, we were astonished that we had left our odd prison; we lay Thomas Müntzer's body on the sand and covered it lightly with salt, according to the words of Luis M. who finally revealed that it was him. River-Tagus had reached the house, and having climbed up a rock it descended, at last, undone, toward the horizon; Thomas Müntzer had become a grain of salt and a grain of sand, we collected him in our mouths which was the place where he could be buried in peace. For our instruction, Alisubbo turned toward the distance, and said:

— This is the sea.

(LX)

We gave, in the most recondite part of the house, a few rooms to Ali-subbo, so he could do his metaphysical experiments there. Alisubbo will send for Alice because his raw material is sea salt, and plants from the sea, or those near the beaches. We thought River-Tagus had left, but when it had already been night for many hours, we heard it brush against the door, and I, barefoot, got up to go and open it convinced it is the desire of the entire Community.

To make it easier for us to escape the inquisitorial perquisitions, we may want to devote ourselves to very simple artisanal techniques requiring pre-alchemical knowledge, such as obtaining dyes to restore old fabrics, or color our cloths.

As for me, they think to elect me Mother of this seemingly closed world, Marguerite, which I did not want. First, because your secret knowledge surpasses mine; second, because I would like for all these women to be Mothers of this knowledge, and exchange its use and powers among themselves. But, if they insist, I will set a limit on my time of service which, unfortunately for you, will be an apprentice-ship. Happily we have Alisubbo and River-Tagus at our side, to hear and destroy. And also Alisubbo's wife, almost blind with her visions, of which she will tell us nothing. On several occasions, obscure texts and events will mislead us. But our distinctiveness is an experimental mysticism.

I advise you, as I still remind myself, to be very careful with your name; because it is still more characteristic of women, rather than men, to worship glory.

(LXI)

Marguerite, you already know what moves me; today, I crossed a room
when I saw a sliver of sun on the ground; the bear hasn't eaten, it only
looks at the operations of the sun, during the day; at those moments,
I read with the depth of its eyes that a steeled danger awaits us, even
though it may not be imminent; where will I keep this manuscript,
or these letters, so no one will read them, not another living soul?;
perhaps I should give them a mysterious language,
or simply not write,
but then how will I communicate with you?

Marguerite,
penetrating the night, I came across a wall where the outside air usually
circulates; sometimes, in very rare moments, I cannot sleep; lying in
bed, I think I will become a corpse, like Müntzer, and I long for an
encounter that will rid me of anguish; mud, cesspit, darkness surround
me aimlessly; I get up, open the door to the room, which isn't allowed
at night, walk in the meanders of the house and, if it isn't too cold,
among the garden's torrents, whose true nature I cannot determine. I
understand, I don't know with what sense, that it must be the wall of
the house belonging to River-Tagus, which has not shown itself for
many days, not as itself, nor in any disguise. I looked in the window but
I did not recognize anything because the night was dense and, inside
the house, the lights were out. But, after a time of contemplation, with
the awareness that my life was shrouded in sackcloth, lights came on
that did not illuminate, as if they were enclosed in a world of waiting.
River-Tagus ran, a small river inside one of those worlds, a true tomb.

Those who possessed their own intimacy had been surrounded by ramparts that night.

I think what was really surprising that night was the nearly unknown departure of River-Tagus. It opened the door, which remained open, looked to either side as if two columns of evil were threatening it; it did not see me because I may not have been recognizable as a woman; the night sank deeper and deeper into its tenebrous marrow. Following it to the core, I had the prescience that it was going to leave.

It gathered several objects that were very valuable to it, a leaf, a miniature boat it sailed in the pond, during its stay in the Convent, and its own death translated into its mask which none of us feared beyond what was strictly necessary because we wanted to remain its subjects. It left the house slowly, after turning around twice when it began to see me, my presence of metal and fire, for I lay, burning, in a heap of stones. Although I was fire, I began to weep its madness of departure. I wept for those of us who move away from one another without a common measure.

Marguerite, it's convenient that you are coming to support me in this writing, and tonight, my experience of death and its multiple deviations begins to become tangible. That Luis M. sends me a letter with a hand of ashes, ruler-straight, my will ebbs away with so many recognitions on the paths we claim as our own.

Anyone who is my friend,

leave me alone. Beyond appearances, there are beings that wish to be with me when the house and garden are completely empty in their phase of stable sun and moving moon; the men's fear made me find these breaths, which I do not want to abandon to their contingency and meaninglessness. If I were to become completely invisible, who would lead them to smell, touch, sight, taste, hearing, and the sixth sense love?

The last words River-Tagus said to our shadow were: — "When I ask you to leave, I am not sending you away; I only ask that you do not remain here, as in this dwelling there is no space, nor grave for you."

If River-Tagus was the water I believed, it would not have deprived us of sleep tonight. But I love it after having to sort out so many enigmas on my own.

(LXII)

The murder of the newly born cats, to save their mother from the darkness, was completely abominable. Placed into a bottle with poison, they were entirely at our mercy, that we pushed them into the narrow space. The bottle closed, there was a moment of chaos. Blanche, my accomplice, said: — How frightening. — I did not speak, taking on all my horrific old age at that moment. On the day of its departure, River-Tagus was suspicious of those eyes, and became motionless with transitory respect. Next to the roots of language, no words were with me. But I must also open my jaws because I am an animal walking upright, no worthier than any feline.

During this incursion into the night, I was accompanied by the *Requiem in Pacis* that Mozart composed for Müntzer. I do not intend for someone to compose a Requiem for me, the measure of my immanence, and your exaltation in it, will be my Requiem.

(LXIII)

Perhaps River-Tagus hasn't left. It was a dream, or a fleeting real fact.

(LXIV)

I went behind the house to feed the chickens; at the entrance to the henhouse, the youngest chicken was dead, a victim of the conflict between the roosters. It must have been dead less than twenty-four hours, as I had seen it alive on the eve. We thought to eat it ourselves and not only give it over to the land. We arrived to heat the water, prepare the ceramic pots, begin to pluck it; but the wounds on its side and chest were many, it had sustained too many pecks to be eaten, which would affect the quality of the meat. We buried it in the garden, I thought about the fall, the separation between wall and rampart, the passion, possibly painful, in which light and darkness confront each other, and the recollection with which I would write, or rather, cast myself into the thinking that transpires.

At lunchtime I was struck by the idea that I shouldn't write a narrative about this dwelling; I have a few pages where I seem to belong to our Community. But I'm increasingly drawn to the life of the hermitage, and what we can be there, disconnected from one another, but exchanging creations. (When I live with the creator spirits, I will realize that only the solitude of true images isn't cruel.) If that happens, Marguerite, I will no longer write to you, I shouldn't put anything down on paper, or perhaps this precaution is excessively strict. Because Alisubbo, who separated the roosters that will be killed, was uneasy about my desire to distance myself, even from this Community, where the written paths are still illusion, and history. He hung the roosters we'll be eating as of tomorrow on two hooks in the woodshed, but not wanting them to be punished but simply killed, I lay them on the ground, near the water and a few kernels of corn.

Did you know I decided to keep my head uncovered, even though this attitude is a serious fault of disobedience and reveals that, in the future,   I must cultivate a sacred perspective?

Ana de Peñalosa told me that Saint John of the Cross and Thomas Müntzer are still separated, that they are contemplating one another in that light, awaiting someone.

Friedrich N. disappeared. None of us have any news of him. A mad river, he will run dry at an inopportune time. Who can safely keep the texts he wrote?

Ana de Peñalosa still suspected that the Poor is his last disguise.

(LXV)

There is yet another journey ahead of us.

Even before leaving, I left in my desire, although other sides of me, lights, shadows, and intelligence, remain in this place, Antwerp and the Plantin-Moretus house, the Vrijdagmarkt and the surrounding streets, where victims of the plague often die in the street, and the capacity of our minds is behind the books; one of the women who I am will be sent in a delegation, to a place or limited duration as yet unknown, to acquire an original that will be published by this printing house, whose importance for these kings and Balthazar has no equal. Ana de Peñalosa surely whispered my name in Plantin-Moretus's ear, otherwise they will find me with enough desire to leave that they will try and stop me. We spoke to one another with nothing between us but the emptiness that allows me to call you.   Forgive me,

Eleanor,

but this time it isn't you I'm addressing; nor will I even attempt to send you this news, because a feeling suspended our exchange of affections, and now I will wander the world myself, with the mission of being granted the rights, for this House, to that book whose pages I suspect... Let me meditate.

(LXVI)

I have dressed in black, and since I will soon leave Antwerp, I go out
tonight for a long walk through the streets, and perhaps I'll go into
a tavern,
which I won't be able to do.

I went into the tavern on the river that corresponds to River-Tagus
— the Scheldt — covered by a hood, and I could be a woman, and
any woman; in the taverns along the port, words, enigmas, sighs, form
a single current; women are not the fabulous animals of the Community; they exist among men as purely imaginary entities, focused only
on them. I stand at the door fearful of my own audacity; but I have
always been driven by the desire to make comparisons, and penetrate
mysteries.

I hear an erratic and protracted breath, then some sad and gentle
sounds. I think I'm outside this world through the force of my concentration but they drag me into the middle. When my hood falls,
they drag the cloak that has fallen to the ground behind me. I hear
someone announce that I am a cross,
it has been said that when one breed of animals is crossed with another,
it will become better. I think I become brilliant and I bend down to
cover myself with the cloak that belongs in the wardrobe at Plantin-Moretus and which, only in a hallucination, did I assume was
there. But as I think, someone utters ironically beside me: — But what
a brilliant lady. — I step back with a splash of real wine on my chest
and see that my usual dress slides down compelled by a collective will,
and that my chest is made up of two parts full of vibration.

For now, I cannot reflect; I cannot do it stretched out on a bench, relieved of my bag, skirts, cap, socks, shoes. They look for my spirit in all the positions of my body, ever more ferociously than what is visible. I want to stop them from that excess but they continue saying "she is shining there, she is even more brilliant there." Perhaps it's true. When nothing remains of me, they sit me down on another bench on top of the table. I sweep my gaze around the tavern, hermetically sealed where the cold dampness of the rivers has already entered. They put a second bench on top of the bench and sit me down higher, reflecting that my body is an imperfect illumination, not denying its origins. Woman once brilliant, woman twice brilliant, woman thrice brilliant, woman frice brilliant. I climb the tower of my agony and exaltation; alone, I am afraid of falling; they throw me to the earth as if I were earth; they cover me or dress me. I stand up. I want to believe I'm still walking, I endeavor to master the pain and to rejoice because my legs move, still. In the inner courtyard of the Plantin-Moretus House, I follow the continuation of the covered gallery, and go into the kitchen. On the table were some glasses typical of that time which, centuries later, will be found in the depths of a cellar, or the mouth of a well. I take off my clothes in my room and, at my waist, I discover a light that shines.

I sit down to write to Ana de Peñalosa,

(LXVII)

mother mine:

I have realized who I am: I am not a woman of the world; but if I were a woman of the world,

either I would love a man,

or he would clothe me in gold.

Because I come from your lineage,

I have lived and relived any number of times, intelligently, what happened to me Monday in the tarven.

They cannot take me for a man, they cannot take me for a woman, they cannot take me for a being that comes from crossing different species, or an unknown animal. In this hot weather that will only continue, there has been a flight pursuing me since early morning, ever since I was possessed at the tavern, which makes me smile for the future of languages...

As for me, I don't want to leave Antwerp, unless they think it necessary for someone to leave; I infiltrate the garden looking for the foundation of those reasons; I know I wanted to fully abandon the dust that covers mortals.

I will meet someone whose name I carry in a sealed letter. A great cartographer like Gemma Frisius? Mercator? Ortelius?

Why did you all presume I know so much about the sea, and give me, for a woman of these times, such a burdensome task? I don't know which face I will depart with, much less which soul; I also don't know who I will meet, nor which fluent work I will bring into print.

Though I cannot help fearing,⠀⠀⠀mother mine so daring,

the hidden dangers of cosmography.

It has already killed so many people on the sea.

(LXVIII)

My ancestors never stopped telling me words full of wisdom and sorrow, difficultly evaluating the singularity of our fate; but their hieratic thought, their love for us, who put an end to their lineage, continues producing its clairvoyant effects.

My grandmother, grandmother of my grandmother, never expected that I wouldn't have children. One day I took a walk with her along the sea, on a northern beach covered with pebbles and coarse sand; I gave her my arm, she tilted her head; she spoke about her mother and her daughter, not daring to speak about me. We sat down in front of the sea that shattered the hardness of the beach and she, who also expressed herself in proverbs, told me: — Daughter, the candlelight that goes forth illuminates twice. — I did not know where that light and this sea were, and I apologized for leaving her without descendants. Grandmother laid her head on her hand, and uttered words of great wisdom: — Everything eventually ends up dying.

(LXIX)

My departure began with a farewell visit to the hospice; I am already wearing my traveling cloak, and the only valuable I carry is a ring that belonged to my mother; it has been so long since I last saw her, I have almost forgotten she is still alive; for a few moments, I confuse her with the old sleeping face of a woman leaning against the door; I step over her without turning my head, immersed in the suffering breaths that stop me in the middle of the room. I think of Saint John of the Cross, of River-Tagus for which I must look, of Müntzer who I cannot for even a moment forget, of the ashes to which I have, in the end, come here to bid farewell.

I am not only like the women in the tavern, and this assignment to leave and meticulously record my journey makes me run the risk of deviating into Glory. To each of the plurifaceted beings that leave with me, I have come to show my final poverty, and that of the poor who cover me in ashes and make me lower my gaze before I leave how immense the promises of Ana de Peñalosa, and I am going, but may the powers of those confines protect me from illusions.

(LXX)

I picked up the Rule of Saint Basil before I left, to try to establish a bridge between opposites; in front of me, our hierarchical superior speaks about the order and subordination of the nine choirs of angels; then I went, for the last time, to the Motherhouse, and she wants me to leave with subjects for my meditation exercises (am I looking for the river or a book, a book or a child, a child or the Poor?), as well as wanting
me to leave with Blanche as company; I reply that she would be burdensome for me on this sort of journey,
my assignment is to look for knowledge rather than prudent virtues; I remind her that she should listen to Ana de Peñalosa, who is above her, and that she shouldn't even apprise the people who remain of my family.

It is an ordinary day, without sun or excessive gloom. As we talk

I often remember the dream I had, today, in my final hours of sleep, the dreams, my dreams, our dreams: a market where I can only see, in a vast plane, trays of vegetables and fruits; faint vegetables and fruit, as if they had only just appeared; among them, and sharing the same nature, there is a box with the writing, and the journey.

Someone asks me: — Bring the tray with the writing. Leaving alone is reckless. — But I reply that I'm not certain.

Someone tells me: — Looking for the river, without the book, isn't for a woman.

In my now-distant thoughts, I tell her that I can return every night, that if she so desires, in obedience to the rule of Saint Basil which is so dear to her, she will see me, at dusk, next to the wall of ivy, at the entrance to the refectory. She replies that this will be impossible, for if I leave on a years-long journey, I cannot return every month, nor every day, there is a tenuous brightness between us on this damp day, most of the flowers are white and lilac, they rise up in the green clinging to the stone.

In a whisper, she reproaches me for being deaf and mute, not even for a moment does she believe that I, every dusk, can return.

(LXXI)

Between the hidden sun,
a downpour of rain at three o'clock in the afternoon,
I spent my final day. I sat down on the promised bench at the back
of the garden, where I can see the magnitude of the green sweeping

over the plants; without my knowing whether they come from the
weather, or the transparent vegetal world; there are a thousand scents,
and trappings of hatred circulating, and a heat tempered with delicacy
and elevation; it becomes clear that I am in my place of return, at dusk,
next to the ivy.

I reply: — If I stay here, I will look for the river.

(LXXII)

I finally reached the banks of the Tigris River, which drank the ashes
of Al-Hallaj; the Tigris is not like the Tagus, or the Scheldt, it winds
brutally through a mountainous region veined with snow; between
the Tigris and Euphrates descending from the mountains of Armenia,
which run side by side for more than a thousand kilometers, I experienced the flood plain, the desert, the Zagros and Taurus mountain
ranges. I arrived one night next to a well

next to a people

next to a well,

surrounded by a mantle of scattered men who spoke with super-ter-
restrial gesticulations,

of a murder they would commit. Next to this well barked three dogs.
I sat down with the old men who continued discussing the byzantine
problem of which son they were going to kill. They had encountered
that horizon in the desert, and although it began to brighten from a
river, they still did not know where they would assemble the torture
machine

over the water,

over the burning wood,
and one of them proposed the brightness itself.
  River-Tagus was not with these rivers,
  or is River-Tagus the one pursued?

(LXXIII)

When I had the prescience to know I was going to leave the humans, a few sailors came ashore; they passed by our sisters who were crying on the dock and one noticed Alice who held back her tears, and brought me her last message: — "Farewell, farewell."

We will see each other again, and I will be the one who, at the hour of my death, with Alisubbo's Alice and Alice of the Cliff on my back at the edge of my bed,
will tell her:
  — "Farewell, farewell." — I don't know if the sisters see that I am here. The leaves that hide me are those from my place of return, the green, the yellow, a beginning of dampness that will rot the leaves.
  They sustain the light and send it back toward all the stones and columns in the cloister; a spiderweb surrounds the leaves, and the sisters, with Alice in the lead, feel a macerated tenderness for it.

(LXXIV)

I climb to the headwaters of the Tigris and Euphrates, sleeping in the cold beneath the trees; again and again throughout the day the light varies in intensity, and the dog I brought with me sniffs out the water as if he were thirsty, and then falls asleep leaving me in peace to read the Rule, to keep it in my forgetfulness. Benedict healed and raised a man who had fallen from a high rampart, I remembered resting for several hours at the edge of a chasm. Then, wanting some fruit I'd never seen before, I also remembered how he had broken a cup where they had left him poison.

This chasm is already so high, and I cannot make out the headwaters of the Tigris and Euphrates; down below, the proportions are so reduced that I have the impression I've grown; I will sleep elsewhere, further away from the fall that happens very quickly here. I decide to eat the unknown fruit,

in the life of Benedict, they say the saint knew through a prophetic spirit that two religious people were eating outside the Convent, how puerile.

Moments bereft of glacial horizons are rare at these heights surrounded by wind and clouds; in the sky drift blocks of ocean where the great rivers I seek make their ascension. I still haven't had the enlightening conversations on genealogy with the old mountain men that I desired; I ask myself where the book is;

it has been said that, in these places, one can remain invisible for at least half their life; I write, with a very cold hand and, on certain occasions, I believe that I'm addressing someone who is there in what I write.

To Eleanor speaking of Eleanor who from these dark snows and suns never stops tempting me:

I am no longer at the extreme limits of that land but close to fulfilling the promise I made you.

(LXXV)

It strikes five o'clock. I am back in the garden; the dampness persists.
My sisters have neglected the flowers, and the living.

In their eagerness to come and see me they forget about them, they
still aren't accustomed to this method. Last night's dew has not yet
gone, and the following night's dew is already appearing. The dampness
persists, and also the fruit from the profusion of trees.
Blanche has the quality of water.
She moves forward with a small trowel in her hand because it is
November 1. She says something in a heliotrope's ear, such as: — "It
is time to bring you inside the Community, because of the dew." —
Blanche is the one to whom the heliotropes belong. She stares at
the garden bench looking for me, while the earth moves away in the
shadow, and I move away also because it's almost six o'clock. So she will
believe I'm real, I leave her a note where I mention the heliotropes:
"Illustrious and lashed blue."

I'm supposed to meet Ortelius. With the thought that his original
projection respects the angles, I stopped in front of the door to the
house, which has heliotropes in the windows along the eastern façade.

I studied the different schools of cosmography before committing
myself to Ortelius. The Portuguese in Sagres, the Germans in Bavaria,
and on the banks of the Rhine. The Flemish, at the time of Antwerp's

great supremacy. Ortelius thought he could enjoy peace here for his knowledge and I come, discreetly, to receive his original which I will deliver to Plantin, or his son-in-law Moretus, at the end of this journey and test. Women are nothing.

They drift like shadows searching for a place,

but if they find it

"Its radiance has no equal,"

Ortelius's daughter told me opening the door for me,

and following in the wake of my body.

Ortelius greeted me sitting down, behind a nearly unfathomable table. The fifty-three charts contain seventy maps and I see the first great universal atlas arranged in front of me. He asks me if I noticed the river, and if it has a different stature than our own. I reply that the being to which he's referring isn't large, nor small, is broad and has volume.

— "It's imprisoned with shackles as if it were a man and every time pain strikes, these maps convulse."

— "I discovered it wants to write to you. Or speak to you." — My instructions hadn't said that I would find Ortelius in person. His originals would be shut away, alone, in a room, placed on the entry table. And he would be absent with his favorite father. They say Ortelius had several fathers. I lean over the maps and and notice that in the place left for the name

Theatrum Orbis Terrarum,

there is a shadow,

Since, after all,

even if I were in an instant a man, a cat, and a heliotrope, all these enigmas would be too burdensome for me,

I give myself over to Ortelius weeping.

I am not a Chimera, but I nourish myself with its truths.

The fire is nearly resting in its ashes; the two of us sit down fraternally, and he murmurs to me that there will come a time when we'll be able to decipher the world as yet unknown. He comforts me: — Mystery does not exist, what exists are Chimeras that we will continue dismembering one by one. — I arrange my dress around my knees, as is my habit. I tell him how I still haven't glimpsed the headwaters of the Tigris and Euphrates, that perhaps in this labyrinth of waterways supporting the present moment, River-Tagus has been lost. — It is like an imbrication, the origin of rivers. — The light that frustrates us falls only on the table and the maps. I can barely make out his profile as a human, and suddenly a kind of racial hatred comes over me, he belongs to a caste of people who are different from the others of my species, and are feminine, like Alice and Eleanor, but without being able to make their fates known. He asks me. — Who are you? Why did Moretus send you to me? — I uncover my hair for him, accentuate the tone of my voice, he is even more upset, as if he were troubled about, in the future, mapping the beings. — But if Moretus sent you, you must be someone interested in gold, and travel routes. — As well as tears. — I sense the hidden meaning of what you want to show me; but my perception is limited. This is why I'm asking you to explain yourself more clearly. — My grandfather had been rich, had eventually fulfilled his desire to toy with the powers of name and money; my maternal and paternal grandmothers were women who I always knew at a kind of pinnacle of their age; within the family they had a prestige and lucidity equal to that of my father and grandfather; I measured myself with this shadow, that is to say, the measurement that confronted me was not calculable, was in darkness.

In this beginning, then, I spoke and tried to see; everything was image and a thoughtful and verbal explanation of the image.

(LXXVI)

On my second visit, he gave me the *Theatrum Orbis Terrarum*. We spoke of predestination. Since the room we were in was amassed with a green that spread over us without any confused consciousness, full of sea and mountain images with simultaneous perspectives of freezes and thaws, I understood that the light had also been chosen and that the hours, passed in silence, expressed their desire for eternal greeting.

I left for Moretus with Ortelius's work. In the house where I'm staying, they gave me this message from Alice:

"At five o'clock I went out to fetch some water and, as I dipped the pitcher into the lake, I dropped it; not a single moment had elapsed and the current was already carrying it off, pushing it further away. Alisubbo's Alice said you had called her: 'Run down to the lake because the person who went to fetch the water is in danger.' She promptly obeyed, and could walk on top of the water as if she were walking on land, to the place where I was drowning. She dragged me by my hair and in a span of uncorrupted time we reached the shore. As soon as she set her feet upon the ground, she marveled at having done something she believed impossible. But I saw, when they took me from the water, your face over me."

I had asked Ortelius: — How many predestined names walk on
the light?

Manuscript after manuscript, day after day,

consecutive separations from what we love,

winter is approaching; there is no nostalgia for its icy paradise, which
does not come to pass; Alisubbo, who has exchanged the convent of
the mothers for his garden, fell ill amidst his autumnal fruits. I feel
myself beyond the cold but run through by it; I must leave Antwerp
on the next vessel departing the port bound for Mesopotamia. What
I have told you about the Tigris and Euphrates was a dream, for in
dreams we prepare life, but now I will have to survive the dream and
make the real river appear.

I asked Ana de Peñalosa if I could return to the house, but she told
me it is my duty to find the Thousand Words that will survive death. I
am conscious of the estuaries and river mouths this statement implies;
I wanted to guide you through doubt, and not through the unknown
which, in these times, reigns over the world.

(LXXVII)

When I was in bed with Ortelius, not even there did I stop thinking,
or writing. Since I felt inarticulate, he told me: — "It's not in your
hands that I seek the joy of love." — Ortelius's eyes are geometrically
conceived and with this vision of the earth he describes the world
precisely. He casts a measured gaze over my breasts asking me to take
off my shirt, and I navigate between my thoughts and his body, with

the irony of those who are distant. Love, Eleanor, is for me a perverse
rapid. At that point, mentally, I wrote a letter to Alice: Dear little Alice:

have you studied the doctrine of predestination?

tell Pegasus, to whom I know you have been speaking:

"torrential is the river, which gives us joy, death, and the beyond."

(LXXVIII)

It has been many days since I last went out wrapped in my cloak, in
the pure air of these summits, and the snow; my earthly figure has
aged and when an idea occurs to me, I get up and walk around the
cave which is vast and corresponds perfectly to my senses; I hope the
headwaters of the Tigris and Euphrates will come to me, which goes
against common sense, but is in keeping with the laws I use to guide
myself; an immense silence excavates the ground and in the subter-
raneans where these narratives seep another purpose always resonates

I hope a gentle melody will counteract the weight of the walls,
it must be at the root of one of these labyrinths that my small rivers
are born; it has been many hours since I last saw myself in the mirror, hours of years; neither books, nor sisters, nor Luis M., nor plants,
nor animals surround me with their paths toward humility; there is a
protracted and expectant cold here, thoughts take on tangible aspects,
and the mordant light will show me the place filled with River-Tagus.

Today the silence is even more copious than usual, as if a crystal
of ice had been broken; I hear nothing and I hear everything in this
silence foreign to knowledge which is my eternal horizon on this day
without month and without year: the rivers think they are alive just

like the living; in these mountains I come into contact with them, with their dense geometric splendor; they open up to me tangibly in the triple aspects of line, surface, and volume; linear paths correspond to itineraries of perennial streams whose turbulence is only expressed in times of flood. Their manifestation in the landscape is a riverbed. Glaciers are real, and they confound.

Their similarity with a certain period of my life does not overwhelm me. They overflow descending through mountains and gorges; when the moment of our investiture arrived, I was moved to smooth out my anger beyond what I expected, the ceremony of possessing little clothing. Garments were assigned to us according to the weather in the places where we would live; and possession was expressed as a conception or desire. A skirt, a dress of uncarded wool, for winter. For summer, the same garments but in a thin, used fabric. During that period, a submerged anger that sustained the order of the world had taken hold of me because of the women and against the women's appearance. What balance could be established between the strength of the current, and the resistance of the sloping riverbed?

They gave me more wool for my hands.

Not even here will I name the color of my habit because I was forbidden from choosing it.

No bodily vestige remained with me from this ceremony of investiture.

Neither a rupture of the hymen, nor different stigmas.

When we left together in the winding line which, by chance, I led with Eleanor, I mentally retained the sign

that the choreography of the river, and its tributaries, was open.

(LXXIX)

Alarming, the results of the wind.

Who wrapped the sunflower that was leaning against the wall and, when it blew restlessly, knocked over the stake holding it up, and broke it in the fall?

When it strikes five o'clock, Alice arrives; this time, rather than me she notices the large flower on the ground, and we suffer the death of a human being.

I confide in her awash in an imaginary sun:

— Give yourself that which already bears your name.

(LXXX)

She needs, that afternoon, to speak about joy; for days, she revealed to me, she has been beset by the idea, whether she is reading, trying to sleep, or walking the narrow paths; an old man happened to pass by, and as she showed him an embroidery of snow, ice from glaciers, snow falling to the ground, ice and snow crystals hanging in the air, a snowy mantle (which is typical of the high plains in Armenia), she named the teachings contained in the *Book of the Dead*. Either I, or him, we tell her:

when the night is completely shadowed, my nocturnal ghosts can eclipse it in the charism of fear; it is an imagined death that will fall short of the fear of death when one is dead;

I will have to pass this test without the feather I use to touch you, taking you for the ferryman; only disfigured images surround, plunging ever deeper into the reality that I will no longer be able to distinguish from their guilt;

in the extreme confusion of signs, in the possession of a bestiary that far exceeds the teeming imaginalia in which you live, you may perhaps believe you have found a limited demiurge.

When Alice asked me to take her to the mountains of Armenia, so we could find the headwaters of the Euphrates, of I and other rivers, we, the older ones, told her that only the rule of death leads, without difficulty, from one day to another; that she is shy and would have to prepare herself to enter different places crowded with people, and train herself to distinguish, in every face seen, what is unknown, uncertain, and dubious; that to come with me implies, more than anything, a constant penetrating; and that, in the end, she would have to abolish her shame, and accept the gleaming parts of the senses where a man touches. When Alice died, a sister suggested, for her epitaph:

— She left today, she arrived here.

(LXXXI)

Without me having any fear of the dead, Alice and I are about to reach the headwaters of the Euphrates. We spent two nights in my refuge, in the mountains of Armenia. When the sun rose we prepared food for the animals, which couldn't be frozen. On the first day, hiding at the edges of the ice, a wolf died. During my absence he fought against his father, Olo, for leadership of the pack. Because of all this, we hardly slept. When the sun rose, we set off toward the headwaters of the Euphrates, which we reached within three days. Alice always wore her ring. We circulated among stones but the diamond she wears on her finger is harder than all the rocks.

The wolves that were born with the Euphrates howl at the edge of the chasm, and to hear them as accurately as possible, I try to distance myself from my human understanding.

The transparency and weightlessness of the river's headwaters cause me to look for Alice, to find what is real in our bones. Night falls but I still hear, with the welling of the water, the whimpering of the young; I stretch out, to calm them down, alongside Alice who slowly warms up in the cold. The wolves howl. If they come to attack us, we must first protect our own, which are our vassals.

We let ourselves be subdued by this landscape. No dwellings, smoke, roads, cultivated fields, or human traces can be glimpsed. All that can be heard is a noise that surrounds us, circulating in the headwaters of the Tigris and Euphrates. Alice and I begin to understand the fire, how it is lit, how it is tended, how it is protected; neither the crossing of the logs, nor their thickness, nor the age of the wood is insignificant; neither their dampness, nor the arrangement of what is burning is insignificant; beyond the log, there is the leaf and the branch and how to place them so they remain lit on the frozen ground.

To relight the fire I must get up and, descending, almost alongside me, I recognize the figure of River-Tagus warming up. It is an intermediate form between wealthy merchant and poor wanderer. Careful observation does not exclude singularity. I knew it would urge me to face the night in order to assess my reason.

This shadow, these young wolves and their mother should have already died of cold.

It is now that the complexity of the images and their thieving wings will take me.

My chances of returning are uncertain, for I feel as though I'm on the side of death in this transfiguration which I describe to you with so few references. Alice, who came with me, is like a thread that binds me to you. A drop of water, another drop of water. I always wanted the Thousand Words to accurately express the beginning of this river. Such an attentive and visionary madness is a munificent gift. Also characteristic of the audacity of this sort of itinerary is that they chose me to attend the birth of a river, be it the Tagus, the Tigris or the Euphrates.

River-Tagus, in its shadow, does not move. When I ask it about the birthplace of the rivers, including the Tigris and Euphrates, it replies that my reason must be imperiled, for rivers are not born, they well up in their symbols.

(LXXXII)

Thus River-Tagus emerged in the shadow, but I did not come to know it any better. I did actually see it but then everything came undone in its contours, and it abandoned me during the night; suspended, I was on the mountain with Alice at my side, either dead, or alive, according to the pauses in her breathing. Fears of all kinds invaded me and I saw our houses, with our sisters, collapse and become dust. Eleanor and the others were transported by a true water which had become furious. We trembled, we died of fear, it was the fall of those who had been rejected by prudence.

(LXXXIII)

If this landscape could give me a better understanding of my son... It is a landscape of those who do not write, it cannot reveal itself as human in a place in space. It is an errant landscape, which is sinking. I write, my sisters, to tell you that I will undoubtedly return to find myself in a less ancient solitude and that, if I came here, it was so that, silently, I could announce Luis M. to you before speaking.

I was imprisoned in the trap sprung on the veranda of the house and, willingly, I abandoned it with Heart of the Bear and my son in my arms, moving through the fields; the veranda opened onto an intense cosmogony that I cannot help remembering. I said quietly, in my son's ear, and to Heart of the Bear who followed us with his sincere shadow, that the earth was an ornate system of fig trees, eucalyptus trees, peach trees, olive trees, and stones surrounding fragrant and empty places. We stopped, there was still discordance among the last shadows, in the privileged place where the setting sun absorbed us in a knowledge that had its own sense. I laid my son on the ground and hesitated, not knowing whether Heart of the Bear, in these westerly places, would remain a bear, or become a wolf. One of our first tasks was to carry branches, with different uses, to the inside of this emptiness, and soon we built a door frame in a wall covered by cistus, rosemary, armfuls of eucalyptus, pennyroyal, savory, which Heart of the Bear brought us as if he had always lived in the West. The first time we slept inside the house, my son lying on the edge of my skirt, there was only that wall, and no other. The heat, pressing down upon us even at night, dried the branches to their core. We noticed the marrow of the plants, and yet we dared not even scrape the marrow of the words that had revealed the vast herbarium of that clearing to us; the scents were the source of the first vocables that Luis M. learned, uttered by me who, inevitably, had the only human voice; "Deep," soon after, in the afternoon, "Intimate," were the names Luis M. gave to the bear who educated him muscularly. The full name he gave him as he played with him was "Intimate Deep Weeds." For a long time, he called me silently bringing me sage. The space where we lived could be seen at a glance; when we left the first space there was a second space, as closed-off as the first, but always with a small opening. We walked entirely covered by these branches, and lit the fire behind that wall, before night fell, waiting to ascertain its different phases; other times, we accumulated only trunks, cutting off their adventitious branches with an axe; still other times, alert, we put out the fire before the rain fell. Together, in the heat of all the bodies, we began to prepare what the child would later write, and which would suffer, mournfully, the slow depreciation of texts. My relationship with Luis M., beyond my having accepted being his mother or his wolf, had hidden roots: I would never only be a trickling source of language for him.

I would be the Nothingness that comes.

I would be the unwanted bird that comes with the Nothingness in the vestiges of the being.

The house had been built, and because when I was coming from far away it looked like a refuge for animals, it remained alive. Low because we lived at the top of an incline sloping several degrees, with a few granite rocks and many materials gathered from nature, stretched out under trees with a wild countenance, it offered me coolness and shade, when I wrote.

I wrote to all of you, through Ana de Peñalosa: "Being the mother of Luis M., who is playing here at my feet, has isolated me from you for some years. Anyone who says that being alone causes you to lose your reason is lying. Besides that, this child only has me to grow up in my image. I don't know what kind of power he is destined for: I always teach him a word, and its shadow; when he comes to offer me a piece of fruit gathered from these trees with a wild appearance and which bear fruit, I always name, after sweet, bitter. With poisons and antidotes seems to be the best way to educate Luis M.

Nonetheless, I am worried about the eventuality of him being alone without having any experience. Walking around the trees, which dared to imitate tall trees, I extend an imaginary thread and, keeping it in my hand, I attach it to the next obstacle, which is also a strategic reference. I foresee that mothers such as I are going to disappear. But Luis M. will find you one day and, among you, he will be the most beautiful human river I have ever known."

I will not grow old here. I learned about his life and, afterward, his texts, which is not the same as his life, as it is with us, the beguines.

My son is a child like the others, but there are no other children in the clearing; at dawn, through the crack in the roof of the house, which we can open and close by moving branches, I saw that I was going to change the usual regularity of my life; the beguines were intending to move to another country that was destined for them and made a discreet reference to the "margins that gathered in the center" and "an uneven line of ships." Ana de Peñalosa also referred to the distance that would begin to come between me and Luis M. and that one night, without me expecting it, a poor man would come looking for him.

Out of an intimate need for defense, over the next few days Luis M. became strange to me. Then, he became close to me. They rewarded this suffering with a candle that had a double flame, or two candles burning in the afternoon. The poor man, when he came, disappeared with Luis M. Without me seeing him arrive, without me seeing him leave.
As in Alice's epitaph.

(LXXXIV)

I sat down on the ground, at the back of the house, in the place I might call "Enclosed garden of animals that fear contact with prudence." As I move away down the hallway toward it, turning my back on the reckless part of the house, I see a woman walking with me, who dampens me, moves toward the space reserved for the plants and animals, and asks:

— Why do they have the right to go in there? — I go in to help them survive, to distribute wet bread mixed with fish and, also, of course, to open other doors to the world where my repose is complete.

The windows in this part of the house, seen from outside, are dark, and Blanche, a cat and not a sister of mine, when the basement she inhabited was empty, brought here, out of reach, her three daughters; this place doesn't look like a ruin, the invasive green of the plants acts as a comfort. I just gave the name Butterfly to an animal that plays with a butterfly, and although the afternoon wanes, bringing cold, I don't want to enter the southern part of the house because it doesn't have the same feeling as it does here, which is, expressed in images, the feeling of someone entering a storeroom at night, a place where firewood is kept, lighting the fire, and preparing the same food for everyone. It could be deliciously simple: toasted bread for me, bread soaked in milk, or water, to give to the chickens, or the cats. Someone then, that is to say, one coming from the human world, would lower their head to fit through the door, would first rest their hand on the threshold, studying the possible fear in my eyes. Reassured by the calm that would emanate from our meal, they should recognize, in themselves, that they do not bear any harm.

From what would it be necessary, myself and these animals, to defend ourselves?

Within our house, facing south, I know how night falls, but I don't know how night falls here; this is why I'd like to light a fire, protect the predisposition of the animals' spirit toward truth. Things would happen because of my insistence on not going to lie down. This world is no less dangerous than the solely human one but there is more coherence in it, and fewer lost images. Through sheer sincerity, or rather, dexterously following the river from its origin, we are protected among ourselves.

The man who remained at the door asks: — Who? — I recognize the Poor from The Remaining Life, and I reply: — I, or Blanche, or Hadewijch, or any of the young women who are here. — He says that one of us, Marguerite, will give Luis M., or John of the Cross, or River-Tagus to this book. — "Do you know this unforgettable river?" — I came here to not hear about myself, and to be in the company of the humblest beings; I understood clearly that a small immortality after death has no relation to the deep absorption in knowledge for which I am looking. I returned from this journey but I had some trepidation about remaining on it. In this, and in other similar places, will the fear of dying be bearable?

3RD PART
THE LADIES
OF COMPLETE LOVE

(LXXXV)

Is it a drama?

No. It is my state of extreme poverty in which I compare myself, through my own experience, to the poorest of the poor, those who need misericordia.

I dwell on that word

                   mise   ri   cordia.

Mise   the impulse;

ri   the musical note outside the seven;

cordia   the heart that invades itself.

I am the note   outside the seven, the community of beguines.

What responsibility do I have to pursue a language with no underpinning,

a thinking language, with a geographical scale?

Cape Espichel, Flanders, Capuchos, Lisbon, Úbeda, the Tigris and Euphrates. What responsibility do I have to have forgotten what kills, and write what lives? What fault do I bear for not loving the broken pitcher of the countries?

If you knew what the island of Ana de Peñalosa means, that this island is, par excellence, the image that is resistance, not because it has defensive cliffs, which would serve as a fortress, but weeds, more weeds, and the line where the lost music note sounds.

There are days, like today, where everything seems enveloped in a not-inconsiderable sorrow of the mountains. I observe it with candor and, if I describe it badly (I barely describe it), it is to penetrate into it with the consciousness of its reality. Is it the absence of human beings that creates the mountain's heavy sorrow? Or is it, rather, the presence of the beings that inflames this place with emptiness?

I see the flame that shines,

but I do not see the candle that burns.

(LXXXVI)

Struck by an unknown evil, we returned to the hospitality of the beguines; the houses scattered among the trees, the door that opens up for me to go in, the chest uncovered because Mary collects our laces of cotton thread and money, the double candle they lit in my honor in the common room, they leave me without a word to say. I sweep my gaze across their faces, some are more wrinkled, in others youth has submitted to the scruples of our own garments.

I sit down at the table touching the porcelain dish where they uncustomarily leave a piece of meat, and slices of pork that I will eat with bread. I sink down in my chair as if its legs were broken, and only my arms could still rise guided by my hands. I reach them out toward a sister called Eulalia who has come once again and who brings me wine in a white cup covered with a napkin. They aren't wondering about anything, they consider my memory empty so I can rest and, although it's still light outside, it is almost time for me to go to bed.

Such care and meticulous order immerse me in a great stillness, and I sleep on the white bed without any movement of my spirit.

The next day they don't let me do any housework, not even the simplest tasks like opening the windows and airing out the clothes. They are quiet in their expectation which they control perfectly, and it transforms into calm; there is a certain serenity resulting from submission to the laws; there is something here similar to snow, with an equally methodical, spotless arrangement. My room has become one of the most beautiful because it has nothing
and it has everything.
It has a bed, a nightstand, a basin and a jug of water on the stand, no mirror, no paper to write, not even a letter. It has a transparency that causes me to vibrate in my weariness, and I find refuge in the many memories I took from here.

Blanche, when she comes in, asks me questions that aren't symbols, nor voices of my invisible friends: "if the water is too cold," "if I slept well," "if the bell is too loud," "your frailty shouldn't be a weakness caused by illness."

(LXXXVII)

I live the days inside my room, removed from all my obligations, my walks, my powers that flow back into River-Tagus, which it gave to me. I put the basin and the jug of water in a corner and sit down at the table with lowered eyes which I will only raise at five o'clock to light the candle. The sisters gathered in my room, remained behind me like a curtain. The wind began to blow with a sharp intonation, a bad omen, and I returned to the chair out of politeness, knowing I should stay in the corner of the room because my sisters had the ferocious mask on their faces that I had seen in old men when they wanted to choose young princes to send off to war.

The candle was, then, behind me, and I heard it strike five o'clock in the morning; Eulalia moved toward my left side and, in an atmosphere that seemed to me to be a nightmare, said that Odile had broken the afternoon, which is why it was already night, even though it was actually five o'clock in the afternoon. Deciding to play her game, I asked her what breaking the afternoon meant, and what evidence she had that the afternoon had been broken.

She told that me she had been scrubbing the floor of the common room, facing the cabinet of provisions, with a stabbing pain in her kidneys. She told me that, at that moment, Odile had come in holding a bundle of candles which she breathed in with delight, and then threw at her feet, not to exalt her but to wound her. She said that, suddenly, the day had set through the objects and trees in the walled enclosure which invaded the room with birds and evil sounds, now nocturnal. She said that, in the meantime, Odile had raised her face, repellant with disgust and tears, from the candles lying on the ground and had begun alluding to an almost island land with another language, geographically in front of the sea, where there was a plague spreading, not of disease but of the stupidity of hatred. She said that Odile had suddenly fallen onto her kidneys like a hammer and had split her into two parts strange to one another, which had taken terrified refuge in the foundations at the two ends of the house. She said that one of the parts, the one that held her eyes, had seen Martha enter calmly and utter, with her illustrious voice that rose in the Chapel, that far away, in Portugal, the Inquisition quartered the dead, and kept the living in a slow agony. She said that Odile had picked up the candles, which were twelve, and had unmade half of them in her hands covering them with wax, as she, Eulalia, repeated that, in Portugal, the beaches were covered with fire, and that they, on those beaches, were expected,

if you, Marguerite, order us to go,

for even though we have hidden it from you,

Ana de Peñalosa, who shared in your decision to make you the chosen one,

went away, agedly,

but did not die.

(LXXXVIII)

— What did Odile say to Eulalia, and Eulalia say to Odile?

— I, who called myself Odile, said to Eulalia, that thus equipped with our visionary power, and in a state of complete poverty, we undressed throwing our clothes to the ground, to be able to traverse the prison of the senses, and be on equal footing with that which is lowest. I understood that our disputes and pains were merely one way for us to state, clearly, the images creating our fates. I said that, if we head toward River-Tagus which, as it happens, also ends in Portugal, as it could have been born to be a dim light in any cave in the world That,

if we head toward River-Tagus which also traverses Portugal,

it cast off its characteristics of water,
as it could have been born to be that light in any cave in the world.

— I, who will call myself Eulalia, said to Odile that when we were all undressed, without any ambiguous gaze or tremble, it would be clear that the next journey was possible.

— But we don't know the language — said Martha.

— Only Eleanor and Marguerite know how to speak it.

— No — said Eleanor. — Only Marguerite knows how to speak it, and I know how to write it.

— What did Odile say to Eulalia, and Eulalia say to Odile?

— I said that the coasts cannot just be destroyed.
We said to one another, in front of Martha, that we must spend some time in expectation; and, if we are all able to learn the language to the point they believe us Portuguese, then we would feel such little joy or sorrow at the moment of our departure.

But I, if not for me and Eleanor, and you, Luis, I will not know how to carry, when we are nude for departure, our cosmogonies.

— Our knowledge about death — said Blanche — is precise. I am a daughter of the living, and a daughter of the dead. — The sun was already bright at that moment. The end of that night; a night when the worst of the best things had happened.

Odile and Eulalia's faces have a common trait, which is a persistent smile when they hit upon the truth; I believe that the voice is a face in the growing darkness like that of today. We had to speak, for a kind of fearful anger could make our futures disappear.

Will I learn to speak this language? And will Eleanor learn to write it? Mentally, I ask her to tell me what she feels, for our intelligence is inseparable.

It was strange. And unusual. That night we learned, with all our senses, that language. It fell from the sky, spread through the air. It grew up with us and, unbeknownst to us, seemed bound to our childhood. It expressed our memories, was present in our most intimate conversations and secrets with an appearance of unfathomable time. If I opened the drawers, and my letters had transmuted into that other speaking and reading, I wouldn't have been surprised; I was, then, given the signal for our departure, and we did not wait for another more perfect knowledge of the stops along River-Tagus, and the places of our fate.

(LXXXIX)

It was a pure and verdant language,
with resonances of a journey,
a well dark in its depths,
an animal lying in the water that I took for a reflected white form,
with fur, wings, and a strong, agile skeleton where I passed by without
finding myself; it was a language still so young and perfectly bright that
I used it to begin thinking about what, in the future, I will write to you.
And, as it was autumn, it fell in leaves in the garden.
It's no wonder that we left almost dazed and without terror; that in this
language terror became relative, and can be tempered. We understood
that we were going to confront enormous disasters, although protected
by this veil that our lover offers us to keep us close to him;

now, that the scales have fallen from our language, and the snake is dead, let us lock up the House behind us.

(XC)

We went into our rooms. Perhaps our departure is still a ways away. Perhaps it isn't. It is surprising, suddenly attaining a new language. It is like conceiving a life within your womb, I mean, mind. — "Let me come in so we can speak" — implored Blanche. — We spoke for the pleasure of speaking while far and near, in the others' rooms, perhaps our Medusa is already rising,   the tight feeling when you are faced with the unknown. Our houses, our fires, our trees? What will we bring? With whom will our animals stay? Our books? Our wisdom in the language we solely spoke until today? This is what we murmured. And, when we said farewell: — "A moment longer."

I, Odile, was responsible for giving a fate to the living.

The cats that populate our territory are many, and their lineage isn't long, but it includes numerous side branches. Before the first mother that reproduced, there was a young white male that Blanche and I found abandoned in Eckhart's mill, and brought back to the house, drawn to him, and pitying his solitude.

He established a principle of genuine disorder in the rooms, for at night he sought out the open windows in order to leave, venturing through the trees and the slippery roof of the greenhouse. He curtailed the sleep of those who did not close their doors, like an Office, and disappeared, perhaps, with a certain disgust for our company.

In the November autumn came Moselle, so baptized for having

been saved from the heights of a tree. To retrieve her, Eleanor broke an arm, and I still see her slip and fall onto the diminishing clarity of the weeds which were covered with splendorous and dull leaves on the Day of All Felines, as we still call it today, because it was the day when Moselle brought us a feline descendancy: Prajna, killed by a child, Bergamote, missing, Cisca, Marguerite, Estelle, Alce, dead, Sancho, Alfonso, Mafalda, Mille Feuille, Rococo, Oc, Pimpinelo I, Jeremiah, Alice, Pimpinelo II, Lilac, Rose, and Jasmine.

I should say that most survived. And that one of the survivors may have been Pimpinelo II, which slept on a stump next to an axe, which is why we put him under the protection of Müntzer, to whom we were finally unable to offer him, because one morning he was no longer inside the walled enclosure, nor in any other part. Two dead and three missing is a weighty fault for those who, like me, look after the living.

I went out tonight to feed the cats. I will still do it a few more times. Everything suddenly appears brown to me and the white one, named Blanche, escapes over the wall when those that seem stronger come near. No more than two cats are born during the summer, but they have unyielding rival qualities. It's true that I don't see very well; but why do I feel plunged into the brown? It is Alisubbo's Alice who will come and look after them.

Would I remain here, if the Rules that maintain our revolt hadn't relentlessly ordered me to enter?

(XCI)

It is necessary to understand the origin of desire;

it moves away like a face disappearing in a mirror. Once again the mirror fills with the same face. I thought that Hadewijch, the luminous shadow of Ana de Peñalosa, was far away, in another distant Community, or had disappeared. But today, when I gathered the first beings (the papers and images of this narrative), and belongings (Luis, thoughts of you) we were supposed to bring, they knocked on the door, and Hadewijch came in with a basket on her arm, head covered by a hood made of a wool once seen in a dress belonging to Ana de Peñalosa.

It was, undoubtedly, her face, her body, her same manner of walking and standing,

but having traveled a path.

The furrows around her eyes indicated a new luminous source, and a quiet experience of darkness that I deemed of an appreciable value to know, as the departure for Portugal startles me at night when we are all together.

Hadewijch set down the basket looking at me

for they suspect I will end up taking Ana de Peñalosa's place which, for now, is vacant. An immense place in these sites of insurrectionary obedience.

Hadewijch, like me, thought about obedience:

— I came because they asked me to. — She had grown pale, she wanted to make me believe that she wasn't Ana de Peñalosa's enemy. And that the reason she had come, I should read it in her unspoken words; the daylight ebbed with great perfection, a perfume spilled out of the basket.

— This basket doesn't contain anything.

We mustn't look, in the end, for any meaning behind her visit. She was, remained, resurrected the presence of Ana de Peñalosa who may have already aged to the edge of death, or even died.

— She is alive — she told me. — She is alive today by chance.

— Which I don't believe in — I replied, trembling to find myself with the two women whom I must join in a knowledge of love.

— I am not an apparition — said Hadewijch still enlightening me, for I had been confused, without the bright spirit that John of the Cross ascribes to me.

She sat down at the table, and her hood slipped down her back; I studied her face intently for some time, completely forgot what I saw on such a boundless landscape because
she took my hand,
and conveyed the request that made me turn my eyes to the window, to the large tree from which Moselle had been saved, to the bench where you, Eleanor, were sitting, to the wall of the enclosure which was now transparent and, in the afternoon, faded.

She smiled to circumscribe my thoughts. Or, in this case, she preferred to say: — I must knock in order to leave.

(XCII)

A man appeared in my sky, a naked man. Facing into the wind, he is in the square of the window, and he is the winged arm of River-Tagus. Bound for the inferno of a new journey, I pick up the basket left by Hadewijch where I put this book
which might remain there, or disappear,
like a night.
These lines, written by several women of mine, of whom I am the

fingernails and head, gather around John,
who is the naked man,
to undress him again.

They kiss him painfully with their nails; in the squares of the windows, an elderly man appears because it is already morning, nearly morning. I call my sisters so they can share my nightmare. They, last night, had horrible dreams and, around five o'clock, by the candle flame, we established the ritual of describing them.

Alice:

I did not think it was possible for a dream about Saint John of the Cross to be a nightmare; we were both stretched out on a sheet of water, and we were supposed to drink the successive waves; Pegasus appeared, and wanted to lie down on the sea; the waves he drank unmade his body, and only his hooves remained.

I clung to Saint John of the Cross who showed me the limits of the horizon; my mouth remained dry despite the amount of water, and I swam toward Pegasus's hooves
which I used to hit Saint John of the Cross in the face.

Eleanor:

I have never seen, of that naked man, of whom you speak, a single image. But I dreamed that he wanted to create with us in this Community. I felt like weeping because he had almost died, wounded by the nails.

Eulalia and Odile were two women who had suffered greatly in their lives outside; before five o'clock they left soundlessly from their small house. Five o'clock in the morning, five o'clock in the afternoon,

matinal or vespertine hour, one or the other with the same brightness propitious to the lighting of the candle flame; they perfumed or
anointed their hands wanting to believe that they were leaving for
an amorous encounter without a man; they closed the door of their
house with a chain, they left a brick in the chimney to warm them
upon their return, which they imagined would be cold according to
the dreams they would tell and hear; "the snow accumulated because
yesterday was the first afternoon of only snow; today is the first day it
has snowed unceasingly; for some years, in the southernmost country
where we are going, snow will no longer be seen; it is, nonetheless,
desirable for it to be replaced by the sea."

The others were already in the room, and while they waited for everyone to arrive, Blanche, confronted with her own anxiety, had rambled:
"we, who are governed by the enlightening fear of our own space
without which the visionary spirit cannot expand, we are filled with
torrents. These rivers that are the space where the vibrating movement
I spoke of evolves. Ana de Peñalosa also spoke in torrents, I feel surrounded by the perpetual birth of assertions. Our dreams have divided
us tonight into different species with identical confines and I propose
that, if this forgotten country wants to create with us...

What future is in store for us, for we who want to leave with so
many images, and so few images of ourselves?"

It was then, with everyone finally present, that Alice recounted her
dream: "I did not think it was possible for a dream about Saint John
of the Cross to be a nightmare; we were both stretched out on a sheet
of water, and we were supposed to drink the successive waves; Pegasus appeared, and wanted to lie down on the sea; the waves he drank

unmade his body, and only his hooves remained.

I clung to Saint John of the Cross who showed me the limits of the horizon; my mouth remained dry despite the amount of water, and I swam toward Pegasus's hooves which I used to hit Saint John of the Cross in the face."

Then, not sitting down with her hands on her knees but standing up, Eleanor followed: "I have never seen, of that naked man, of whom you speak, a single image. But I dreamed that he wanted to create with us in this Community. I felt like weeping because he had almost died, wounded by the nails."

(XCIII)

the air clear and cold, and even more clear and cold beyond the windows, we heard the voices that describe the dreams and that, in this almost Chapter-like visiting room, take on noble intonations; they had different tones than those they usually had when speaking or reading; Hadewijch who remained among us, Martha and Eulalia are standing; Mary, Odile, Eleanor, Alice are sitting; Blanche walks with small steps; I, resting on my elbows, lean over the table full of images; this diversity of positions gives a certain aspect of restiveness to the room which, in its stone architecture, is methodical.

through the half-closed windows, the snow now falls brightly in the night and, in the depths of Eulalia's voice, which was alluding to her nightmare, the Chapel's organ music sounds; we understand that Alisubbo is playing for us, or Luis M., or Nietzsche, or Saint John of the Cross, or River-Tagus which encompasses all of us and, among the passions revealed in the dreams, we add to our Rules the obligation to give refuge to River-Tagus.

(XCIV)

Our departure is approaching; we take our places in two carriages; I appreciate the strength of the horses and think, constrained, about their tireless march; we leave Brabant in winter, and at the end of the year; we will greet the New Year along the way, we will see long stretches of road, and inns; we will see different houses, we will be able to look at our faces languidly, sitting down facing one another, we will see the journey measure itself against what we say; I think to tell them a bit about the journeys of my life, I open myself up to them with my voice. Blanche, Eulalia, and Alice travel with me, and we remember the nostalgia of our homes.

Thus are we women.

The horses have now stopped, and we abandon the last forests of Flanders, with Brabant already behind us;

like our past life;

we close the windows hermetically, and Alice opens her mouth in the new language. — If we spoke according to the second language — she says. Sitting between us is a passenger who has come from Portugal to show us the way and who seems to have lived in a time much farther at the future than our own; "at the future" shouldn't be said, if the language were always immaculate; outwardly she is not pleasing but her speaking, yes, is almost enticing: — My country is a country of poor rebels. By day, they are miserable; by night, opulent on the island of loves. — It was then that Nietzsche revealed himself sitting among us in our carriage. He traveled pressed between Alice and Eulalia. He still loathed women, but not us, who continued swaying on the road and who were what remains of women. He said to us: — "The truth? Oh, you don't know the truth. Is it not an attack on all our modesty?" — He spoke among women, as if he were also a woman. But he looked at us suspiciously, our hoods starched, and exalted; he told us a donkey couldn't be tragic and, when the carriage turned onto the right path, he disappeared through Alice's face. She, after a pause, conveyed to us that the last murmur she had heard from him had been that, since knowledge placed boundaries on wisdom, there were many things he never wanted to know. Cecilia, who had come with the intention of taking us to Portugal, did not let silence fall: — I want her to be as invisible to you as you are to me invisible. — The carriage had stopped; they had reached an inn.

Today it isn't cold, it seems less wintry, and the rooms in this inn look toward the country where Saint John of the Cross was born; Cecilia's country, where we're going already knowing its language, is farther to the West and I imagine we'll still have to cross green valleys, almost deserted plains, land, land, land. Cecilia either speaks at length, or is silent, a binary rhythm brings her to us, and takes her away from us; because I told her she had similarities to the sea   its waves   as I offered her a sip of water from the pitcher sitting on the windowsill which overlooked the arid soils of Saint John of the Cross, she confessed that she had also known him, through companionship in love and writing, that he had been the only man she'd ever loved,
although she had always lived far away from him, except on the day

he'd come to sit down, lower, at her side, and she had ultimately been unable to speak, only write the text he dictated; his face, when it was near, was always what she saw when she was far away, and he had an unexpected way of commanding her to write, or rather, making her understand his movement of voices, gestures, the tilting of his head which, out of all the parts of his body, put everything into words; I feared losing this subtle, and strong fluidity, and leaned toward him, ever nearer to his closed fists. And, at a certain point, he got up to go to the window that overlooked this same landscape, or one almost identical to it, and told me that I, either now or later, must accompany you to Portugal, and that he gave you his hand. I accepted it for you, not for me, though I had always loved him, and his hand remained on the windowsill, the hand itself, not its shadow, and he left with his bloodied wrist hidden in his sleeve and murmuring to me, when he departed, "the writing grows," he consoled me.

I beg your pardon for being,   Alice began to say when, at the meeting in the inn which replaced that of the Chapter, she came to show us her nightmares.
I offered her a tree branch to say that I would support her.
Dearest Alice,
tonight, in the place for your head, I had a dream: that you lived inside a small glass; that's why you were eager. When I asked if you would, soon, die,
they replied that you would live until the rim of the glass.

(XCV)

Since the snow continued falling heavily, and the wind never stopped
accumulating ever more wind, we had to interrupt

this part of the journey; at the inn there are many rooms, and particularly storerooms, vacant places, where straw and abandoned agricultural
tools accumulate; when the snow advances through the half-open
doors I notice, on my walks, that there are dark and sheltered corners
where velvety and delicate beings, full of hunger and perspicacity, hide
themselves. We are not yet talking about dying, for his eyes illuminate
my path to those that run away as soon as I arrive, although they never
stop watching me. I remember sitting halfway down a staircase, in the
ideal time of my childhood, but this has nothing to do with childhood, they are real forms of another thought; I sometimes close the
difficult-to-close door behind me, for the wind blows and a barrier
of ice has been created, always being careful to leave enough space so
that those beings can leave; they are dark in color, light, in-between
without a shadow and I give them food to eat with only a minimum
of water so they don't freeze. I give them names that guide me and
I decide to speak about them to my sisters who, like me, are eager.

perhaps these beings are related to River-Tagus, are its tributaries or
children that have become ancestors; in this crude language of images,
a restorative rhythm is revealed which I read in the eyes of those future
beings, banished in their own time; I called them posthumous, each
with their own name to be able to describe them; there is Blanche,
Boat, and Mote; when I enter that hidden part of the inn I always know
that a tree, in my spirit, is going to fall; those beings do not tremble
when they hear me, the only commonalities they have with humans

are their eyes, and even those are more lucid or distant; Boat will allow me into its solitary understanding.

my visits are always short because it's cold, which chills me, and I'm afraid to impose my human presence upon them; I never wanted to bother them humanly, and I lean back against the wall without any noise or images in my gestures; they are hesitant, move closer to the food I brought them, and wait for me to leave, to recreate the movements that are pure currents of water.

we couldn't yet leave; in the forced immobility, the snow became a breath of monotony.

I, who lose myself easily in this white darkness, reconstruct my life; we are halfway to where we are supposed to return; I, Eleanor, remain with Marguerite after so many separations, disillusioned by being near, without any words to write to one another; the slope is a perfect path, and we are both at the threshold of the beings where only I can enter. Yet behind me, she brings the food that she looks at as if it were a distant horizon. The monotony of her pace is an effect of the snow; I invite her to meet them because I suspect that the consequences of her presence on these intuitive beings may be almost nothing; there is an odor of straw decomposing, of substances that live. These beings that proliferate in the snow, run away into the snow, take shelter inside the house, itself abandoned.

Setting the food on the ground, we remain standing; it is even colder here, but we barely breathe out of respect for these beings which believe that our movements may be a sword striking them.

We stop. Years are not enough to measure my desire to penetrate time;

Marguerite's face clouded, darkened, filled with shadow; I wanted to make this language traverse all languages until it became, at last, shadow and silence. I speak to you with passion, Marguerite, to your shadow so you will answer me,

make me see,

so that this place won't be an end to movement.

I know that, among us, there is the equivalent in hatred; but I wanted to tell you that where those confines lie, the bodies are in a place, and surrounded by other bodies.   The beings gleamed, they couldn't hide themselves, no longer be seen by the women.   they are being burned in the autos-da-fé that terrorize Lisbon today. They left through a side door where one of the beings thought to hide; warned by its light, they found themselves outside, always cold.

they were in Portugal, in a church called São Domingos, in the Largo de São Domingos, and Marguerite thought, when she heard Eleanor speak, "when this end is reached, the origins are near."

As beyond created things are uncreated things, a fishmonger attending the Mass saw a luminous crown envelop Christ's head and whispered to those who were near: "Miracle." "Miracle," Marguerite eventually realized a woman was saying in her ear.

As when the miracle arrives the decline began long ago, Eleanor murmured nothing;

and, as the people rose to shout, they remained seated, close to one another, but without uttering a word.

From the lips of a man who was almost at the back of the church, and who could not escape, they heard the truth: — Listen to what I'm saying: it is only the candle's reflection. — But two Dominican friars had already called it a monster of heresy, and everyone fell upon its body; they immediately made a fire, and burned this being.

Marguerite and Eleanor moved away from this smoke hand in hand, lost in one another; they entwined their fingers so as not to weep and, before it was time, make themselves known. They stumbled through the spruces of Flanders and Brabant, although they were in Lisbon, and they did not see the signs proclaiming: "praise be forever the Blessed Sacrament" on the walls in the last city along River-Tagus; when Marguerite was able to weep, she explained to Eleanor, in the new language which they now always spoke, that it was in atonement for the church of Santa Engracia having been robbed, and the sacred host stolen; a new Christian had already been beheaded, and burned without any proof.

— It was under these circumstances — said Eleanor — that Marguerite and I awoke from the same nightmare — when she finished recounting it to the gathered sisters; a letter had arrived from Luis M., which was given to them by Odile and she, and all those on the path of return, were already aware of the news.

EPILOGUE

The poor entered the House, the kitchen became promiscuous. Each of them is my Master. The poor, in the country of this language, are threadbare, even more despised than they are anywhere else. Able to teach us much about the weft of life, they have opinions about everyday events that they express in lapidary and hereditary phrases.

Comuns is a poor man between forty and fifty years old, who is still considered an orphan, who doesn't give age the least importance, who knows the Thousand Words, and who sits facing the sea only holding out his hands to eat. The face invaded by his beard is dark, with white spots, I walk close to him without the shudder I sometimes feel in the presence of men, particularly Alisubbo. At night, he stretches out in the same place, nights and days pass with Comuns studying his apparent lifelessness. He follows me with his eyes, exudes a pungent odor, utters his lapidary phrases — proverbs and premonitions.

Among the poor hide some of those who are persecuted. It is bitter, for those who aren't poor, to take on the inconspicuous and monotone physiognomy of the poor. It is bitter to live sitting on the ground with the specter of fire and torture. Those who can be killed by fire do not love, as we do, the candle flame. Ever since we arrived, we still haven't lit it for the ritual contemplation at five o'clock. We limit ourselves to contemplating the candle flames burning routinely on the altar. We have a single altar, also surrounded by the poor who work for us praying Ave Marias, and whispering. At night I lie down with my head heavy from this whisper, my spirit obtuse, the smallest images of silence lost.

Even by my bed, on another shorter but equally massive bed, there is a sick woman sleeping who sighs, with the accuracy of a clock, at every hour of the night. At five o'clock we get up, I wash my face in the common basin, I kneel in the chapel among these miserable ones, who sleep. Miserable ones worthy of misericordia, motionless sleeping and awake, who are many of the Faithful of Love for whom we were looking.

Our long day, then, begins: our Rules have become more cohesive and rigorous, as if we had gone back in time. Arising at Matins, we go back to bed, so as not to sleep. We finally get up with the sun, again wash our faces in the common water of the basin.

Knowing that other hands have plunged into it, it is, for me, a singular water. I am Eleanor, if I haven't yet said.

Some meters from the house, we have the sea: a sloping path, a mantle of sand, and the saline smell. All along the path are the poor, who wait, who greet us from afar, and then become immobile to wait for a long time. They do not have a family name. Here, the names surprise me, Silva, Oliveira, Romão, Rosa, Loureiro. Stick, thorn, flower, fruit. One of these poor brought me an offering in his grimy hand, several shellfish that had been caught on a rock and still moved between his fingers, more alive than dead. I opened my handkerchief to put them inside, and the poor man asked me if there was another poor man called Comuns, that he was called Laranjeiro, and came from the North, slowly traveling dry lands. We are south of the Tagus and I speak this language so clearly that no one can imagine I am a foreigner.

I reply that, in fact, there was a man called Comuns who had arrived several days ago saying little about himself. — He has an illness — said the newly arrived poor man — which takes hold when he breathes words. — That may be true. Let us go and find him. — He is sitting in the same place, face impassive, and gaze vacant. — The smells from the kitchen reach us before him — observed Laranjeiro. I still have the mollusks in my handkerchief, I should hurry to my place in the Chapel, sing in the choir.

I decide to stay with them, and later confess the failure in the Chapter of Faults. I look at one, I look at the other, I hope they're going to speak. The first asks the second: — How is the weather, and the drought? — The second replies: — Everything is fine. — Not another word is said, they no longer look at me, nor want to see me. I think about attending to my obligations in the Chapel, to be able to hold onto my discretion in the Chapter of Faults.

Except for the presence of the sea, which crashes, which repeats, which amplifies amidst this promiscuity, the silence is total, a true silence of solitude. The voices don't become scarce, the movement, the orders, the care, the fears, the eyes on the faces of the beggars and sick who may only be unprotected, or also persecuted; Marguerite tries to keep , her spirit calm and sits down, at times, for a few moments in front of the sea, not on the beach but near the window; only speaking one language clearly isn't enough, that's what I believe she is thinking; and this sea is a lost continent, and this soil a rock. Our eroticism and that of our sisters has become acute, the more mysterious and mute they are, the more we desire these poor; their dusky complexion has no limits.

I am here, and not in Flanders, in front of Comuns who today has become livid. I do not know if this manuscript will ever see the light of sea, the light of land, or the light of sun. Marguerite, who also can be intelligent/cruel, calls me, almost in silence, the lady of Comuns. I am, in fact, the lady of the sick man who is lying here. If not for the hollow cheeks, the body losing the occasion to stay with us, the tongue immobile at every moment, one might think that, under the blanket, he is resting. He only rests in the glaucous light. In the moments when his lividity becomes attenuated, his dark complexion causes me to move my hand; why must I always confuse desire, and peace of mind. The lamplight shares the room. I do not know if I am at the bedside of a man, or an image. From time to time, Marguerite's figure appears at the doorway; I do not know if she is watching over me, or watching over it. If Comuns were a persecuted man, and not only a poor one, if Comuns were an envoy, and not only a man, if Comuns had lived in heresy creating new heresy, what auspicious funerals would we give him?

As soon as Laranjeiro left, undeceived by the death sweats, I knew who Comuns was: — I came with a message for you from River-Tagus... — crossed his lips without him speaking and I, afraid of distorting the said with the unsaid, stood up in Marguerite's wake. I did not have to go far because she was still with the poor, deeply weary with the feelings of our night. She tells me, on the way, that he is more water than man, a moribund sign.

An hour later, Luis Comuns raised his right right; grasped Marguerite's wrist, not mine; looked at me as if rereading: — I came with a message for you from River-Tagus...

— Who? — asked our sisters in the end. — What killed him?

I tremble as if he had sealed that message; I notice I am hungry; it became brighter. Marguerite is still holding his wrist. She will be, in the Chapter, the intermediary for what only she was able to read: "Everywhere it dared become visible, River-Tagus appeared as the figure of a poor man. A poor messenger, a poor man like Comuns. In 1646, in Lisbon, they burned that apparition in an auto-da-fé. That was the day Comuns died among us and Heart of the Bear, who had witnessed the act, told us how the justice of darkness had been served. It had been impossible to burn the water but, nonetheless, possible."

Description of November 18, 1646:

Heart of the Bear wanted to become tiny and accompany me in my body where he had embedded a kind of place for traveling. I was with Marguerite, and the others in the Community.

The day had dawned in a final silence and the Tagus River, from the spot where I was, could be seen moving populated with boats, the larger vessels in the distance, the eternal seagulls gliding and ignoring those who were inside or outside the circle of heresy.

From time to time, either a spectator or a condemned felt a shiver down their spine; but the others, only spectators, shouted delightedly into the wind from the river, "finish them off."

We, Comuns and I, and I, and I in Comuns, and Heart of the Bear who, after Müntzer, coalesced with River-Tagus, did not know this city was volatile. We were more accustomed to the cold ones, to countries where the snow covers almost the country itself, making the territory the snow itself.

Apostille,
or annotation
to this writing:

being only the woman who writes is impossible:

I will keep existing, for I am no longer alive, but a total instrument of writing; bound to Portugal I am its hopeless prey, and I believe I can only come back to life there; how could all this happen to me after so much time away, and as a result of a single journey?

Being only the woman who writes is impossible; a landscape perpetually deluged with thoughts keeps me as its slave. In the language of Comuns, I would say it is the slave who has enslaved me, but now the Convent of the Capuchos, in the Sintra hills, unsettles me from the back of the room, is an imperfect incident for a book. I see the first scene being born between tears, the king suspected of being a dreamer speaks with a friar who is his spiritual superior. I am with them, in the small forecourt, noting the gathers of his voice, and what kind of morning it was, as well as finding myself disguised in the same cave where the farewell was taking place:

— My Lord — said the friar — considering that everything passes, everything has already passed us by.

— The sufferings I will endure — said the king — I already know them.

— That's why you came to spend the night in this cell, tonight, and the following nights, after your departure.

— I know you're right — said the king. — But you must add something to this poor Cork convent, a monument still unknown to us.

— Which one? — asked the friar.

— A monument still unknown to us: the entrance under two cliffs — repeated the king moving toward the opening, which was the dizzying entrance to the Sintra hills that could be seen everywhere.

— Tomorrow you will only see the sea; and not this courtyard of

Cedars—added the friar.

— Tomorrow I will only see this Convent drifting in the waters; no matter where I go, the Sintra hills will be before my eyes; who would image that it is to win them or lose them that I am going to fight in Africa. — The hills were so lush that the fact that a single tree was within reach of the king surprised me.

— Liege — said the friar — as always here, the morning is damp and cold. Do not let yourself be overcome by a terrifying fear.

— Bring my horse — said the king. — If I lose to the enemy, if any evil comes to me, this evil will come to you.

— This evil is already here — said the friar. — Even though our cells have such small openings.

The Road to Flanders, July 6, 1977
The House in Jodoigne, August 18, 1979

LLANSOL, POET OF THE POSTHUMOUS

Benjamin Moser

Everyone in this book is dead. Not because they lived in the past, though they did: Friedrich Nietzsche died a long time ago; and so did Saint John of the Cross; and so did the radical Protestant Thomas Müntzer, decapitated in the sixteenth century.

In biography or history — not to mention in our own common understanding — death circumscribes life. But in *Geography of Rebels*, death hardly even impinges upon it. Müntzer carries around his severed head while participating fully in whatever "action" can be said to unfold in this book; and John of the Cross remembers his own death as a floating departure, akin to the bodily levitation he has mastered with his spiritual exercises.

Characters' names are no more attached to their bodies than those bodies' parts are attached to each other. In this oneiric world, time loosens its bonds, and lets people who lived centuries apart chat like neighbors bumping into each other on the street. Here, heads split from necks, and hands from arms; sentences snap into fragments, breaking the painstakingly "logical" constructions that, at least in literature, we expect to bind one thought to the next.

★

In this theater of the casually dead, the deadest figure of all is its creator, Maria Gabriela Llansol. This is not because she is, in fact, dead. (She died in Portugal in 2008, at seventy-six.) Needless to say, she was not dead when she wrote these books.

They were composed over a five-year period from 1974 to 1979. At the time, she was living in a small Belgian town called Jodoigne. She had left her homeland in 1965, at the beginning of the last agonizing decade of Salazar's dictatorship. That regime, founded in 1926, predated her birth, in 1931, and proved to be one of the twentieth century's most tenacious: it only succumbed in 1974, the year Llansol began *Geography of Rebels*.

Perhaps the year is not a coincidence. She was forty-three, but a writer who would become notably prolific had hardly published anything: there was a book of short stories in 1962, *Os Pregos na Erva*, and its sequel, which appeared in 1973. Under the suffocating regime, her silence was typical. Poverty and oppression had forced tens of thousands of Portuguese into exile. There were the villages full of impoverished regular people, who became concierges in Paris or bakers in Rio. Political dissenters left because they had to; artists and intellectuals left for places where they could work in freedom.

Llansol was one such exile. Her husband, Augusto Joaquim, had refused to participate in the cruel colonial wars that Portugal was waging in Africa, and deserted. They went to Belgium. "I came with great daring," she wrote, "and also with an enormous thirst for freedom, for novelty, for reaching the core of being. No one can possibly have even a pale image of the thickness of the air that we breathed down there, in the tiny closed cells of our lives. I was trying to escape in order to write."

Belgium gave her freedom. There, she discovered an institution peculiar to the Low Countries: the beguinage, medieval hostels that offered a refuge to spiritually inclined laypeople. These cells offered not captivity but freedom; and in the thirteenth-century beguinage of Bruges, Llansol suddenly understood that "several levels of reality were deepening their roots, coexisting without any intervention from time." As it happens, this is a good description of *Geography of Rebels*: of its structure, which abolishes time to merge life and death; and of its cast of mystic seekers, who inhabit the murky borders between apparently incompatible levels of reality.

Alongside this timeless spiritual world, this book reflects Llansol's, and Portugal's, concrete political situation. Under Salazar, Portugal's ancient culture had been reduced to the "three f's": futebol, fado, and Fátima; sports, folk music, and repressive Catholicism. In the thick air of a country like this, an eccentric artist like Llansol could not possibly have had a career.

*

Yet this was a kind of blessing. Joseph Brodsky once observed that censorship is bad for artists but good for art. This is questionable, and more than a bit romantic. But to read *Geography of Rebels* is to wonder whether a work such as this, with its severed body parts and abruptly severed sentences, could have ever been written, or written like this, for a country where it might possibly ever have been published.

One can easily imagine the despair that a writer would feel at finding herself exiled and unpublishable in middle age. Literary history offers abundant examples of people in similar situations who gave up on art, and on life. Only a woman of uncommon strength could have made virtues of those necessities, and one is constantly amazed by the courage that it must have taken Llansol to write like this. To write like this, she has had to give up on writing as a career; to accept that a lifetime of work may be destined for the rubbish-heap — and to go ahead anyway.

That is why, in some way, we feel that Llansol is dead: that she has accepted that much of this work would only be read after her death, or not at all. Perhaps it is this choice, taken while it was yet day, that the figures in her books are constantly pondering. "As he became dust, Thomas Müntzer heard the trampling of the horses farther and farther away. He had never died before."

Living through death while remaining fully alive: the theme appears on nearly every page of these books. To choose a living death is a choice that only a saint could make. The conscious embrace of oblivion is, after all, a spiritual choice, not an artistic one. And from the spiritual perspective this embrace is not a restriction but — like the freely chosen monastic cell — an opening, a freedom. In the dark of what night, and at what personal cost, did Llansol accept that freedom?

★

By the time she began writing these books, Portugal was taking its first steps toward rejoining the democratic nations. Many of Llansol's books would eventually be published, but even today her archive in Sintra is stuffed with thousands of pages of unpublished writings. A broader readership eluded her until after her death, and it is not hard to understand why. She was not young when she began writing in earnest. She was even less young when, in 1985, she finally returned to her homeland. The pact with the posthumous had already been forged.

Throughout her life, Llansol translated French, German, and English poets, including Hölderlin, Rimbaud, Éluard, and Rilke. One is hardly surprised to find the patroness of posthumous poets, Emily Dickinson, on the list, too. Dickinson, like Llansol, seems to have been writing only for herself—and, perhaps but not necessarily, for some future reader, yet unborn. This gave them the freedom to slash at the language they inherited: Dickinson with her dashes, Llansol with the strange pauses that break expected patterns and create a spooky and addictive rhythm. But unlike Dickinson's poems, which often require close study to reveal their meanings, Llansol's writings are musical; their flavor emerging best when read aloud.

Another writer's spirit hovers still more urgently over these writings. This is the ghost of the great Brazilian, Clarice Lispector, who was still alive when Llansol began but who, in 1977, when Llansol was still working on these books, had taken up her place among the legendary dead. Clarice's witchlike power over her readers is surely unlike that of any other modern writer, and her devotees more like the votaries of a saint than the admirers of a famous artist. This power has often been described, not least by the present writer.

But if her power over readers is well known, Clarice's power over writers has never quite been described. With its unsurpassed beauty and its uncanny emotional power, her language offers a nearly irresistible example to anyone writing in Portuguese, and especially to young writers. Alas: imitating her nearly always leads to catastrophe. And for a critic to suggest a comparison to a writer who dominates her language as completely as Clarice Lispector dominates modern Portuguese is to diminish that writer, even when the intent is to praise.

Yet if anyone might be profitably compared to Clarice, it might well be Maria Gabriela Llansol. This is because of the fundamentally mystical impulse that animates them both, their conception of writing as a sacred act, a prayer: their idea that it was through writing that a person can reach "the core of being." This core becomes an equivalence of life — all life, any life — with God. When Llansol says that her writing "is a kind of luminous and generalized communication between all the intermediaries or figures, without any privilege for humans," she approaches the Spinozistic pantheism that received its most fulminant illustration in Clarice Lispector's *The Passion According to G.H.*, published in Brazil in 1964.

These books more closely resemble the interior monologue of *Água Viva*, published a decade after G.H., the year Llansol began *Geography of Rebels*. The authors share favorite metaphors (the desert, the body, the writer), and a desire to surpass the structure of the traditional novel. This abolition, to which the authors of the nouveau roman also aspired, is one consequence of doing away with linear time — though the French writers lacked the mystical impulse present in Clarice and Llansol, and though Clarice never goes so far as to abolish the line between life and death. For her, death would always remain the great mystery.

Llansol's writings also illustrate the dangers of abolishing the structure of the traditional novel. In a novel, the reader — and she did always have at least some readers, especially after her return to Portugal — needs some way of knowing where he or she is, of knowing who is talking, of understanding why this story is being told, if any story is being told: if, that is, this is a novel at all. But the longer one inhabits Llansol's world, the more one sees what it might mean to write against the novel, to create prose that could aspire to the status of a living being. "The new being was also not a book. Ana de Peñalosa did not love books; she loved how they became a visible source of energy when she discovered images and images in a succession of descriptions and concepts."

And so it is not for plot or character that we read Maria Gabriela Llansol. It is for the source of energy that her books contain. Open them to any page, like a volume of poetry; and listen to these dead people s cats, dogs, and beings of immortal originalities.

MARIA GABRIELA LLANSOL (1931–2008) is a singular figure in Portuguese literature, one of the greatest writers of the 20th century, yet never before translated into English. Although entirely unknown in the United States, she twice won the award for best novel from the Portuguese Writer's Association with her textually idiosyncratic, fragmentary, and densely poetic writing; other recipients of this prize include José Saramago and António Lobo Antunes. In 1965, Llansol and her husband moved to Belgium to escape from António de Oliveira Salazar's regime, where she spent the next twenty years in voluntary exile, teaching at the local school, translating Rimbaud and Baudelaire, and reading medieval mystics. Upon her death in 2008, she left behind twenty-seven published books and more than seventy unpublished notebooks, all of which evade any traditional definitions of genre.

AUDREY YOUNG is a translator, researcher, and archivist. She received a Fulbright grant to research non-theatrical film in Portugal and studied Portuguese language and culture at the University of Lisbon with a scholarship from the Instituto Camões. She has worked at the Getty Research Institute, the Cineteca Nacional México, and the Arquivo Nacional do Brasil, among other archives.

Thank you all
for your support.
We do this for you,
and could not do
it without you.

DEEP
VELLUM

DEAR READERS,

Deep Vellum Publishing is a 501c3 nonprofit literary arts organization founded in 2013 with a threefold mission: to publish international literature in English translation; to foster the art and craft of translation; and to build a more vibrant book culture in Dallas and beyond. We are dedicated to broadening cultural connections across the English-reading world by connecting readers, in new and creative ways, with the work of international authors. We strive for diversity in publishing authors from various languages, viewpoints, genders, sexual orientations, countries, continents, and literary styles, whose works provide lasting cultural value and build bridges with foreign cultures while expanding our understanding of how the world thinks, feels, and experiences the human condition.

Operating as a nonprofit means that we rely on the generosity of tax-deductible donations from individual donors, cultural organizations, government institutions, and foundations. Your donations provide the basis of our operational budget as we seek out and publish exciting literary works from around the globe and build a vibrant and active literary arts community both locally and within the global society. Deep Vellum offers multiple donor levels, including LIGA DE ORO ($5,000+) and LIGA DEL SIGLO ($1,000+). Donors at various levels receive personalized benefits for their donations, including books and Deep Vellum merchandise, invitations to special events, and recognition in each book and on our website.

In addition to donations, we rely on subscriptions from readers like you to provide an invaluable ongoing investment in Deep Vellum that demonstrates a commitment to our editorial vision and mission. Subscribers are the bedrock of our support as we grow the readership for these amazing works of literature from every corner of the world. The investment our subscribers make allows us to demonstrate to potential donors and bookstores alike the support and demand for Deep Vellum's literature across a broad readership and gives us the ability to grow our mission in ever-new, ever-innovative ways.

In partnership with our sister company and bookstore, Deep Vellum Books, located in the historic cultural district of Deep Ellum in central Dallas, we organize and host literary programming such as author readings, translator workshops, creative writing classes, spoken word performances, and interdisciplinary arts events for writers, translators, and artists from across the globe. Our goal is to enrich and connect the world through the power of the written and spoken word, and we have been recognized for our efforts by being named one of the "Five Small Presses Changing the Face of the Industry" by *Flavorwire* and honored as Dallas's Best Publisher by *D Magazine*.

If you would like to get involved with Deep Vellum as a donor, subscriber, or volunteer, please contact us at deepvellum.org. We would love to hear from you.

Thank you all. Enjoy reading.
Will Evans, Founder & Publisher, Deep Vellum Publishing

PARTNERS

LIGA DE ORO ($5,000+)

Anonymous (2)

LIGA DEL SIGLO ($1,000+)

Allred Capital Management
Ben & Sharon Fountain
David Tomlinson
& Kathryn Berry
Judy Pollock
Life in Deep Ellum

Loretta Siciliano
Lori Feathers
Mary Ann Thompson-Frenk
& Joshua Frenk
Matthew Rittmayer

Meriwether Evans
Pixel and Texel
Nick Storch
Social Venture Partners Dallas
Stephen Bullock

DONORS

Adam Rekerdres
Alan Shockley
Amrit Dhir
Anonymous (4)
Andrew Yorke
Anthony Messenger
Bob Appel
Bob & Katherine Penn
Brandon Childress
Brandon Kennedy
Caitlin Baker
Caroline Casey
Charles Dee Mitchell
Charley Mitcherson
Chilton Thomson

Cheryl Thompson
Christie Tull
Cone Johnson
CS Maynard
Cullen Schaar
Daniel J. Hale
Dori Boone-Costantino
Ed Nawotka
Elizabeth Gillette
Rev. Elizabeth
& Neil Moseley
Ester & Matt Harrison
Farley Houston
Garth Hallberg
Grace Kenney

Greg McConeghy
Jeff Waxman
JJ Italiano
Justin Childress
Kay Cattarulla
Kelly Falconer
Lea Courington
Leigh Ann Pike
Linda Nell Evans
Lissa Dunlay
Maaza Mengiste
Marian Schwartz
& Reid Minot
Mark Haber
Marlo D. Cruz Pagan

Mary Cline
Maynard Thomson
Michael Reklis
Mike Kaminsky
Mokhtar Ramadan
Nikki & Dennis Gibson
Olga Kislova
Patrick Kukucka
Patrick Kutcher

Richard Meyer
Sherry Perry
Steve Bullock
Suejean Kim
Susan Carp
Susan Ernst
Stephen Harding
Symphonic Source
Theater Jones

Thomas DiPiero
Tim Perttula
Tony Thomson

SUBSCRIBERS

Ali Bolcakan
Amanda Harvey
Andre Habet
Andrew Bowles
Anita Tarar
Anonymous
Ben Fountain
Ben Nichols
Blair Bullock
Charles Dee Mitchell
Chris Sweet
Christie Tull
Courtney Sheedy
Daniel Galindo
David Tomlinson
  & Kathryn Berry
David Weinberger
Dawn Wilburn-Saboe

Elizabeth Johnson
Geoffrey Young
Holly LaFon
James Tierney
Jeffrey Collins
Jill Kelly
Joe Milazzo
John Schmerein
John Winkelman
Kevin Winter
Kimberly Alexander
Lesley Conzelman
M.J. Malooly
Margaret Terwey
Martha Gifford
Mary Brockson
Michael Elliott
Michael Filippone

Mies de Vries
Neal Chuang
Nhan Ho
Nicholas R. Theis
Patrick Shirak
Peter McCambridge
Rainer Schulte
Robert Keefe
Ronald Morton
Shelby Vincent
Suzanne Fischer
Sydney Mantrom
Tim Kindseth
Todd Jailer
Tom Bowden
Tracy Shapley
William Fletcher
William Pate

AVAILABLE NOW FROM DEEP VELLUM

MICHÈLE AUDIN · *One Hundred Twenty-One Days*
translated by Christiana Hills · FRANCE

ANOUD, WAJDI AL-AHDAL, CRISTINA ALI FARAH, NAJWA BIN SHATWAN,
RANIA MAMOUN, FERESHTEH MOLAVI, & ZAHER OMAREEN ·
BANTHOLOGY: Stories from Banned Nations·
translated by Ruth Ahmedzai Kemp, Basma Ghalayini, Perween Richards,
Sawad Hussain, William M. Hutchins, & Hope Campbell Gustafson · IRAN,
IRAQ, LIBYA, SYRIA, SOMALIA, SUDAN, & YEMEN

CARMEN BOULLOSA · *Texas: The Great Theft* · *Before* · *Heavens on Earth*
translated by Samantha Schnee, Peter Bush, Shelby Vincent · MEXICO

LEILA S. CHUDORI · *Home*
translated by John H. McGlynn · INDONESIA

ANANDA DEVI · *Eve Out of Her Ruins*
translated by Jeffrey Zuckerman · MAURITIUS

ALISA GANIEVA · *The Mountain and the Wall* · *Bride & Groom*
translated by Carol Apollonio · RUSSIA

ANNE GARRÉTA · *Sphinx* · *Not One Day*
translated by Emma Ramadan · FRANCE

JÓN GNARR · *The Indian* · *The Pirate* · *The Outlaw*
translated by Lytton Smith· ICELAND

NOEMI JAFFE · *What are the Blind Men Dreaming?*
translated by Julia Sanches & Ellen Elias-Bursac · BRAZIL

CLAUDIA SALAZAR JIMÉNEZ · *Blood of the Dawn*
translated by Elizabeth Bryer · PERU

JOSEFINE KLOUGART · *Of Darkness*
translated by Martin Aitken · DENMARK

YANICK LAHENS · *Moonbath*
translated by Emily Gogolak · HAITI

FORTHCOMING FROM DEEP VELLUM

EDUARDO BERTI · *The Imagined Land*
translated by Charlotte Coombe · ARGENTINA

GOETHE · *The Golden Goblet: Selected Poems of Goethe*
translated by Zsuzsanna Ozsváth & Frederick Turner · GERMANY

KIM YIDEUM · *Blood Sisters*
translated by Jiyoon Lee · SOUTH KOREA

PABLO MARTÍN SÁNCHEZ · *The Anarchist Who Shared My Name*
translated by Jeff Diteman · SPAIN

DOROTA MASŁOWSKA · *Honey, I Killed the Cats*
translated by Benjamin Paloff · POLAND

BRICE MATTHIEUSSENT · *Revenge of the Translator*
translated by Emma Ramadan · FRANCE

SERGIO PITOL · *Mephisto's Waltz: Selected Short Stories*
translated by George Henson · MEXICO

SERGIO PITOL · *Carnival Triptych: The Love Parade;*
Taming the Divine Heron; Married Life
translated by George Henson · MEXICO

ZAHIA RAHMANI · *"Muslim": A Novel*
translated by Matt Reeck · ALGERIA/FRANCE

JESSICA SCHIEFAUER · *Girls Lost*
TRANSLATED BY SASKIA VOGEL · SWEDEN

ÓFEIGUR SIGURÐSSON · *Öræfi: The Wasteland*
translated by Lytton Smith · ICELAND

DEEP
VELLUM